ORBIT

LEIGH HELLMAN

ORBIT
Copyright © 2018 by Leigh Hellman

First Edition.

Published by Snowy Wings Publishing
www.snowywingspublishing.com

Cover design by Najla Qamber Designs.
Interior design by Dorothy Dreyer.

ISBN (paperback): 978-1-946202-81-9
ISBN (hardcover): 978-1-946202-82-6
eISBN: 978-1-946202-83-3
Library of Congress Control Number: 2018910622

*For Rachel B.—without you, this would still be a
what-if.*

[PROLOGUE]
78 YEARS LATER

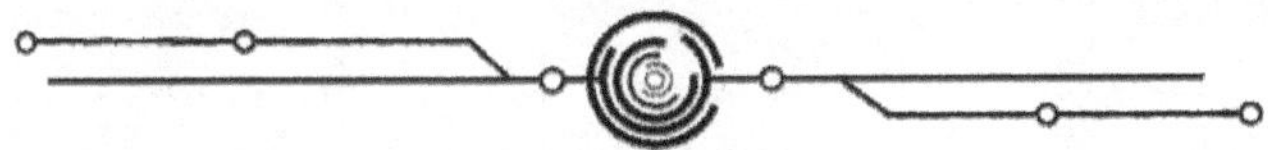

NIGHT HAD ALREADY CREPT across Toi and the Earth loomed—huge and menacing and beautiful—just past the crooked rooftops, as it slowly consumed the sky. Across Toi's dented metal streets two sets of footsteps pounded out a frenzied rhythm that echoed just slightly, like a spring rain over tin shingles.

I've got to lose him, was all that Ciaan could think. The words looped through her mind: *I've got to lose him, I've got to lose him, I've got to lose him.*

She didn't care where she was; she barely noticed when the buildings began to shift from the shiny, newly-seamed ones of her neighborhood to the rusted, warped

1

clusters she'd been warned about. She didn't care that she couldn't remember how long it'd been since she heard the curfew alarm; she'd still been racing past gleaming lacquered storefronts then. All that mattered now was getting as much distance between Melean and herself as her stubby legs could manage.

"Run all you want, greenie! You're not gonna get away from me!" Melean's threat was broken up by his wheezing breaths.

Ciaan scanned the street directly in front of her, noting sharp turns at small intersections or down narrow alleys that she thought of taking always a second too late. Fear began gnawing sharp in the pit of her stomach as she realized that all the thick acrylic windows were closed and most likely locked here. No one would hear her scream; or if they did, they wouldn't care.

She decided, as she missed another possible turn, that her best bet was to stay on this main street. No one was going to come out of their house to help her, but she might run into some straggler coming back past curfew. And eventually they'd be out of this sector and then maybe she'd be able to scream. At any rate, the main road kept her visible and out of dark dead-ends where she'd really be in trouble.

She listened behind her for Melean's heavy breathing and footfalls, trying to gauge how far apart they were and whether or not it would be safe to slow down a bit. Her own breathing had become ragged and forced and her legs were shaking beneath her. She'd never really been a runner—despite her school's mandatory rote physical drills. She could manage shorter distances well enough, but long distances always gave her side cramps. Plus, she'd never had to run for her life in organized athletics, so this was a whole other thing entirely.

The good news was that Melean seemed to be just as bad at murderous chasing as Ciaan was at terrified running. He wasn't big in either muscles or fat, nor was he thin and gangly like many of the other boys on Toi, so she'd assumed he'd be better at it. He was, Ciaan imagined, what Earth boys looked like: tall enough, strong enough, handsome enough. The only thing he was too much of was mean. That's what made him a p-kid.

Ciaan, on the other hand, looked exactly like a p-kid. Dark-skinned like Melean (but blotchy where he was smooth) with an undergrown, slightly disproportionate body that someone could look at and not quite be able to put their finger on what was off. Only they could with her, because of the one stark difference between her and the other p-kids: her hair. She could feel it slapping against her neck as she ran, thick woven braids of bright, gold-pale hair. The color they all said only Earth people could grow, the color she had never seen on any head but her own. The color that branded her forever as someone who wasn't a real p-kid. Melean, with his close-cropped black braids, knew what that color meant—that it meant soft and weak and vulnerable and green like the wilting Earth where it came from—and that was why he tormented her every chance he got. That was why he was chasing her, and that was why she couldn't let him catch her.

"Come on you…filthy…little…brat!" Melean's voice sounded gummy—like he had too much saliva in his mouth, or not enough.

Ciaan's vision blurred and she struggled to blink it clear. Her eyes refocused, searching ahead. To her growing horror the buildings seemed to only get worse; huge cracks in the steel shot up the walls, and front steps were sunken and scratched away. People in this sector didn't even seem to care about lacquering their homes to hide the fact that this was a whole planet made of metal. The buildings were thinner and more tightly stacked together, like the street had decided to compress and forgot to tell the houses about it. It made the second-floor apartment that Ciaan and her father, second mother, and the rest of their children shared seem like an Earth mansion.

Sweat was running from the back of Ciaan's head down her neck and under her loose shirt collar, tickling her buzzing skin. She knew that she'd have to stop soon or risk fainting dead in the street. She could no longer hear Melean behind her—her blood throbbed too loudly in her ears—but she knew he was still there. She knew that if she turned around, he'd be just a few inches past arm's length away. She didn't want to, but the tears had been stinging her eyes for a while now, so she let them run down her face. They wouldn't look like anything more than another trail of sweat anyway.

Suddenly, a flash of sharp light cut out from the street ahead. It was a curfew patrol, she realized, and now she was caught either way. She considered flagging it down, turning herself in, and facing her father and second mother at home. She'd only been caught by a patrol once before—when she was eight or nine—and between her obvious panic and her second mother's desperate begging, the soldier had let her off without a note on her record. This time she probably wouldn't be that lucky, even if she wasn't out late by choice, but a curfew violation was definitely better than the alternative of Melean. Every ounce of better judgment told her this. So, like a typical thirteen year-old, she did the exact opposite of what her better judgment recommended and ducked away from the approaching headlight into a dank alley.

She quickly—but not quite quickly enough—realized

her mistake. This was just the type of place she'd been trying to avoid by staying on the main street. Narrow at the front, it tapered even more as it pushed farther back to where the houses were the most warped and pressed together. Trash chutes lined the walls at about shoulder-height, and the whole place reeked of three-day-old garbage that had probably already been rotten when it'd been thrown out. The only legal animals on Toi were the few that people kept as standard pets, registered and restricted to indoors. Still, people bred rodents and other small scavengers illegally, though for what reason Ciaan couldn't imagine. She tried to ignore the scuttling sounds that shot out between tattered trash bags.

Of course the worst part of this decision was Ciaan's particular choice of alley; she'd turned into one with a dead end. She was trapped, plain and simple, and the best she'd get out of this now would be some dark bruises and chipped teeth. She didn't want to think about what the worst would be. P-kids played rough, and they didn't play fair.

She didn't have to turn around to know Melean was there. She could hear his breathing—gasping and tight like hers—and knew he was doubled over like she was, waiting to catch his breath before the fight started. Finally, their gasps slowed. Ciaan sucked in a long gulp of sour air and her stomach clenched against it.

The first blow hit her like a brick to the side. She stumbled back a few steps, clutching at her waist. She'd expected a little gloating before he started; he was probably pissed that she'd actually made him chase her.

"Thought you could outrun me, didn't you?" He swung at her shoulder; she leapt back and he only caught a fistful of foul alley air. He paused then chuckled, but there wasn't any humor in it. "You almost did, too, you greenie trash. But not quite. You should already know that p-kids are faster than greenies, but I guess you're too damn stupid with your shrunken greenie brain to remember that, huh?"

"I told you I'm not a greenie." She muttered it through her teeth, too bound up with anger and fear to say it out loud. That got her a kick to the ankles that didn't fully connect but threw her off balance enough to send her crashing down onto the cold metal ground. She fell into a garbage bag with a thick splat. Something pale blue and curdled oozed out beneath her, sticking to her in clumps as she pulled herself up.

"What was that, *greenie?*" Melean sneered above her.

"I'm not a damn greenie, you bastard!" She kicked a booted foot at his stomach and he was too busy sneering to dodge it. He doubled over with a curse and she knew she'd done it now; if he was going to let her off easy before, he wasn't anymore. Now he was going to decimate her.

She knew she should've thought first and kicked second, but she didn't really regret it—not yet anyway. If she was gonna get beat up in some lost little hellhole of an alley, she wanted to at least get one good hit in.

He lunged at her fast and brutal, grabbing her tightly by the collar. She stared up at him, focused on the black centers of his eyes. She wasn't going to let him know how much he scared her.

"You know, ever since the first time I saw you—the first time you waddled into primary grades—I hated you." His voice was low and cruel and even though she didn't want to, Ciaan flinched. "You know why? Because you think you're better than us. I didn't care that you said you were a p-kid, or that you made friends with p-kids, or that your dad was a p-man himself. Because I knew that deep down, no matter what, you thought you were better. You and your whore Earth mom. Where'd that dirtbitch go anyway? Got sick of raising a halfie and went back to her precious greenie planet, didn't she?"

That was it. If Melean was going to fight dirty, then so was Ciaan. She thrust her knee up with all the strength she had left and smashed it into his crotch. He yelped and reeled away, giving her a clear escape route back to the main street—back to her second-floor apartment, back to her p-man father and p-woman second mother.

I should go, she thought, without making a move.

Melean lay on the ground curled in on himself—a cocooned, whimpering mass. She should've felt compassion for him, should've apologized. That was what an Earth kid, a *greenie* would do. But Ciaan wasn't an Earth kid—she'd never even *been* to Earth—and she had just this one chance to prove that to him. She kicked him hard in the back, then again in the side. He cried out and pleaded, raising his arms in a pitiful self-defense. She took the opportunity to stamp on his chest, grinding her heel into his sternum.

With each kick her anger seemed to grow instead of diffuse. She started to relish it, grinning down at his huddled body as it began to blend in with the garbage.

"Pl—please..." Melean choked and sputtered, shielding his head with his shaking hands. He tried to say something that got muffled with blood and tears and Ciaan could only make out one word:

"...mercy..."

Mercy, she mused. *What a funny idea. When was I ever given mercy? If it was me on the ground instead of you, what would you do?* She knew the answer and stamped him hard between the shoulder blades for it, careful to avoid any strikes at his head or neck. She didn't want a malicious death on her record.

Ciaan paused to regain her balance and as she stared down at the little pools of blood collecting in the crevices of the alley seams, she wondered if life was like this on Earth. Her mother—her first mother, her *real* mother—had said that people were people everywhere, good and bad. Ciaan wasn't so sure that she believed that. P-people, she thought, must've forgotten some part of what it meant to be human a long time ago. 78 years ago—when the Earth governments launched the first phrase of their initiative to help deal with overpopulation and housing crises by unsubsidizing public homes, demolishing the Earth ghettos, and sending the initial wave of poor, now homeless, humans out to live on their first project (or p-)planet, Toi—could they have anticipated what would happen? 78 years later, with seven metal housing planets now in orbit around the Earth, did they know that they were creating a new race of people—meaner, angrier, and hungrier for something that had been taken from them generations ago?

Or maybe just more bitter and lonelier, like Ciaan had once thought. But the more she saw and learned and became like other p-people, the more she had to believe that something was missing in them—that green part of Earth, the bit of fertile ground in humans and their planet that let something reckless and beautiful grow. P-people didn't have that and it made them colder, like the dead space just beyond their artificial atmosphere.

Well, Ciaan thought viciously, *it's better to be cold than dead.* She stomped on Melean's forearms, just above the wrist.

Her momentary pause gave him a chance to regroup too, and he grabbed her ankle when it came within reach. She pulled away, but not before he had a chance to claw across her skin, leaving three or four thin red gashes. It was times like this that she wished regulation pants came down to their feet instead of just their knees. She winced and hissed, smashing down on his hand before hobbling back herself. She caught her other foot in a loose piece of garbage and landed on the ground with a loud thud.

Melean was up again before she was. He flew at her and hit her in the one place she'd avoided with him—the face. She thought it would be a smack, hard and sharp and embarrassing mostly but otherwise not too damaging, but he punched her instead. She felt her whole face crumble under his fist, cracking and shattering before her mind could really register the blow. He was laughing again, high and hysterical like he'd really lost it, and for the first time that night she seriously considered the possibility that he actually wanted to kill her. She didn't know whether it was the adrenaline surge or her survival response kicking in, but her arms suddenly started flailing wildly, trying to lash out at him any way they could. A scream—primal and desperate—ripped itself out of her tightening throat.

Suddenly a new voice sliced through the alley and echoed off its walls, drowning out everything else: "That is quite enough!"

Ciaan suddenly recalled the stories her first mother had told her about some of the old Earth religions—how they believed that, when you died, magical things called angels took you to paradise. This voice didn't sound especially sweet, but Ciaan had to believe that not all angels talked like tiny bells.

"If you do not stop immediately, I will not hesitate to use force against you!"

Melean froze and Ciaan was sure he was going to finish her right there. But he wavered for too long, bruised knuckles hovering in the air, and was heaved off of Ciaan like he was just another sack of garbage. Ciaan blinked past tears and fuzzy double-vision as a different face came into view, a rigid and vaguely translucent one with two dark eyes devoid of any emotion other than professional irritation.

"Are you all right, girl?" A gloved hand clasped Ciaan's arm and brought her staggering to her feet.

Ciaan shook her head, couldn't tell if that was a yes or no herself.

"Both of you are in very serious trouble." The voice, which Ciaan now understood went with the face and the gloved hand, belonged to an Artificial patrol soldier. Her p-partner, who stood almost a head shorter than her, glared at Melean. "Not only are you in violation of curfew, but you have engaged in acts of public aggression that have led to injury. We will not have any choice but to add these violations to your records."

Ciaan didn't know much about Artificials; she'd never had more than a brief, passing interaction with one. She knew that technically all Artificials were soldiers—at least accordingly to the history books her first mother had kept stacked next to her nightstand. She knew that they were a sub-race of artificially-grown humans who'd been popular during some Earth fad decades ago but must've gone out of fashion since then because now they were funneled into administrative academies and security force units. She knew that most p-people thought they were weird and that—while they worked in partnerships and mixed groups—most Artificials only socialized amongst themselves.

This Artificial didn't seem strange so much as stiff and frustrated; she looked from Ciaan to Melean and back again, then sighed and rubbed her forehead. Ciaan noticed how tired she looked and wondered what time it actually was.

"I think it would be best for you to be taken to a medical unit and scanned for serious injuries." She rounded on Melean. "What is your name, boy?"

He narrowed his eyes; a muscle ticked in his jaw. From behind the Artificial soldier her p-partner barked, "Lieutenant 2719 has asked you a question, boy. What's your name?"

"Melean, sir." He muttered it, dropped his eyes to the alley floor.

"Well, Melean," Lieutenant 2719 continued, "you will go with Sergeant 0919. And you, girl, will come with me."

Without glancing back at Melean, Ciaan nodded and followed the lieutenant to the patrol craft in silence.

"My name is Ciaan."

They had been speeding along streets that Ciaan didn't recognize for nearly ten minutes without speaking, and she thought she might as well break the ice with the person who'd more-or-less saved her life.

"I don't remember asking for your name, girl." The lieutenant's tone was brusque; it deflated any remaining adrenaline Ciaan had.

Her neck flushed and she swallowed down her sudden shame. The whirl of the engine grated against her eardrums and she reconciled herself to an uncomfortably quiet ride to the medical unit.

But the lieutenant must have been uncomfortable too, because after a few minutes she cleared her throat quietly like she was getting ready to say something that was both very important and very awkward.

"Your hair isn't regulation length."

Ciaan sputtered and crossed her arms—was this all going to be about her hair? She closed her eyes and felt the sweat-sticky wisps of curls cooling at the nape of her neck and thought suddenly about the first home they had, when her first mother had still been on Toi. It had been a real home, a full building, or at least half of one cut straight down the middle. It had had different floors at any rate—something that Ciaan missed—and broad, open corners. Shelves lined the walls, just out of reach and stacked with antique scientific journals and delicate silver contraptions that Ciaan could imagine a hundred explanations for—remnants of her first mother's past life on Earth. Colorful trinkets from the local artisans' market dotted the walls, pieces of her father elbowing their way into the décor. They had always made Ciaan smile.

Ciaan had loved to climb up and down the spiral

steps, from the second floor where her parents slept to the third floor where her room was. She'd stop at each floor—pretending that she was a confused guest who couldn't find the right apartment—and would apologize to her mother in funny accents that she'd heard on the Information Channels, where delegates from the different Earth Unions came on and talked for what felt like hours about significant Earth concerns. Her favorite accent was the one that the delegate from the Northern Asian Union had; it was all ups and downs like he was trying to catch a fly with his throat. Her mother loved it too, and they would laugh and laugh when Ciaan burst into the kitchen trying to imitate it. Those were the days when Ciaan's mother would plead with her not to cut her hair so short and close to her head, which was against regulations, and urge her to be proud of her pale braids. They were, her mother had said with a smile, the same as her grandmother's. Those were the days when Ciaan would listen and let her braids grow long, so they brushed against the small of her back when she walked. That was before her mother had left on a transport for a week's Earth leave—the first Ciaan could remember her taking—and had never come back.

Now Ciaan's second mother pleaded that she keep her hair at regulation length, but Ciaan didn't listen. It wasn't that her second mother was a hateful sort of person; she was kind and patient with Ciaan, sometimes even in ways that her first mother hadn't been. But her second mother wasn't her first mother, and so it didn't matter.

The patrol craft decelerated for a turning transport vehicle and Ciaan shook herself out of her memories.

"Then why don't you write it up on my record? It doesn't matter now." Ciaan immediately regretted snapping at a soldier, tried to cover it with a cough.

But the lieutenant seemed to barely hear her. "You got that color, I think, from your grandmother."

Ciaan shifted in her seat. How did the lieutenant know that? Was it in her records somewhere? Why would this soldier be going through her records? And what else was in her records, she wondered.

After another minute or two of a tenser silence, the lieutenant spoke again. "I wasn't sure about it at first, but now I'm almost positive."

Ciaan looked over at her. The lieutenant smiled, just slightly, but it made her strange skin warm up at the edges.

"I knew your mother."

"What?" Ciaan bolted up in her seat. "When? Where? Who are you?"

"Calm down, Ciaan. You're still a criminal in here." The lieutenant tried to sound severe, but she was still smiling and Ciaan thought she might be younger than the stern set of her features suggested. "I knew your mother on Earth, back when I was stationed there. She was a very…significant woman—and you"—she glanced over at Ciaan with sharp, quick eyes—"you are a very significant child."

"What?" That was all Ciaan could manage. She had so many questions—too many—and her brain couldn't sort out one from the rest. The lieutenant started to say something else but stopped abruptly when a bright green light began blinking on the control board.

The patrol craft came to an abrupt stop; Ciaan would've been thrown against the front window if she hadn't been strapped in. That stern shadow stretched back over the lieutenant's face as she turned the vehicle completely around and sent it zooming off in the opposite direction.

"You need to stay in the patrol craft. Something has come up that I have to supervise."

Ciaan nodded faintly. She knew they were stopped in front of a port—in fact they had to be at the Central Port Zone of Toi. Enclosed and separated docking stations were set up one after the other with nothing but two layers of artificial atmosphere barriers between people and void. The sky holograms didn't extend over ports and Ciaan gazed out at the true blackness of space, vast in ways that she hadn't even tried to imagine before. The hairs on her forearms pricked up.

The lieutenant reached up to close the patrol craft door and seal Ciaan in. An unsettling thought occurred to her. "You're coming back, right?"

The lieutenant's hand rested on the edge of the doorway. "Another soldier will escort you to the medical unit and then home. Upon consideration I feel that you were only exercising reasonable self-defense against an imminent physical threat, and therefore I have decided not to submit the fight onto your record. The curfew violation, however, will be noted."

Ciaan should've been relieved by this unexpected moment of mercy, but for some reason a nervousness still lingered. "Am I going to see you again?"

The lieutenant smiled, but this time it didn't quite warm her features and Ciaan knew what she was going to say before she said it.

"I don't know. Perhaps."

Ciaan slumped in her seat.

The lieutenant reverted back to her professional tone. "If and when I return to Toi, I will make every effort to see you at least once, so that we can talk more fully about your mother. That is what you want, isn't it?"

Ciaan nodded. The lieutenant leveled her gaze at Ciaan but didn't say anything else.

"Do you know where my mother is?" Ciaan hadn't meant to ask it, and she definitely hadn't meant to ask it so abruptly. But now that the question was out there she thought she might've wanted to know the answer after all.

The lieutenant stiffened. She pursed her lips, her hand lingering impatiently near the door button. The stillness made Ciaan fluttery, like her skin had just grown a thousand wings and they had all started flapping at once. The lieutenant exhaled, smooth and controlled. Ciaan—not knowing what else to do—did the same.

"Ciaan." The lines of the lieutenant's face were firm, but Ciaan thought she caught a simmer of emotion behind her icy composure. "Your mother is dead."

All the wings that had just been beating so hard stopped midflight; a long shiver ran from Ciaan's toes to her ears. She thought about bursting into tears, then decided against it. It felt like too intense and smothering a response, like something an Earth kid would do. So Ciaan blinked once, twice, three times and let all the pain and shock wither and drip off of her.

"I'm very sorry, mainly that you had to find out this

way. She could have been something else, if the worlds had been different," said the lieutenant. For a second, it looked like a shimmer of tears had welled up in the lieutenant's dark, impassive eyes. But then it disappeared and Ciaan wondered if it'd just been the flickering shadows.

The lieutenant was probably expecting Ciaan to babble nonsense or demand details. Or maybe to sob and throw herself into a strange soldier's arms as some sort of replacement for her dead mother. Ciaan half-expected one of those reactions herself, so she was a little surprised by what came out of her mouth instead.

"What's your name?"

The lieutenant paused and stared at Ciaan like she had just lifted her head off her shoulders. Then she cleared her throat, steady and official, and answered, "Lieutenant 2719. My registered name is Kwe NAU 27198607."

Ciaan shook her head, felt the pain from the fight claw up her neck. "What's your real name? The name that they gave you in the training facilities, or that you gave yourself?"

Lieutenant 2719 looked Ciaan up and down appraisingly, like she was scanning her for weapons. Finally, she conceded. "Aaniin. It means *good day*."

"It's pretty." Ciaan held out her hand, only half-mocking regulation manners. "It was nice to meet you, Aaniin. I hope that I will see you again sometime."

At that, Aaniin laughed outright.

"Well, Ciaan. It was a pleasure meeting you as well, even if it was under somewhat less-than-legal circumstances. I hope that we will meet again too." With that she turned towards the door button and pressed it. As the patrol craft door slid shut, Ciaan thought she heard a whisper: "You are your mother's daughter."

Then the door was closed and sealed and all Ciaan could see was Aaniin's rigid frame retreating as she approached the first dock. A small crowd of people huddled there, surrounding a young woman who couldn't be more than a few years older than Ciaan and was obviously heavily pregnant. Aaniin took the young woman's arm and opened the docking platform door. People in the crowd waved and wept and a few had to be held back by the others, but the young woman walked forward and through the clear doors without looking back. Somehow Ciaan knew that if the woman turned and looked at her family, she'd never be able to leave.

That night, after her father and second mother had

yelled and lectured and hugged her for almost two hours straight, she lay wide awake in her bed and listened to the tin-patter rhythms of breathing that filled their second floor apartment. She tugged idly at her pale hair and watched a braid glimmer in the bright moonlight.

Tomorrow, she vowed, she would throw away her shears and let her hair grow to regulation length again— and longer. She closed her eyes and breathed in deep the cool, metallic, artificial air. She thought for just a moment that she tasted the tang of blood on her tongue, but then it was gone. She let her hand fall from her hair.

Tomorrow, she thought, *I won't miss the green parts anymore.*

[ONE]

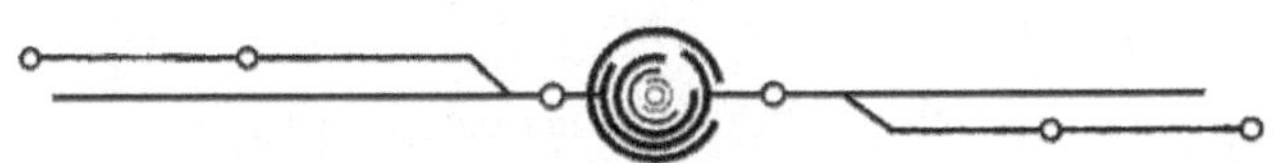

"GENNETT, CIAAN." THE CLERK—grim-faced and shaped like an overstuffed cushion—didn't look up from shuffling his forms as Ciaan moved to stand behind the courtroom partition.

Two judicial secretaries sat on either side of the main screen, positioned ten feet or so in front of the electrified field that separated the court officers from the accused criminals. With the rise of nano-technological personal weapons, the government began installing what they called "shock walls"—panels lined with electrical currents that activated if the initial barrier was breeched. The governmental buildings had been the first to shock up, then the courts. Now everything from banks to patrol crafts to elementary schools had them. Ciaan had even heard of a few of the richest p-planet homes hiring government-leased security agencies to shock up their homes, though she couldn't imagine anyone but the emigrated politicians having enough money for that.

But in spite of the price—or maybe because of it—the shock walls were effective, even she had to admit that. Not once in her twenty years had Ciaan heard of a shock wall anywhere being successfully punctured. The only complaints people normally had were that they tinted everything on the other side neon blue and warped the image like looking through an eerie, wrong-set window.

In front of Ciaan now were two blue-tinged secretaries, one blue-tinged clerk, and a long desk covered in slumping piles of loose paper that had yet to be entered into the digital court system. They each took less than a second to assess her and, within a minute or two, the main screen flickered on.

"You are Ciaan Gennett of Toi Sector C-22. Your census number is 371113. You are a female adult human currently aged twenty." The judge looked crisp on the video feed, like he could've been sitting in the courtroom with them instead of in some secured office several stories above them.

"You have pleaded guilty to the crime of vandalism

of civilian property and intimidation with the intent to harm." His upper lip curled slightly—the only hint of emotion he offered. "Is that correct?"

Ciaan spoke into the small microphone mounted on the shock wall. "Yes, sir."

The judge nodded. "Do you have any remarks to make before I announce sentencing?"

The secretaries and clerk turned to Ciaan; she could feel their condescension prick against her skin. She leaned forward to say *no*, but her second mother jumped up from the visitor benches and wedged in next to her before she had the chance to get it out.

"Please, Your Honor." Her second mother's voice sounded shaky and small and Ciaan thought, not for the first time, that she must be slowly killing this woman. Her second mother had come to every court hearing, trial, and sentencing that Ciaan had racked up over the past six years. She'd come to detainment centers at all hours of the night with the last of her paychecks to bail Ciaan out so she'd never have to spend the night in jail. She'd lectured and sobbed and begged Ciaan to stop trying to burn the world down. And when her father had refused to help Ciaan out anymore, when he'd threatened to throw her out of their apartment and never speak to her again, her second mother had been the one who'd kept him from making good on those promises.

For three years after that things had been almost okay, but then this happened. Ciaan almost wished her second mother would give up too, just so she wouldn't have to feel so damn guilty about what she was doing to her.

"Please, Your Honor," her second mother repeated, wiped off a tear before it hit her cheek. "My daughter is not a criminal. She has broken the law, and I understand that she must be punished for that, but please don't send her away from her father and me. Without her family, Ciaan will be completely lost."

The judge raised an eyebrow. "Are you this girl's mother?"

Her second mother paused and Ciaan's gut clenched.

"I am her—her mother was separated from the family when Ciaan was very young. I am her father's second wife. But, regardless of the circumstances, she's my daughter. I raised her as my own and I consider her as much my child as any of our others." Her words were full of an earnest fury that tore at the pit of Ciaan's stomach.

"You are—" One of the secretaries scanned his file screen, adjusted his glasses at the glare. "Illonde Tohannson, married to Rouan Tohannson of Toi Sector C-22?"

Next to her, Ciaan could feel her second mother's joints stiffen.

"She took her mother's maiden name instead of her father's family one."

The secretary peered at Ciaan, eyes narrow behind his thin frames, for a few seconds before minimizing her second mother's file. "Mrs. Tohannson, you do realize that you have substantially less control over your daughter's fate now that she is legally of age, correct?"

Her second mother brushed her fingers against Ciaan's wrist; Ciaan pulled back, folded her hands in front of her instead. She didn't reach for Ciaan again. "Yes, I understand. It's just that she's still so young and she hasn't had an easy life and it would break my—break both her father's and my—hearts if she were sentenced to a detention facility. She's made her mistakes, but that doesn't mean she's a monster."

Ciaan tossed those final words—*a monster*—around in her head, didn't have her second mother's conviction on that subject.

The whole courtroom rustled, waiting to see if her second mother was finished pleading for leniency. If Ciaan thought her own pleas and wailing might help sway the judge's decision, she would've gladly put on a show herself. But she'd been through this enough times to realize that nothing anyone said on the criminal side of the shock wall really mattered to the people on the court side. Her second mother should've known that too;

maybe the same part of her that thought she could save Ciaan from herself also told her that hope would prevail across the board. *It's the only rational explanation for it,* Ciaan thought.

After the brief hush, her second mother quietly thanked the court for allowing her to speak and shuffled back over to the hard-paneled benches.

The judge cleared his throat over the monitor. "The court appreciates Mrs. Tohannson's passionate remarks on her daughter's behalf and sincerely hopes that Ms. Gennett grasps the significance of such selfless familial support."

Ciaan bit at the inside of her cheek to stop herself from rolling her eyes. If her second mother was a different kind of woman, she might've fed off her perpetual martyrdom on Ciaan's behalf. But she wasn't; she just cared about Ciaan and that made it so much harder to endure.

The judge continued: "If this were a first-time offense, or a crime of lesser severity, the court may be inclined to exercise mercy and grant Ms. Gennett probation. However, as Ms. Gennett's disconcertingly long record shows, probation does not appear to act as a suitable deterrent for her."

That, Ciaan mused, was really more the court's fault than her own. The only punishment available for a nonviolent offense committed by a youth was probation and it didn't act as much of a deterrent for anyone nowadays.

"And furthermore, as this crime showed signs of escalating aggression with a potential for violent behavior, the court does not feel that probation is a severe enough punishment in this case."

Behind Ciaan, her second mother sucked in a sharp breath.

"However, in taking into consideration the requests of Mrs. Tohannson, this court feels that a detention sentence indefinitely separating Ms. Gennett from her family would be ill-advised."

That was a load of shit; the courts didn't want to ship Ciaan off Toi because the transport fees were staggering. Besides, there were plenty of detention facilities on-planet that were close enough for daily visits if her second mother was really that dedicated.

"Also, considering that intimidation is not legally considered a violent offense and noting that Ms. Gennett has not been arrested since she was seventeen, this court is willing to abstain from sentencing her to a detention facility under the strict condition that this be the last time she graces *any* courts with her presence."

That did surprise Ciaan; she'd been preparing herself for a prison term since she pled guilty to vandalizing an abandoned storefront and arguing with a patrol soldier over it three months ago. She gritted her teeth and waited for the final decision, not sure if she should be relieved or apprehensive. The video feed flickered, briefly distorting the judge's face.

"Therefore, it is the ruling of the First Rank Court of Toi that Ciaan Gennett be sentenced to two years labor service in the government reserves. She is ordered to serve no less than one year but may be released early if she demonstrates exceptionally good behavior. She will serve her time at the Central Port Zone Base and may continue to reside at her parents' home if they so choose. Otherwise, she will live in the base barracks with the other reserves. She is also hereafter restricted from associating with any known criminals for the duration of five years, under penalty of her labor sentence being immediately commuted to a detention facility term. During those five years she will not be allowed to leave Toi except under the orders of her reserve superiors or in circumstances of extreme and imminent planetary danger." The judge stopped, stared directly at Ciaan for the first time since he'd appeared onscreen. "Do you understand these terms?"

"Yes, sir."

"Then the defendant shall proceed to the Processing Room for final documentation and record revision."

Ciaan nodded politely to the judge once and then

hurried out of the courtroom as fast as she could, barely giving her second mother a chance to catch up. As the exit doors slid open she heard the clerk hack out a loud cough—preparing to call the next alleged criminal to the shock wall—but the doors closed and sealed before she could hear who it was.

"I've been trying to call and send direct messages to your Right Hand all day, but it kept saying that access to the account was denied!" Tidoris's agitated face flickered in and out on the old computer monitor that her father had purchased from some Earth goods resale shop years ago.

Ciaan had sworn up and down that she couldn't get the computer to work—that she only wanted it because the antique circuitry was interesting to pick around in— so she'd been able to keep it around without any questions, even though Tidoris had fixed it and wired it into the main digital planetary system a week after Ciaan had wrestled it out of her father's packrat piles. That was around the same time her father had said she needed her own room partitions for privacy; she hadn't argued with him. The privacy and the computer had both come in handy a lot over the past four or five years, especially when her parents confiscated her personal digital assistant (which most people just called a "Right Hand") as punishment.

All p-people—Artificials and humans alike—and probably all Earth people too, had a Right Hand designated to them. Ciaan missed hers now, but she'd had it taken away enough times already to know how to improvise without it. Her solution was usually just relying on the computer for all her digital and network needs, despite its low memory and sludge-slow speed, and since Tidoris was the only person she ever really talked to outside of her family she felt like her secret was safe enough with him.

"Where have you been? How did the sentencing go?" Tidoris was nervous and jumpy on his best days—he had been ever since they'd first met at their sector's primary school—so the fragmented and pixilated image that came over the monitor didn't seem too far from normal.

"I've been worried."

Ciaan smiled, lips tight and teeth pressing into the back of them. "You're always worried." Tidoris opened his mouth to protest, but she cut him off.

"I didn't get probation, but I didn't really expect to either. And I didn't get a detention term, which was probably the most shocking part." She paused, hoping he'd say something scathing like she felt she deserved.

Instead, he pursed his lips and avoided direct eye contact with her.

"Well?"

"I got labor service in the reserves. Two years—one if I play nice." She kicked at the sheets on her unmade bed. "Plus five years' probation. No more hanging out with criminal menaces or revolutionary plotting 'til I'm twenty-five."

She laughed, brittle and bitter but not loud enough for the rest of her family to hear in the other room.

"Damn it, Ciaan! This isn't funny, you know. It's serious stuff. How're you going to get a job with a record like that? How're you ever going to get out of your parents' apartment, or do anything with your life?" Tidoris's voice cracked like a craft skidding to a stop. "Do you know how lucky you are that they didn't lock you up for real this time?"

Ciaan scoffed. "It's not enough that I have a crusading second mother, now you want to go and be my third? Shit, Dori, why don't you just sign me up for the colony expeditions? You have the family connections, after all."

An awkward silence hissed through the monitor screen. Ciaan wanted to apologize but only managed to mutter, "How's your family?"

"Same as always, I guess." Tidoris's expression

loosened at its pinched edges. "Dad's still lining the pockets of émigré politicians to boost government stock in his company, and Mom's still smiling her way through second-tier galas in the First Sector. And both of them are still sufficiently disappointed in their spineless second son." He tried to cover his hurt tone with a chuckle, but Ciaan caught it.

"And what about their first son?"

"Melean?" Tidoris looked surprised by the question; Ciaan figured it was because she rarely mentioned his brother, much less expressed any interest in his wellbeing. Tidoris knew that they had a history, but he almost never asked about it.

"Oh, he's still spouting off the same p-pride propaganda garbage. I think he fancies himself to be a young politico now, since he's always going on and on about how there needs to be legislation to establish our inherent superiority over the weakened Earth race, blah blah blah." Tidoris mimicked a gag.

Ciaan scratched at the back of her neck. "Not our inherent superiority, Dori, *your* inherent superiority. I'm a worthless halfie, remember?"

"Don't say things like that, Ciaan," Tidoris snapped at her from the flickering screen. "It's trash, all that stuff about superiority and inferiority, and you know it. Only idiots listen to it."

"Yeah, too bad our world is run by idiots," Ciaan bit back coldly. "That's why Melean has such a promising career in politics, right?"

"No, my brother has such a promising career in politics because our father is paving the way for him with bribes. And even that can't get him a straight shot to the top. Why do you think he's been an under-clerk at the sector office for a year and a half now?"

Ciaan grunted noncommittally.

"Anyway"—Tidoris glanced down from the screen—"labor service isn't that bad. Is it on Toi?"

"Yeah, at the Central Port Zone base. The judge said I could live at home if my parents let me, and knowing my second mother, they will."

"The CPZ base?" Tidoris's eyebrows shot up. "Really?"

"Yeah. Why?" Ciaan squinted at him. "Is there something I need to know about it?"

"Only that we might be seeing more of each other than initially expected." A grin broke across Tidoris's face. "I've been commissioned as a Technical Advisor there."

"A Technical Advisor?" It came out louder than Ciaan had wanted it to, and she held her breath as shadows moved on the other side of the partition. When they faded away, she turned back and whispered, "When did that happen?"

"I got the letter a day or two ago." Tidoris beamed. "I thought that maybe Dad had pulled some strings for it, but he swears that he wouldn't have spent one p-bill on getting me such a pathetic excuse for a job."

He glanced down again and made a show of scratching his ear. "I mean, it isn't the most glamorous position and I won't really be in close proximity to the reserve workers, but it's something."

"Yeah." Ciaan agreed softly. "It's something, Dori. Hell, that's more than something—that's great! Now I won't want to kill myself for having to work there every day and I'll have company for the commute. And"—she leaned in a bit closer—"you get to do something you actually want to do, away from your *stimulating* family life. Win all around."

"Yes, well…" Tidoris trailed off, chewing at his bottom lip. "Actually, it *is* going to be away from my family life. The, um, the job requires me to be available at all times so I've been assigned living quarters there."

The last sentence tumbled out of his mouth so fast that it took a second before Ciaan could fully understand it. He watched her with apprehension, picking at his fingertips.

"Oh." Ciaan reconsidered her possibilities. She wouldn't say that life in her father and second mother's apartment was a joyride—especially not now that she was pushing on into her adult years—but it was safe and free and she didn't have to worry about new personalities showing up there and throwing off the balance. It was familiar. Barracks would mean uprooting her whole life, something she'd only done once before—when her first mother had left. She hadn't really cared for the experience then and she couldn't imagine it being any better this time around.

Then again, Tidoris was right. When was she going to leave home and get any sort of experience outside of her family? He was her only legitimate friend; everyone else she'd ever known had either been a bully or a thug. As each year passed people she'd known as p-kids grew up and disappeared, just like her first mother.

No, she corrected herself. Not like her first mother. But the end result was the same. They'd been there and then they weren't and meanwhile she kept staying, kept getting left behind. Sooner or later she'd turn around and the only person still there would be her, and then she didn't know what she would do.

"Well, then, I guess I'm going too." Ciaan folded her arms across her chest and repositioned herself at the edge of the bed. "I mean, I can't just leave you all alone out there. Who knows what'd happen? You'd probably get kidnapped by space pirates or something."

"There are no space pirates, Ciaan," Tidoris corrected her with his prim, intellectual tone—but the wide flush that spread across his cheeks ruined the effect. "It's only commissioned rogue ships that still comply with the government contracts they've signed."

"My mistake." Ciaan bowed in mock deference. "You'd probably get kidnapped by rogue ship captains who still comply with the government contracts they've signed, only that doesn't keep them from snatching up a defenseless, handsome young civilian every now and again for those lonely space nights."

"Yeah, probably." Tidoris toyed with his thick glasses but his mouth twitched at the corners. "So when do you start?"

"First thing next week. You?"

"Technically, I don't start for another two weeks, but I'm sure they'd let me move in early. After all, I only hold the entire fate of their interplanetary network devices in my hands."

Ciaan snorted. "Careful, Mr. Technical Advisor. You don't want all that power rushing to your head right away. I won't deal with another Melean in your family."

Tidoris snickered, then looked behind him, following the sound of a muffled voice. He turned back to the screen apologetically. "Guess that means it's dinner time for me. Are you going to be okay?"

"Yes, third mother." Ciaan rolled her eyes. "In a few days, I'll have no one but you nagging me. I'll probably want to strangle you before the month is over."

"Not if I want to strangle you first." Tidoris's hand disappeared behind the screen.

"Night, Ciaan."

"Night, Dori. Don't let your brother brainwash you in your sleep."

Tidoris chuckled one last time before the screen sputtered and went black. Ciaan caught her own dark reflection mirrored in the dead machine—it wavered there, trapped between stasis and motion.

The world was changing fast, and Ciaan wasn't sure if she'd be able to keep up with it.

[TWO]

"WAKE UP, CIAAN." A metallic voice sliced through Ciaan's sleep-muffled mind, and she groaned out into the stuffy darkness of the CPZ reserve barracks. "It is 5:45 in the morning on Monday the first of April. You have two new direct messages. Should I play them?"

Ciaan burrowed her face into the scratchy sheets of her barracks cot, pressed her pillow against the side of her head and tried to convince herself that she could trick her Right Hand into thinking she was already awake. It wasn't a great plan, but that hadn't stopped her from trying it on all the other mornings of her life.

"Your response time has lapsed. Please request *Delay* if you want to reschedule my alarm."

Ciaan exhaled, hot and sour, into the lumps of her pillow. If she hit *Delay*, she'd be late to first call and her superior officers would pitch a fit. She should move, should get up and get ready.

Instead, she curled up deeper in the sheets.

"Should I play your two new direct messages, Ciaan?"

"Fine!" she shouted at the device; it blinked back at her innocently from its secured dock on her locker lid at the foot of her bed. A few other recruits eyed her maliciously from across the room at the commotion, and the poor kid on the bed next to hers jolted awake and tumbled in a heap onto the floor.

She cleared her throat and lowered her voice. "Play messages."

A low, garbled sound started up and Ciaan quickly added, "Expand display."

The enlarged head of her younger step-sister filled the projected image, playing at the end of her cot like an old-fashioned movie theater. She dropped into the message midsentence.

"—weird around here and everyone says they miss you, even Briette. She did come over today and said we should get a pet now that there's room, though. But don't worry, Mom and Dad said we didn't need a pet and you weren't going to be gone forever. They really miss you too. I'm not supposed to tell you this, but Mom cried all day after you left. Even Dad couldn't cheer her up. Eerick is just glad that you aren't going to prison. He was so afraid that you'd get traded to space pirates and he'd never see you again, but I told him that was stupid because you said there aren't any space pirates. Well, it's almost time for breakfast so I'd better go. DM me when you can; I know Mom and Dad want to hear from you. Oh, and if anyone makes fun of your hair, make sure you punch them in the nose for me! But…don't do that if it'll get you in trouble. Maybe just say they fell down in the showers or something. Okay, well…bye, Ciaan!" The toothy smile of her fifteen year old step-sister faded out. Ciaan glared at the few people staring at her nearby, daring them to start something for waking them up.

Her second mother had already had two daughters from her first marriage before she'd met Ciaan's father. Briette had been nine when her mother had married again; Helona had only been four. Ciaan had been eight. The girls' first father had divorced their mother and Briette had spent the better part of their first year together as a new family not speaking to Ciaan or her father. She'd come around to him eventually but never really made her peace with Ciaan. In the beginning, Ciaan had held on to the secret hope that Briette would actually want to be her new big sister. But after a while, that hope crumpled and now Ciaan couldn't say who avoided who more. When Briette had announced last year that she was moving into her own apartment one sector over to be closer to her professional instruction facility, Ciaan had only shrugged. Briette was going to be a nurse, even though no one but Ciaan seemed to remember that Briette always said she hated being around sick people.

At least their parents could be proud of their oldest kid.

When their half-brother Eerick was born, Briette finally seemed to warm up to her second father. It was around that same time that Ciaan began to pull back, started spending more time with the nastier p-kids in their sector. If there was a cause and effect there, Briette and Ciaan both ignored it.

Eerick was eleven now and despite the family strains—or maybe because of them—he worried about his sisters like another father, always asking if they'd remembered their jackets and eaten more for breakfast than a supplement bar. Ciaan wasn't as close to her half-brother as she sometimes wished she could be, so she tried not to brush off his fussing too much. At least, not to his face.

But out of all the messages she could've woken up to, she was glad it was one from Helona, who'd always seemed to love her no matter how she acted. Ciaan could still remember the very first day her second mother and step-sisters had moved in—Briette stood there like a statue with big, silent tears running down her cheeks, clutching her tattered blanket and looking like this was the end of the world, while Helona walked right up to her step-sister with the strange light hair and threw her little arms around Ciaan's hips.

She'd shrieked gleefully, "Hello, new sister!"

Ciaan still chuckled at the memory.

"Should I store or delete this message?" her Right Hand repeated, snapping Ciaan back to the barracks and away from the hazy lost chances of her childhood.

"Store," she answered brusquely. "Play next message."

Tidoris's face, apprehensive and jittery, filled the empty air. "Hey, Ciaan. Sorry I couldn't get the transfer sooner. I know I said that before, but I'm gonna say it again so you know I'm really sorry. Anyway, I haven't heard anything about you getting yourself into trouble during your first two weeks in the reserves, so I don't feel too bad. Uh, anyway, I'm just DMing to remind you that I'll be coming onto the CPZ base at 7 this morning in case you want to see me or…whatever. They're running my orientation sessions this afternoon, so I should have time to move into my quarters and get familiar with the place before that. Maybe you can get a work assignment to assist me? I don't know how that works—but hey, it's worth suggesting, right? Oh, and I found out that my quarters are actually really close to the reserve barracks—and I pretty much have free schedules for eating and decompression time—so I could definitely eat with you and stuff. Yeah, so…I guess I'll see you soon? DM if your plans change." His face flickered darkly for a second, and Ciaan leaned in towards the projected screen. "And one last thing: my dad insisted that I have official transport to the base because no son of his was gonna show up for work in a shuttlecraft, blah blah blah. But, um, my official escort…Dad is making Melean escort me. Just so you know. I don't know if that's…a big deal…or anything…but I thought I'd give you a heads up. Later."

The screen went static and then blank; Ciaan swore under her breath.

"Should I store or delete this message?"

She was already out of her cot and tossing around scattered pieces of clothing before she shouted a muffled, "Delete!" *Where are my clean uniform sets?* she wondered frantically. "Right Hand, what time is it?"

"It is 5:56 morning time, Ciaan."

"Shit!"

Her second mother nagged her all the time about

being more organized, and if she could've seen Ciaan's barracks space, she would've been ashamed. Ciaan kept telling herself that she was going to at least start making two piles—one for used uniforms and one for clean ones—but somehow everything still managed to get shoved together under her cot.

First call was at 6:15 morning time and if a recruit wasn't there exactly on time, they were marked as "Unreported/Missing for Duty." One UMD mark got a recruit double chores and no decomp time the next day. Two UMD marks got that for a week. Three or more UMDs got the recruit a disciplinary hearing in front of their superiors and the base commanders, and if that went bad it could even get the recruit expelled. That meant jail for Ciaan. She'd only been seriously close to a UMD once when she'd slept through her morning alarm on the second day. She'd run into line just as they'd begun roll call. Since then she'd kept her alarm on maximum volume and slept more fitfully, dreaming about window-less rooms with figures in dark hoods all pointing ominous fingers at her. After a while, she got used to the fatigue and she hadn't had to race for first call since that day.

Just as she was about to grab a used uniform in desperation, Ciaan remembered the one spare pack that all reserves had in their lockers. She skidded to the end of her bed and fumbled with the lock code, promising herself that she'd sort through her stuff before she went to bed that night. The keypad finally beeped; she threw open the locker lid and dug around for the unopened plastic-sealed package. She found it at the very bottom of the container—under a dog-eared book on Earth fashions of the last century that her father had given her for her fifteenth birthday—and ripped it open, shredding the packaging before successfully getting the uniform out. Then it was down with the lid, on with the uniform, a quick ruffle of her sheets, and a swift kick of everything still on the floor under her bed again. She grabbed her Right Hand and ran past the cots of a few still-sleeping recruits, tearing off their blankets and barking at them to get up as she flew past.

At this rate, she thought to herself, *I might still be able to wash up and send a short message to Helona before first call.*

She was suddenly feeling more optimistic than usual and Tidoris's arrival had a lot to do with that. Every time the initial isolation and jarring strangeness of her new life away from home had started to choke her—usually late at night when she couldn't see anything in the blackness but her own fears—she told herself, *Dori is only a few days away.* Now that wait was over and she couldn't help but be a little eager about it. The only ugly spot in the whole thing was Melean, but Ciaan wasn't gonna let him ruin this for her.

She was so excited that it wasn't until she stepped into a puddle of cold water in the washroom and felt it seep through her socks that she realized she'd forgotten to grab her boots on the way out.

At 7 the entrance gates didn't open for any official transport vehicles. At 7:15, Ciaan began to flick her fingertips in irritation. By 7:30 she was pacing back and forth in the parking zone, waffling between frustrated and frightened. She wasn't really worried about an accident; p-planet transit collisions were so rare that she couldn't remember the last time she'd heard of one actually happening. What she was worried about were Tidoris's parents, particularly his father, changing their minds at the last minute and refusing to let him work as a lowly CPZ Technical Advisor. She was also hungry; she'd skipped breakfast after first call to go wait by the gates so that she'd be sure she was there when he arrived. She was just about ready to abandon her position and head to the mess hall when, at 7:47, the gates finally opened and a sleek black government craft pulled into the base.

Ciaan stood at attention; she didn't want to start screaming at the occupants until she was sure at least one of them was Tidoris. When she caught sight of his thick-framed glasses her shoulders relaxed and her hands balled into fists.

Tidoris saw her and sprinted around to the other side of the craft, already holding his arms out in defense.

"Look, Ciaan, I know we're late, but it isn't our fault…" He stopped a few feet in front of her like he was hesitant about getting any closer.

"Do you know how long I've been out here waiting?" she growled. "Breakfast only runs 'til eight, and thanks to you I'm gonna miss it."

"I know, I know, I'm sorry." Tidoris took a small step forward, squeaking his soles across the metal ground. "Maybe Melean can ask the shift commander if you can have a little more time?"

Ciaan glared at him. "Don't you dare. I don't want any favors from *him*."

"Well, technically it wouldn't really be a favor since it's sort of his fault that we're late." Tidoris chewed at the corner of his lip.

Ciaan hooked up one eyebrow. "What?"

"He, um, got held up at his sector office this morning and then couldn't get the craft released until almost 7. I tried to take a shuttle, but Dad—"

"Fine!" Ciaan hissed, cutting him off sharp. "Whatever."

Tidoris's mouth clamped shut.

Ciaan closed her eyes and blinked slowly once, twice, three times. She breathed out hot through her teeth. "There's nothing we can do about it now. At least you got here in one piece and your dad hasn't gotten you fired or anything. Yet."

Tidoris exhaled too, faster than her, and let out a nervous chuckle. "Yeah, well, we'll see if his connections still have reach in here. But for now let's get my stuff unpacked and…"

He trailed off as the steady click of crisp-heeled shoes approached them. They hit the metal ground with a clack that echoed just inside Ciaan's ears. Tidoris glanced between her and toes of his scuffed boots and back again.

"I see that you still don't feel like the regulations apply to you and your *special* hair, Miss Gennett." The way Melean talked now seemed so different from how he'd sounded seven years ago. His voice had been full of bubbling rage then, crude and coarse and hateful. Ciaan could still hear that hatefulness—she wondered if it'd ever really go away—but it was coated now with a hollow layer of sophistication and culture. *He must've picked up some tricks from rubbing elbows at his father's political functions and his mother's galas*, she thought sourly. Now that he had the superficial air of an important p-person, he could afford to be patronizingly polite to his inferiors.

Pulling at his fingers, Tidoris muttered, "Shut up."

Melean didn't acknowledge his brother's retort; he was pinpoint-focused on Ciaan.

They were almost the same height now —he'd stopped growing just around the time she'd started— although both of them were still shorter than Tidoris (who everyone said was tall even by Earth standards). Melean's clean-pressed brown suit blended against his skin, which was lighter than his brother's, and his thick braids were trimmed at precise regulation length.

Tidoris had thinner braids, unevenly spaced with a few strands of thick curled hair escaping out of them, which added to his usual frazzled appearance. He was still in his civilian clothes; he probably wouldn't have to even wear the same rust-colored uniform that was assigned to the reserves.

Against the muddy red-brown of that uniform, Ciaan's light braids—which now hung to the middle of her back when she didn't bundle them on top of her head—stood out even more. It'd been the first thing the other reserves noticed—it was the first thing that everyone noticed—and some of them still made occasional comments about it. And even though they were now wound into a tight and secure bun set high on her head, it was the first thing Melean saw too.

It's probably the only thing he sees, she told herself.

"Last I heard, Official von Ulger, was that you were an underclerk for sector street maintenance and not actually in charge of regulating what I do with my person," she replied, the same sugar-fake politeness as him. Tidoris gaped at her. "Please correct me if I'm wrong."

"You're not wrong—at least not about my position." He tried to mask it with smugness, but Ciaan could still hear the edge of defensiveness in his tone. "However, as a faithful servant of our planet's government, it is my duty to promote compliance with *all* of our laws. It's the only way to ensure that order and security is maintained."

Ciaan snorted. "I suppose you'd like to cut my braids to regulation length yourself then, since they're such a threat to the stability of our society?"

Melean smiled, familiar and cruel. He dropped his voice to just above a whisper. "Oh, Miss Gennett, I'd like to do more than just *cut* your braids."

Ciaan gritted her teeth and swallowed against a dry throat. "Are you threatening me?"

"Not at all." His smile peeled back to a contemptuous smirk. "Really, it isn't my place to enforce personal appearance regulations. That should come from your own sense of dignity and decency. If I were you, I'd be embarrassed by the color—it's such a pathetic cry for attention—and just dye it. Then again, your hair isn't the only way you strive for attention, is it? I mean, just by looking at your arrest and conviction record, it's clear—"

"That's enough, Melean!" Tidoris shouted, his gangly limbs shaking like overwound tethers. Melean jolted, obviously surprised by his brother's reaction, and leaned back from Ciaan.

Tidoris squared his shoulders and sighed. "Just…stop it."

As the three of them stood there in an uncomfortable silence, Ciaan started feeling a little guilty for upsetting Tidoris so much. After all these years she didn't really consider what'd happened between her and Melean to be anything more than a twisted sort of game, but Tidoris took most things at face value and he seemed to feel their attacks more acutely than either one of the actual players did. She wanted Melean to leave so she could apologize to Tidoris without looking soft to his brother, but no one was making the first move. After a long beat, Tidoris offered her a sad half-smile.

"I'm sorry you missed breakfast because of us, Ciaan. I'll talk to your supervisor about getting you more time—or at least letting you to eat during your chores, if you want."

Ciaan rubbed at a kink in her shoulder. "Don't worry about it. I won't starve to death before lunch."

Suddenly—like someone had dumped a bucket of ice water on him—Melean turned sharp and stormed away. The click of his shoes was quicker now, more agitated, and Ciaan and Tidoris both watched his dark coat flutter out behind him.

"I'm sorry about all that, Dori. I didn't think it'd get that bad that fast." Ciaan didn't look at Tidoris, but instead stared behind him where Melean was discussing something with a base commander. "We haven't seen each other in so long…but I guess neither one of us really outgrew our bad blood."

Tidoris shrugged like it wasn't a big deal, even though Ciaan knew it was. "It's actually kind of nice to see him act like a dumb twenty-two-year-old every once in a while, instead of some clone of Dad. He's always so dead at home, and everywhere else really, so a little bit of emotion out of him is refreshing." Tidoris paused. "Even if it's a bad kind of emotion."

"I'm just glad that didn't end in a fistfight like last time." Ciaan chuckled; Tidoris didn't. She'd forgotten that she never told him what'd really happened between her and Melean that night seven years ago. His eyes were wide like moons behind his glasses.

"Don't look at me like that. You might as well know now that I began my life of violent crime courtesy of your brother when I was thirteen." She grimaced; her jaw twinged with a phantom hit. "He was a dirty fighter then and he's a dirty fighter now."

Tidoris took another tentative step forward, like he might be making some sort of move to comfort her. Without meaning to, she flinched. He froze, turned his attention back to his boots. The two of them stood there, stiff and awkward, until Ciaan heard someone calling her name.

"Gennett!" The base commander who'd been talking with Melean was waving her over. She grabbed Tidoris's sleeve and dragged him away from the craft, desperately hoping that Melean hadn't used what little sway he had to get her removed from the reserves.

"Private Gennett," repeated the base commander when they reached him. Ciaan saluted him and stood at attention, holding her breath. "Have you had breakfast?"

"Uh." The question caught her off guard, made her sputter. "No, no I have not, sir."

"Why is that, Gennett?"

"Because I was waiting for Tid—Technical Advisor von Ulger. He was scheduled to arrive at 7 morning time but was delayed until 7:45, sir."

"Was that an assignment of yours, Private Gennett?"

"No, sir." Ciaan's blood pounded in her ears.

"Then why were you waiting for him?" The base commander didn't sound angry, so Ciaan decided to take a chance and tell him the truth.

"Because he's my friend, sir, and I promised him that I would help him move in."

"On your own time?"

Ciaan dug her nails into the palms of her fists. "Yes, sir."

"Well, then, private, your request for an extra thirty minutes for breakfast is approved. Report to your superior no later than 8:30 for your chores. Understood?"

Ciaan didn't really understand, since she was being approved for a request she hadn't even made yet, but she nodded anyway. "Yes, sir."

"Good. You can thank your friend here for persuading me." The commander dropped a hand on Melean's shoulder, knocking him forward. Melean cringed slightly but flashed a full-teeth smile at the superior officer. "Now go to the mess hall before I change my mind."

"Uh, but, sir…" Ciaan stuttered out; the commander raised an eyebrow. "What about TA von Ulger's move in?"

"You can assist TA von Ulger on your own time— when you have it again." The commander squeezed

Melean's shoulder. "I'm sure he'll get all the help he needs right now from his brother."

Tidoris looked between her and Melean, baffled, and honestly Ciaan wasn't that far behind him. But before either of them could come up with something coherent to say, Melean stepped forward and slid his arm across Tidoris's back, maneuvering them both towards the parking zone.

As they walked away, Ciaan could hear Melean talking smooth and soothing to his brother: "I'll help you get settled now, and you'll see her at lunch in a few hours anyway. Besides, you need to check in with your own supervisor and pick up all your equipment…you'll be so busy that it'll be lunchtime before you know it…" His coaxing trailed off and Ciaan could feel the insistent gaze of the base commander behind her.

Unable to make any sense out of what just happened, Ciaan decided to follow her new orders for now and analyze the rest of it later. She turned and saluted the commander once more, then marched off towards the mess hall.

Maybe it's just hunger playing games with my head, she mused. *Because otherwise, Melean just did something nice for me and there is no sane explanation for that.*

If she was a little less cynical, or if Melean was a little less…Melean, she might've taken a kind gesture like this at face value. Or maybe as a sign that she ought to reevaluate his character and its flaws, reconsider his potential for growth. But she *was* cynical and he *was* Melean and this whole thing felt more like some sort of devious plan disguised as benevolence than a genuine olive branch. If he couldn't kill her with his bare hands, he might as well try to rip her apart in more subtle and complicated ways.

She mulled it over as she chewed at the soggy breakfast leftovers, so distracted that she didn't realize it was 8:27 until the kitchen workers began stacking up the chairs to get ready for lunch prep. She gulped down the rest of the meal and—for the second time that day—Ciaan found herself running for a call and frantically trying not to get a UMD, cursing Melean in the worst ways she knew how the whole way there.

[THREE]

"**C**HECK THE AIR FILTERS and vitals tanks and unload the second cargo compartment." A wide man draped in bright, exotic sashes crooned at Ciaan and the other recruits milling near the port gate. She guessed that he was a fabrics merchant—probably with a stock of illegal dyes and definitely with a fashion flair that First-tier wives would drool over—but she hadn't seen anyone as gaudy as him since she started her training a few months ago. He had to be one though, since no one else would've been allowed to break clothing codes so brazenly—especially on a Port base.

"Ah, my dear friend! There you are!" The merchant swung his heavy arms open, waiting for an approaching official, and almost knocked over a passing reserve worker.

The official—clean-cut and all sharp angles, with a sleek government suit and shiny tight braids—smiled like a snarl. He waved off his security flanks and held his arms open too, though not as wide as the merchant's.

They embraced, firm but cold, and the merchant chuckled. "Perhaps I shouldn't address you so informally here, High Official Yeager."

There wasn't any wind in the base but the sashes fluttered, following his exaggerated gestures.

"Perhaps you shouldn't." Yeager was darker than his friend and wore his age more elegantly. He nodded in Ciaan's direction; the merchant spun towards her.

"You, basic! What are you staring at? Didn't I give you enough work to do?" The merchant's face flushed red and purple, stained like one of his scarves. It was only then that Ciaan realized the rest of the recruits had already scattered to start working on the ship, while she'd been standing around staring and getting herself blatantly caught.

She was just about to turn and duck into the gate when the high official glanced at her again. This time his eyes lingered, gaze hardening with a familiar disdain.

"What's your census number, girl?"

The condescending *girl* stung more than the rude *basic*, and Ciaan felt her temper creeping up, prickled with fear. She stuffed them down both and stood up straighter.

"My apologies, High Official. And to you, sir." She nodded deferentially towards the merchant, who'd crossed his arms over as much of his large frame as he could.

"I got lost in my thoughts for a minute—I meant no offense."

The merchant shifted to a broader, more imposing stance. She stumbled on with her explanation.

"And if I may speak frankly"—she pitched her tone up, hoped that it sounded convincingly awestruck—"I was admiring your sashes. As I'm sure you can tell, I've lived on this p-planet my whole life and I've never seen such…"

She grasped for the most effective word.

"…*superior* clothing before."

The merchant's lips twitched up at the corners and his arms went a little looser. Yeager didn't seem as moved by Ciaan's speech, so she doubled down on his friend.

"I know that's no excuse, though, since you probably get this kind of reaction everywhere you trade." Ciaan went for the full effect and bit her lip. "I mean, except Earth. You must blend right in there."

At the comparison to an Earth human—flattery that worked on even the nastiest p-people—a soppy, patronizing smile spread across the merchant's face.

"So sad—pitiful, really." He looked sympathetically at Yeager, who raised one thin eyebrow in return. "It makes you want to *do* something for them, doesn't it? After all, we come from the same place—these project planets—"

The merchant paused. His expression soured, like the phrase left a bad taste in his mouth.

"And even if you and I did make something better for ourselves, I still feel a bit of guilt for leaving others to wallow in this…this menial life." He gestured at everything and nothing, but Ciaan knew what he meant. And she agreed with him, but not enough to want his pity.

"I don't know, Moises, this one seems to be doing all right for herself." Yeager shot her a brief, penetrating look. "We never did get your name or number, recruit."

"Well, sir…" Ciaan searched for a distraction, something to deflect the official's knife-edge instincts.

He reminded her of Melean in a way, or at least what she knew Melean aspired to be. What he'd never achieve unless he let go of his warm, human rage.

Huddled near the control rooms, Ciaan spotted Tidoris chatting with another recruit. The girl was long and lean and her uniform set wasn't spotted with unidentified smudges and the occasional unmended tear, which meant that either she wasn't a labor recruit or she was just clean and organized. Either way, it meant she wasn't like Ciaan.

Tidoris held his bulky work Right Hand—the one provided for all non-recruit employees and designated for CPZ base-related use only—against his chest and bounced on his heels. He was nervous and Ciaan could see why: the recruit was pretty. Her dark, glossy braids were loose and swung soft against her ears and forehead, and when she laughed her eyes wrinkled up like Ciaan's dirty nightshirts.

It bothered her, but not because Tidoris was flirting with some other girl. It bothered her because he was flirting with some other girl instead of coming and helping get her out of this interrogation.

The other basics in her unit were still working on the merchant's ship, a little too enthusiastic for her liking. It was just after lunch and most of the officers and staff had decomp time, so the base was quiet and—as her luck always seemed to have it—distraction-free. At the far end of the ports, a group of people—mostly, from what Ciaan could tell, young women—were being loaded onto a waiting ship. They were making a lot of fuss, but no one was paying any attention to it.

Probably being shipped off to a detention center or labor site, she thought bitterly.

Ciaan was about ready to break down and ask if she was being reported when a thick shadow blotted out the stars above the artificial atmosphere layers.

Ships were restricted from flying directly over the base for security reasons; special docking channels had been designed to prevent it, but that didn't stop inexperienced or regulation-bending captains from ignoring them and the port zone protocols. It still threw Ciaan off guard when it happened, though, and she noticed that even Yeager glanced up as the shadow slid off of him.

The space gate next to the merchant's port started beeping, loud and urgent, as a derelict cargo ship pulled up to hover in front of it. Ciaan looked around to see who was going to take this docking; when no one stepped up to the gate, she realized this was the perfect distraction and rushed over to the port switches without waiting to be dismissed.

She held down the intercom signal until the line crackled through. "Vessel, this is Toi Central Port Zone base gate 13. Please identify your captain or commanding officer and state your docking purpose."

Static buzzed on the other end for a few seconds before a voice cut in.

"Gate 13, this is the EAU registered cargo ship *Maelstrom* and I am Captain Mael Moon. Our purpose is refueling and minor repairs. Estimated docking time is two days, one night."

"Copy, Captain Moon." Ciaan groaned at the captain's name; the biggest crime of space travel had to be the stupid puns it inspired.

She put in her ear plugs and entered the space gate code, waited for the blast of combustion and metal coming in from the suck of space. For all the frenzy its name implied, the *Maelstrom* puttered and hiccupped its way to the dock and finally let itself down with a rusty wheeze. Ciaan punched in a few more codes and initiated the locking gears.

A hand dropped suddenly on her shoulder and Ciaan whirled around, fist already cocked back. Tidoris dodged fast and raised his arms, half in surrender and half in protection.

She shook out her fist and pulled out her ear plugs, shouting over the clatter of the ship powering down. "Shit, Dori! You scared the hell out of me. You saw me docking that ship, right?"

Tidoris nodded sheepishly, then held out his Right Hand.

Ciaan snorted. "Are you my third mother *and* my supervisor now?"

Regulations stated that vessel names, registration codes, and crew manifests had to be entered into the base's digital system before a ship was cleared, but since recruits usually monitored docking and none of them had base Right Hands, things usually got filed after the fact. Tidoris kept nagging her to document her dockings right away in case any problems came up later—that way, she wouldn't be blamed for them—so most days he shoved his base Right Hand at her at least once.

She grabbed it from him with a grunt.

"I do outrank you," he muttered, wiping the exhaust off his glasses.

Ciaan rolled her eyes and started typing in the information she had. She got through the ship's and captain's names and was just getting to the Union registration when she felt Tidoris go rigid next to her; she looked up from the screen.

High Official Yeager and his merchant friend Moises were walking towards them. Ciaan had assumed—had *hoped*—that they'd lose interest in her, but apparently, they hadn't.

"High Official Yeager, good afternoon." Tidoris bowed low—customary from one official to their senior— and Yeager acknowledged him with a nod.

"Tidoris von Ulger, I thought that was you. The last I heard, your father was hoping to send you to the High Technical Training Academy." He scanned Tidoris up and down with small, dispassionate eyes. "What are you doing here?”

“I’m a Technical Advisor for this base, sir,” he said, the hint of pride in his soft voice making Ciaan bite back a smile. After a beat, he added, “I got the position by myself.”

“Ah.” Yeager paused, like the topic had turned distasteful. His eyes flicked to Ciaan.

“Do you know this basic?”

Tidoris started at the term; Ciaan jabbed a warning elbow at his ribs. He coughed a little to hide to jostle between them.

“This recruit is a friendly acquaintance from primary grades.” Tidoris cleared his throat. “Is there an issue with her?”

Whether Dori knew what he was doing or not, Ciaan silently thanked him for not revealing her name.

The merchant, obviously distressed by being left out of a conversation, interrupted loudly.

“No, no, no issue with her. The poor child was merely mesmerized by luxury items that have clearly been out of reach in her life.” He smoothed a thick hand over his sashes.

“Yes,” Tidoris answered slowly. “Most p-people can’t imagine owning such…colorful pieces.”

Behind them, something teetered and crashed. The merchant flailed his arms, howling like a crate of rare imported birds.

"What do you think you're doing, you brainless little basic?! Do you have any idea how much these cost? Who'll be wearing them?" The merchant stormed back to his port dock, where one of the recruits had dropped a cheap-looking chest overstuffed with ruffles.

He loomed over the cowering boy—a year or two younger than Ciaan at least—and jabbed a finger in his face. "I could buy your life for half the price of one of these fabrics, and sell it for even less!"

Disgust welled up from deep within Ciaan; she wanted to march over and snap that fat finger in half. She might've done it, too, if something at her own half-processed port hadn't started obnoxiously clanging.

A stubby, only partially groomed man stood on the other side of the port gate. His face looked like it'd tried to grow several small patches of beard without much success, and he was bald except for a thin ring of hair between his ears and uneven sideburns.

He blinked twice then yelled, "Can you open this door now?!"

Ciaan looked back at Tidoris, and they both turned to Yeager.

"I'm afraid that I need to supervise this recruit with her docking. She's only in her fifth month of training." Tidoris feigned an apology, adjusting his glasses. The lens glinted in the hard, artificial light. "You know how it is, High Official Yeager."

"Yes I do, TA von Ulger." Yeager's words weren't contemptuous per se, but they didn't sound nice either. He continued brusquely, "I'll see you later, no doubt. Give your father my regards and tell him that he and your mother will be expected at this year's Earth Gala."

"I will, sir." Tidoris bowed once more; Yeager didn't return it.

As soon as the high official was gone, Ciaan raced over to the port and entered the door code, grateful for Dori—even if he did occasionally flirt with other recruits instead of bothering her.

"So what was *that* all about?"

Tidoris and Ciaan were trailing after the squat, disheveled man—one of the grubby civilian crew members from the cargo ship. People who wanted to travel and weren't too picky about accommodations usually signed up for short runs; Ciaan would've assumed that this man was from the p-planets, except that his tufts of hair were matted instead of braided.

I guess even Earth humans get dirty sometimes, she

mused.

"What was what all about?" Ciaan tapped a few random keys on the Right Hand screen, trying to look like she was busy and not dodging his question.

"You know what."

They ducked under a wing and stopped short. The crewman held out a grimy hand and scanned the area, more like a reflex than a warning.

"Wait." The man lowered his arm slow, craned his neck around to look at them. "Here."

Ciaan scoffed at the dramatics as the crewman waddled away and disappeared behind the hull.

"You know what," Tidoris repeated, a little more emphatically. "You and HO Yeager. Why were you stirring up trouble with him?"

"Thanks for the support, Dori," Ciaan bit out. "What makes you think that I was the one stirring up trouble?"

Tidoris sighed. "Because you're always the one stirring up trouble, Ciaan. And even if you weren't stirring up trouble, Yeager isn't someone you want *disagreeing* with you. He's not even really someone that you want *agreeing* with you."

Ciaan grunted noncommittally and kept punching in the ship's specifications.

Tidoris grabbed her arm, hard and fast, and she

jolted in surprise—not really because of the gesture so much as because it was Tidoris doing it.

His eyes were bright and fixed on her.

"I'm serious. Official Yeager is a cunning officer and a ruthless man. He's destroyed people's lives just because they irritated him. If you knew some of the stories my father's heard about him…and you know how my father is himself…" Tidoris trailed off with a small shudder. "My father wouldn't let Melean accept a position under Yeager, so that should tell you something."

It did, though Ciaan wasn't sure exactly what. She patted Tidoris's hand and he loosened his grip.

"Promise me you'll avoid him as much as you can. Like, completely, if at all possible." He squeezed her arm for emphasis, then let go.

Ciaan met his gaze and held it. "I promise. As long as he doesn't wear any bright scarves."

She laughed and—after trying to stifle it under sternness—Tidoris did too.

"So what was *your* thing all about? Back by the control rooms?" Ciaan poked him in the shoulder.

Tidoris cocked his head to the side. "What?"

"You know what." She pointed at the control rooms, waggled her eyebrows.

He stared at her blankly. "No, I actually don't."

"She was pretty." Ciaan offered, trying to sound

casual. She flipped through some tabs on the Right Hand screen.

After a few awkward moments, she groaned loud and exasperated. "The recruit! The one you were talking to—or flirting with, really."

Tidoris's mouth dropped open; she let out a couple hard laughs as tension she didn't know she had rushed out of her body.

"Oh, God, Dori, don't look so offended. It's not like flirting is against regulations, even if you're bad at it."

It was a cruel thing to say and not even totally accurate—Ciaan knew that—but it was out before she could stop herself, before she could decide if she really wanted to say it or not. The tips of Tidoris's ears reddened, but against his dark skin, it was barely noticeable.

The grin slipped from Ciaan's face. She chewed on the inside of her cheek until it was raw.

"Sorry."

Out of all the people in the world who Ciaan had owed apologies to over the years, Tidoris was the only person who always got a sincere one. She told herself that that meant something, to both of them. At least it meant that he always forgave her, even if she sometimes thought she didn't deserve it.

"You don't have to apologize—not for what you said

about my flirting, anyway." He half-smiled, his ears redder. "It *is* pretty pathetic."

"Inexperienced," Ciaan countered.

He chuckled. "I will, however, accept the apology for your misunderstanding, because I wasn't flirting with that recruit."

Ciaan tilted her head. "Really?"

"Yes, really." Tidoris crossed his arms, mimicking his official stance. "We were just discussing the damaged wiring between the control rooms and the Administrative Headquarters. It's been a huge headache for all the technical recruits and AH has really been on us about how to fix it, because they can't get accurate docking records except from manual uploads from individual Right Hands now." His forehead wrinkled; it was his best Serious Technical Advisor expression. "But the thing is, we can't do anything about the wiring without authorization from the sector communications office and to do that, AH has to request an inspection from them, which they don't want to do because they think it's undermining their authority on the base..."

He trailed off with an angry groan and Ciaan wondered, not for the first time, why someone like Dori would choose to work in the government. But she didn't really feel like getting into a rant about bureaucratic bullshit at the moment, so she waited quietly for him to recollect himself.

After a long minute of Tidoris silently fuming, Ciaan prompted him. "Anyway."

"Yeah, anyway." He shook off his annoyance. "Anyway, that was what we were talking about. You must've confused my work anxiety for…another kind of anxiety." Tidoris added sarcastically, "It's an easy mistake to make, I know."

She smirked.

"And for your information," Tidoris continued, "if I was looking for someone to flirt successfully with, it wouldn't be Private Sidthe. She's alternative."

Ciaan perked up. "Oh, so I can try my luck then?"

Tidoris huffed, "Like you'd be any better at it."

She shoved him away playfully.

"Now that's something I'd like to see," a new voice boomed behind them, bold and just a little mocking. They both jumped at it.

Ciaan fumbled to catch the Right Hand she'd almost dropped while Tidoris rubbed at the back of his head where he'd hit it on the ship's wing. When Ciaan turned around, she saw an Earth man grinning smugly behind them.

His hair was dark, but not like Tidoris's; it was straight and floppy and cut into blunt layers that hung over one side of his forehead. The rest was short like black needles—so short on the sides that she could see his scalp. His body was solid but not bulky or tall; he was shorter than Tidoris by almost a head. He was wearing what looked like an old, red pilot's jacket and a military set with thick, low boots. The colors were faded and mismatched and the jacket hung open, exposing a tight, graying undershirt. The fabric clung to him and shaped his body—unlike the formless recruit uniform sets or even the officer sets that Tidoris was allowed to wear—and made him look both appealing and untrustworthy.

But the biggest difference was his face. His skin was paler than the stubby crewman's, though that might've just been because he washed it more frequently. He was tan, and a few scars dotted his cheeks and neck. His face seemed open and vast—with sharp, dark eyes and a broad nose anchoring his features. He looked different than anyone she'd ever seen before, but Ciaan wasn't sure that she could explain how if someone asked her.

The stranger glanced between the two of them, lingering on Ciaan's hair and Tidoris's face. It felt like he was waiting for them to do something, and when they didn't, he just shook his head.

"Why are you two looking at me like you've never seen an Earth person before?"

Ciaan suddenly realized what that vague difference was—she *hadn't* seen an Earth person before, not really.

At least not an Earth person who actually looked like what she'd always imagined them to be.

"Who are you?" Tidoris muttered it like a little kid, but at least he'd said something. Ciaan was glad that he'd been the one to sound stupid first.

"Ah, thank you! One of them can actually talk." He made an elaborate flourish with his hand. "I'm Mael Moon—*Captain* Mael Moon—and this is my ship."

He propped one hand on his hip and slapped the other on the rusted hull then paused, tilting his chin up at a haughty angle. He wasn't looking *at* them now, but *past* them, with a wistful gaze.

Tentatively, Tidoris turned and glanced behind them too. Ciaan rolled her eyes and kept silent. Eventually, the captain's expression started to wilt and he dropped his hand from the hull.

"Well, you two are just buckets of fun, aren't you?" He grimaced but didn't wait for an answer. "Did I talk to one of you over the intercom? If not, could you please direct me to that more intelligent life form?"

Indignation sparked in Ciaan and she couldn't choke it down.

"You're not so charming yourself, Moon." She hadn't meant to bark the words or use such an informal title, but it was too late now. The captain stared at her in surprise and Tidoris shot her a warning look—base regulations stated that all titled persons be addressed as such unless they requested otherwise.

Ciaan supposed that included arrogant cargo ship junker captains too.

She gritted her teeth, swallowed down the burn of her temper. "I was the recruit who docked you, Captain Moon. If you'd prefer, I can request a change of liaison for the short duration of your docking."

She started marching to the port door, hoping to get out of being bullied by a glorified space cargo-craft driver for the next few days.

"Wait!"

Damn it—Ciaan stopped just out of reach of the port door switches—*almost made it*. She turned and walked back to where Tidoris was still standing, mouth slightly open.

Ciaan glared at him—*You owe me*.

"I don't want to change recruits." Moon schmoozed like Melean, she thought, sly and self-satisfied. "I like you."

"I'm flattered," Ciaan replied, not even trying to sound genuine. "But I don't think likeability is the most suitable quality for a docking supervisor. I'm sure I can find a more competent and experienced recruit for you."

She caught Tidoris's eye and nodded towards the port gate. He hesitated, shifting from foot to foot.

"What's the matter?" Moon prodded. "Do you not like *me*?"

The question tripped Ciaan up; she hadn't been expecting it. But his confidence, the way he said it like he already knew the answer, set her straight again.

"I don't even know you." She spoke cool and dismissive.

A grin spread across the captain's face like an infection. His eyes flicked to Tidoris.

"What about you? Do *you* like me?"

Tidoris blinked fast like his eyes were on fire, fiddled with the rims of his glasses and, for some reason, Ciaan remembered what he'd said about flirting.

"I—I," he stuttered, then cleared his throat and drew himself up to his full height. "I don't believe that is an appropriate question for a Central Port Zone base officer or, for that matter, a recruit. But, *Captain Moon*, if you'd like a truthful answer then no—I don't like you."

For a moment the air sizzled between the three of them, then the captain laughed out rich and loud. "I like you too."

If she hadn't been so annoyed by the captain, Ciaan probably would've been laughing at Tidoris's stunned expression too. Moon clapped a hand on Tidoris's shoulder—Tidoris winced at the force of it—and they all stood there while the captain's guffaws slowed to wheezes.

When he finally caught his breath again Captain Moon put his hands back on his hips and said seriously, "All right then. Where can a space captain get some fuel around here?"

[FOUR]

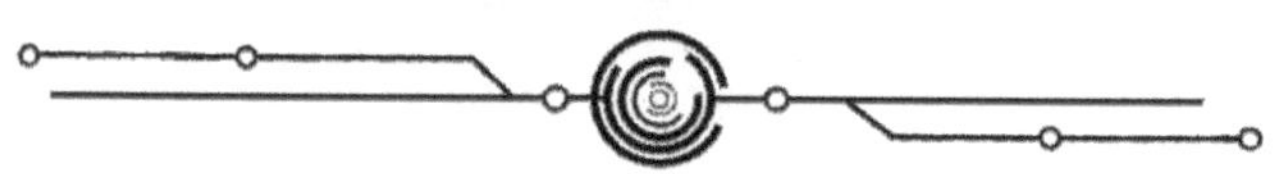

"I DON'T LIKE THIS, CIAAN." Tidoris jittered next to her, whispering pinched and breathy.

They stood watching the handful of scraggly crew members unload dented barrels and chipped shipping containers; on the other side of the ship, a first-week recruit was prepping the tank for refueling.

"Yeah, you said that already, Dori." Ciaan typed in shorthand notes—size, color, shape, condition—for each of the cargo pieces. A couple feet away from them, two of the crew members were fumbling with the port weight scale.

"Hey! You two! Don't drop containers on the scale like that!" Ciaan waved frantically at them, tried to sound strict and authoritative. "I don't care how light they are; it's gonna be my ass if they get broken—so please, keep it gentle."

They muttered something too low for her to hear, but eased the next cargo piece onto the scale. She nudged Tidoris, flashed him a cocky smile, and saw the stress lines etch across his forehead.

She sighed heavy through her nose.

"What's the big deal? Yeah, that captain's a pain in the ass, but so are like 90% of the other captains we deal with. Something about flying around in space and egomania, right?"

Something popped out and rattled inside the hull. Ciaan shouted to the new recruit, "Everything okay over there?"

A small, greasy fist peeked out from behind the ship with a thumbs-up.

"Just slipped the latch!" a muffled voice called back.

Ciaan rubbed her temples. Each new monthly batch of recruits seemed worse than the last; she was sure she'd never been as useless as some of them.

Tidoris shifted next to her, tinkered with the pocket flaps on his uniform set. Ciaan nudged him again and he shrugged.

"I mean, who talks to officers and recruits like that?"

Ciaan scoffed. "Everyone. And you'd know that if you didn't spend most of your time in the tunnels fixing fuses. You know, Dori, I think you just don't like him and you're looking for any excuse you can find to justify it."

"I am not." Tidoris's voice cracked; he coughed it out, hitting his chest a few times with his fist. "I mean, it's true that I don't like him, but he's done more than enough to justify that on his own."

Ciaan hummed vaguely in agreement.

"No, it's something else..." Tidoris continued, shaking his head. "We don't know anything about him—or his ship. What's in those containers? We don't know. They could be banned animals or chemical substances or—or children! He could be a space pirate!"

Tidoris jutted his jaw out stubbornly, but only sounded half-convinced himself.

Ciaan didn't look up from her data input screen. "Yes, a space pirate. You got it. And he's come here to our little p-planet just to bother you."

Tidoris huffed and Ciaan finally closed the file, telling herself that she'd finish it before decomp. She nodded at the *Maelstrom*.

"Speaking of our space pirate, where'd he go?"

They both scanned the area, suddenly aware of the captain's absence.

"He's probably gone to commandeer some of our base supplies." Tidoris crossed his arms in a pout.

Ciaan ignored him.

She flagged down the stubby crewman they'd met before; he seemed to be in charge of the others.

"Crewperson, where is Captain Moon?"

The man wiped a smear of sweat off his forehead. "Don't know. Probably on the ship with the first officer. They like to negotiate deliveries on arrival."

Ciaan scratched at the scalp between her braids—she thought this man *was* the first officer.

"How far are you traveling with this ship?"

"This is it." He gestured to the base, and Toi, collectively. "Just took a short run—one month. But that's longer than the rest of these fools. Most of 'em got on at our last Earth stop. And we all get off here—captain's orders."

"But this is just a refueling, right? Why would Captain Moon change his whole crew here?" Suspicions started to itch at the back of Ciaan's mind, but she pushed them out.

She'd been listening to Tidoris too much.

"The captain likes to keep his crew small and refreshed." The man sounded a lot less worried about the situation. "If he's not taking full cargo, he'll only have two or three crew members. And if he's got no cargo, then it's just him and the first officer. As for short runs, well, the longer a crewmate rides the more time they have to get in trouble—and the captain'll get the blame for that. Besides, a crew's gotta be fed and insured and that takes money."

"And Captain Moon doesn't have money?" Ciaan asked doubtfully.

"Oh, money he's got." The man grinned with only half a mouthful of teeth. "He just wants to keep as much of it as he can."

Ah, Ciaan nodded. *That makes more sense.*

"Anyway, we're unloading here and he'll have an empty cargo bay, so that means—"

"An empty crew list." Ciaan finished the sentence for him. "You know a lot about Captain Moon's habits, don't you?"

The man shrugged, face blank. "Been on a few runs with him, that's all. Paid me fair, always been decent to the crews, and he keeps a good ship."

"Well, thank you for this information." Ciaan started moving towards the main deck hatch. "I think I'll go and take a look around the ship myself, just for a standard protocols check."

"Sure, but be careful."

Ciaan hesitated at the man's wary tone.

"The captain doesn't like people messin' with his ship and makin' problems. The *Maelstrom*'s all his pride in the worlds." He patted the re-seamed hull affectionately.

"I'm sure it is," Ciaan mumbled.

The man squinted at her but she didn't say anything else. Instead, she checked that Tidoris was still managing the unloading process and reached up to release the hatch handle before ducking inside.

Ciaan's cheap reserve boots thudded against the metal walkways, echoing in the confined space of the ship. It was larger than it looked from outside—though it definitely wasn't spacious—and there was no lacquer or ornamentation, which surprised Ciaan. She'd expected someone like Captain Moon to be just as flashy with his interior design as he was with his personality. But the halls were bare: clean and well-lit but also old and a little worse for wear. Her second mother would've called it quaint; Ciaan called it a totally unspecial, completely average cargo ship.

She wandered around—found the cargo hatch, the cramped dining hall, the crew bunks, the communal bathroom—and noted that it felt eerily similar to the reserve barracks, only more compact. Some of the newer or more luxurious ships had things like Enjoyment

Rooms with transmission archives and interplanetary coms, but the *Maelstrom* didn't. Ciaan supposed that an ER probably wasn't really budget-friendly for an independently-owned cargo ship.

She made her way to the front of the ship, hoping that Moon and his mysterious first officer were on the bridge so she wouldn't have to go poking around in his private quarters. As she got closer to the bow, she could make out two voices—one boisterous and familiar and the other flat and hard. She thought she might've heard that second voice before, but she couldn't remember where.

"—if we make it by next week, that should still give us enough time. I can't believe they'd give us shit for that, not after all the favors we've done for them," the captain snapped. He sounded anxious.

"All the same, I don't think it's wise to make promises and then break them."

Standing with her ear pressed to the bridge door, Ciaan was *sure* she'd heard that voice before. It reminded her of the tang of metallic blood in her mouth.

"There would be very serious repercussions if any of this was leaked." That voice was even like steel beams. "I'm risking a lot."

The captain's tone softened. "I know you are—so am I."

Ciaan was suddenly extremely aware of her own breathing, the huffs of hot air against the heavy metal door and the silence inside that swallowed it. She knocked; no one inside moved.

"Captain Moon?" Ciaan's voice sliced awkward through the thickness. "Are you on the deck?"

One set of heels tapped swift across the bridge and the door whizzed opened.

A pale, almost translucent face appeared with two wide, deep-set eyes staring down at her. Thin lips opened and the voice that came out was strange—something Ciaan remembered—like fingers on a manual keyboard or rain on crooked tin roofs.

"Orders were given to DM the captain when the unloading was finished." Those eyes belonged to a soldier—or maybe an ex-soldier, given the outdated security forces uniform—and they assessed Ciaan from braids to boots without stopping to linger anywhere. "I don't believe that ship inspection is one of the base labor recruit duties."

The soldier stood between Ciaan and the bridge—between Ciaan and Moon. Ciaan took the hint, knew that was a line she wasn't supposed to cross.

She stared back at the soldier.

"I need some statistics for the filework that the crew was unable to provide, so I had to find the captain."

Ciaan spoke cautious and precise. "Which would've been easier if he'd stayed on the dock as requested."

The soldier didn't move, didn't blink. "The captain had business matters that needed to be finalized."

"Yes, I heard." Ciaan thought she saw the soldier's jaw clench, so she corrected, "From the crew members. Something about negotiating deliveries on arrival. You know, the base Administrative Headquarters strongly discourages that practice, since it causes them a lot of tracking headaches."

The soldier pressed her lips together like she was trying to suffocate whatever she wanted to say next. Ciaan took a very small step into her space.

"You're an Artificial."

The soldier's hands flexed like she wanted to curl them into fists.

"Yes, she is." Captain Moon's voice boomed from behind the Artificial. "She's also this ship's first officer."

Ciaan couldn't see it, but she knew he was smirking.

"Officer." She gave the customary salute; the Artificial nodded in return.

Ciaan realized now that she didn't know this soldier—of course she didn't.

P-people (and probably, Ciaan thought, Earth humans too) said that all Artificials looked the same; something about being created in labs reminded people of copies and clones. But Artificials were neither—they weren't copies of anybody—and for most people that made them less than a copy of a human.

They were only a copy of the idea of a human.

Ciaan had probably seen more Artificials in her twenty years than most p-people saw in their entire lives, though Lieutenant 2719 was the only one she'd spent more than a few minutes interacting with. Artificials were relegated to patrols and military training and administration on the p-planets, with the occasional court or Planetary Assembly assignments. Most Artificials were stationed on the far larger Earth, or designated for space missions. Ciaan didn't know what specific work they did on those missions, but she knew that they weren't usually first officers on cargo ships.

This Artificial didn't look like Lieutenant 2719— *Aaniin*. Ciaan had forgotten that name until just now.

Aaniin's face had been cut at high angles, but this Artificial's face was round with a strong chin. Her eyes were bigger and set closer than Aaniin's and her body stretched out more in every direction. Her hair was a dull, burlap-brown—cropped short and slicked back in the standard Artificial style. Her uniform was more rumpled than Aaniin's had been, but that was probably just a side effect of prolonged space travel.

This Artificial was nothing like Aaniin, except for her

voice. It was the same, or almost the same, close enough to remind Ciaan of the way Aaniin had spoken to her. The way she'd spoken about her first mother. That same uncanny calm, like sliding a palm down the freshly waxed wall of a metal building. Feelings that Ciaan had shut away pooled molten at the bottom of her stomach.

"You've met an Artificial before?" Captain Moon's face popped up, half-blocked, behind his first officer's shoulder.

"Yes," Ciaan said, hazy like she'd just woken up. "When I was young. I got in a fight and she…"

Ciaan paused, searching for the right phrase.

"She set me free."

For a gummy second, the bridge went silent.

Then Captain Moon laughed loud like he just got the joke and smacked his first officer hard on her back. "See, I told you I liked her! She's got…*something*. I don't know what, but she's full of it."

"Yes, Captain." The Artificial looked skeptical.

"What's your name? I know it's not just Recruit." He eyed Ciaan like she was a particularly profitable piece of cargo.

"What's it to you?" Ciaan retorted. The Artificial started and she amended, "What's it to you, Captain Moon? Are you trying to get some blackmail leverage?

"Of course." His eyes glinted.

Ciaan suddenly felt like she'd stumbled into an Earth game she didn't know, didn't have any interest in playing. She pulled herself back from these two strangers who—like Tidoris said—she didn't really know anything about, and tried to steer them all back towards a more official conversation.

"Regarding your ship's cargo, if you plan on negotiating sales or deliveries from this port, you'll need to get authorization from AH. That usually takes about a day and a half, so I suggest you upload your filework as soon as possible. You'll also need to update some of your cargo containers to comply with the new standards. I'll need a catalogue of all your containers, including weight and an inventory of items, before you can be cleared for departure. TA von Ulger is supervising your ship's repairs assessment. I'll leave a copy of my primary report with your crew or I can give it to you directly if you come down to the dock before my shift ends."

Ciaan paused to breathe and noticed that the captain and the first officer both looked faintly impressed with her debrief.

"And if you'd like to address me, my title is Private Gennett. I have a few more details to add to my report, so if you don't mind…"—she nodded curtly—"Captain, Officer."

She spun around and stalked back to the main deck

hatch before she could decide whether she'd won or lost this Earth captain's obnoxious game of chicken.

Outside, Tidoris was hovering over four or five nervous recruits all huddled in front of the open engine panel.

"No, that's the alternate reactor," Tidoris explained, exasperated. The vein in his neck pulsed as he swatted the recruits' hands away from the mechanism. "You don't want to touch that. In fact, you probably don't want to touch anything. Who here is a mechanics and maintenance trainee?"

The same girl who'd suggested the reactor in the first place raised a tentative hand. Tidoris rubbed his eyes and groaned.

"Never mind. Just go around the back and mark down the gauge readings."

The group started to scatter as he called out after them, "And, please, for the love of god, don't touch anything!"

Ciaan wandered over and gave him a brief, consolatory shoulder squeeze.

"I don't know who keeps giving me untrained newbies for workers." He looked haggard; Ciaan wondered how long he'd been trying to give those idiots an engine check lesson.

"The same people who give you extra filework and

ask you to pick up extra chores. The people who know you won't say *no* to anything and take advantage of it."

Tidoris's mouth twisted sour, but he didn't deny it.

Ciaan sighed. "They won't stop until you make them stop. That's how p-people are."

Tidoris shook his head but didn't look at her. "Not everyone."

"Yes." She ground out, cold and sure. "Everyone."

Tidoris rubbed at his knuckles uncomfortably while Ciaan glanced around for someone who could give her a list of the cargo container weigh-ins. She was about ready to order one of the new basics to do it when a hatch opened behind them and two sets of boots dropped onto the dock.

"Private Gennett," Captain Moon called out, casual like they hadn't just been in a standoff on the bridge. The Artificial stood a few inches behind him, looking a lot less relaxed.

Maybe that's just her regular expression, Ciaan mused.

"And you must be TA von Ulger," he continued. Tidoris bristled and Captain Moon smiled at him, one corner of his mouth stretched higher than the other. "Your friend let that one slip."

Ciaan balled her fists; her short nails bit into her palm.

The captain seemed to sense the atmosphere shifting

and raised his hands appeasingly. "Now, let's all relax here. I don't want to cement any bad first impressions."

Tidoris grumbled something under his breath; the captain ignored it.

"In fact, I'd like for us to be on a first-name basis. So from now on, just call me Mael." He paused for effect, and Ciaan wondered if he anticipated applause after his speeches. If he encouraged it from his crew.

At any rate, no one indulged him here.

The Artificial stepped forward, clasped her hands behind her back like she was waiting for a performance review. Ciaan considered again why an Artificial soldier had been assigned to some overcompensating cargo hauler.

Mael presented her. "This is my first officer, Kwe EU 11198706. You can call her 1119."

Ciaan's eyebrows shot up. "She has a name—a real name—doesn't she?"

She turned to that odd, silver-white face. "Don't you?"

"She does," Mael conceded. "And so do you."

Ciaan narrowed her eyes. She knew his strategy now, could follow his goading tricks. Playing for egos and one-ups was something that p-people did too.

She weighed her odds.

"Ciaan." She spat it out like poison then looked over

at Tidoris, who wasn't quite following the conversation. "His name's not mine to tell."

Mael nodded and glanced at 1119. "Neither is hers. But two first names is a start."

1119 stepped back, having said nothing for herself at all.

Rage flared up under Ciaan's lungs; she'd lost this round.

"Listen, *Mael*, I'm done with your little games and with your little...*you*." She sneered down at him and that, satisfyingly, seemed to strike a nerve; the smirk fell from his broad Earth face. "I don't know what it is you want from me and really, I couldn't give less of a shit. You've got my name now—although honestly, you could've filed a complaint with just my recruit number. So go on and do that if you want to. If not, get me the stats I need and leave me and Tidoris the hell alon—"

His name was out before she even knew she was saying it.

She berated herself—*stupid, reckless, never knowing when to shut up*—and the temper tantrum that'd probably just gotten her a decompression suspension and Tidoris a complaint mark on his pristine record. She was going to suck it up and apologize but stopped short at Mael's voice, no longer light and mocking, much closer to her than it'd been before.

"You don't have to like me." Mael growled low and dark, like space past the far side of Earth. "But for as long as my ship's docked here, you're gonna be dealing with me. So you'd better start practicing my name because if we can't work together, a complaint's gonna be the *least* of your problems, Ciaan."

[FIVE]

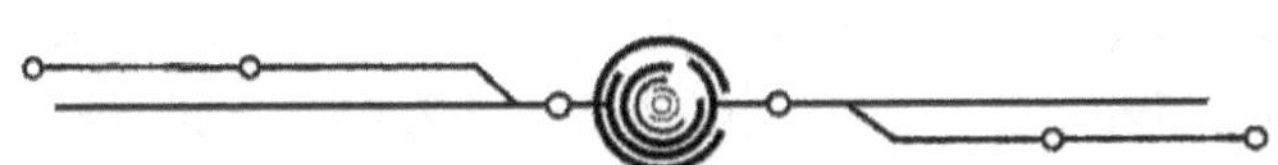

T HE AIR BETWEEN THEM simmered, just on the edge of a boil. Ciaan glared at Mael but he was unreadable, his expression thick and smooth like a slab of polished marble. Inside, Ciaan fought both the urge to run away and the urge to punch him square in the middle of his handsome Earth face.

"Are you threatening us?" Tidoris challenged and Ciaan wondered what'd gotten into him. Something about this ship and its captain seemed to push every last one of his buttons, even the ones Ciaan usually managed to avoid.

The idea rattled around in her head that maybe this was some part of himself that he shared with Melean— something distinctively von Ulger. He used his extra inches to loom over Mael so that the captain had to crane his neck to look up at him.

"I will remind you that Private Gennett and I are both members of the base forces and as such are employed directly under the security and transportation sector. We are backed by the Bi-Lateral Interplanetary Agreements and failure to comply with our orders or attempted intimidation of our persons are offenses punishable not only through the CPZ base AH, but also the p-planet High Courts and the Interplanetary Commission."

His icy, controlled tone made Ciaan squirm.

"So I suggest you reconsider your language, Captain, and reassess your professional attitude."

Mael blinked at him; if their height difference dented his confidence, he didn't show it. Tidoris, on the other hand, wasn't used to being menacing and started to fidget under the scrutiny. Ciaan could feel him trembling next to her and waited for Mael to call his bluff.

Instead, the captain laughed. Tidoris reeled back like he'd been sucker-punched.

"I know I keep saying it, but I really like you two." Mael wagged a finger at them. "You've got a lot of spunk, that's what it is. Every port we go to is either full of high and mighty bureaucratic asskissers or bumbling new recruits who always look like they've never even seen a spaceship before. It's the same everywhere—Earth, p-planets, stopover outposts—and I was starting to worry that the bases had lowered their qualifications standards." He grinned at 1119; she didn't return it. "But maybe I've just been getting the wrong kind of docking supervisors."

He winked at Ciaan and Tidoris, who both gaped back at him.

"I honestly have no idea what your objectives are." Tidoris started, fluttery and nervous again. "Or what you're talking about."

Mael leaned in. "TA von Ulger, you don't actually think I'm stupid enough to threaten the people in charge of taking care of and eventually releasing my ship, do you? I'm just trying to get you to loosen up a little, you know, pop the top uniform buttons open. Coercion isn't my style—too much margin for error. No, I'll take friendly favors over that any day."

"You want to bribe us?" Ciaan cut in, less offended than she tried to sound.

"Mutual aid." Mael corrected with a toothy grin. "You weld my seams, etcetera."

"If you think you can buy us with some cheap Earth liquor and banned adult publications—" Tidoris stopped short.

Mael quirked up a suggestive eyebrow, but he shook it off and continued.

"That's right, I saw what was in those containers! You know that restricted items have to be declared before they leave the base and we're not gonna just sit by and let you blatantly circumvent regulations!"

Mael tossed up his hands. "P-people need to have some fun too. Besides, most of the cargo is perfectly bland and unrestricted. Towels, flower pots, wood paneling. Folks take pride in the upkeep of their planet and they can't do that without Earth materials."

Tidoris held his Inspection Scanner at his hip like a nano-gun; Mael brushed it away.

"Go scan for yourself, if you don't believe me."

"Oh, I will." Tidoris marched off in a huff.

"He'll do it, you know." Ciaan watched as Tidoris ordered the few lingering crew members to show him where the digital barcodes were. The old containers had them stamped on haphazardly, which was part of the reason why upgrades were now being required.

"I hope so." Mael chuckled sharp. "He's an upstanding one, your friend Tidoris."

"Yeah, he is." Ciaan felt two sets of eyes—one quick and narrow and the other deep and swallowing—studying her. She added in a quieter voice, "You should leave him alone. He's not used to being teased like that."

"I wasn't teasing him," Mael said simply. "Or you. You p-people are so suspicious of everything."

The Artificial—1119—cleared her throat. "She's right. We've played around for long enough."

Her tone was as clipped as it'd been on the bridge, but noticeably less spiny.

She turned to Ciaan. "I can do the filework for the restricted items and unregistered deliveries, but there is another issue that we'll need your help with."

"What issue?" Ciaan wanted to snap—wanted to make it clear that she wasn't some silly little p-kid they could walk all over—but it came out more curious than anything else.

"Our stabilization system has been damaged. We can't fly safely without extensive repairs."

Ciaan didn't see what that had to do with her. "So why didn't you dock at a damages port before coming here? You know the bases don't do large repairs—we don't have the specialized officers or resources for it."

"You've got *him*." Mael pointed at Tidoris, who was arguing with a crewman over some inconsistent specs.

Ciaan and 1119 continued their conversation around him.

"Damage ports take money and time—a lot of both," said 1119. "And the wait would've been even more strenuous on the supporting systems."

Ciaan narrowed her eyes. "You didn't want to double-pay the entrance fees and miss your delivery window."

Damage ports—set up on the small, grimy outposts that dotted the routes between the p-planets and Earth—also operated as independent hubs for various illegal or questionably-legal businesses. Since they weren't under strict governmental oversight, they could get away with charging pretty much whatever they wanted for their services. If a ship's crew had to eat or sleep at their derelict facilities (which was usually the case, since the most common stopover reason was major repairs) they were hit with high fees on top of their repair bill. Seasoned captains and crew members referred to DPs as hell's rest stops, and it was even worse for cargo ships that had to pay a second immigration and customs fee if they unloaded any cargo at a p-planet port.

"You knew that if spontaneous damage was found after docking the base would *have* to complete your repairs before authorizing you for departure." Ciaan stared at 1119 accusingly.

The Artificial didn't respond—no angry jaw tic, no guilty flush, not even a blink or two. Nothing.

Ciaan crossed her arms loose against her wrinkled uniform jacket. "So what do you want us to do? Not report you?"

Mael sidled in. "Of course, that'd be nice."

1119 glanced around like she was worried about

being overheard. "This needs to be kept quiet. It's a tricky situation for us—and for you, now that you know about it."

Ciaan suddenly remembered how serious 1119 had sounded on the other side of the bridge door.

"Well"—Ciaan looked between the captain and his first officer—"how am I supposed to be able to get your repairs done if I can't talk about them?"

Mael gestured, with a little flourish, to Tidoris.

"No. *No.*" Ciaan's eyes widened; she waved the idea away. "Tidor—*TA von Ulger*—is a Technical Advisor, not a Mechanics Officer. He doesn't know the first thing about actually fixing an engine."

"Well, then, it's a good thing that our engine doesn't need to be fixed," Mael countered. "He knows how to fix electronic systems, right? Because that's what's wrong with our ship."

Ciaan hesitated, shook her head without much conviction. "I don't know. I mean, he could probably work on the digital infrastructure, but I'm not sure if he could really repair a ship's stabilization system. I don't think he's ever even tried doing something like that."

"What's the big deal?" Mael shrugged. "It's all just wires and fuses, right?"

When Ciaan didn't respond, he spun on his heel.

"Okay then, let's just ask him and see what he says.

TA von Ulger!"

Tidoris looked up from where he was trying to pry a container's security panel open. Ciaan yanked Mael back hard, hoping to jar the smirk off his face.

"Fine, fine! I'll talk to him about it and try to convince him. Better me than you anyway—at least with me, there's a chance he might actually agree to it." She jabbed a finger at 1119. "You'd better have that filework uploaded *tonight*. I'm gonna have to make up some excuse for a docking extension because there's no way you'll be repaired and cleared by tomorrow, and it's gonna be an even bigger pain in the ass if I have to deal with a bunch of questions about missing documentation."

1119 pursed her lips and nodded, frowning at the finger in her face.

Ciaan headed towards Tidoris and the mound of precariously stacked cargo containers; hissing out one last demand behind her: "—and you'd better have a damn good bribe for me once all of this is over!"

"You agreed to *what*?" Tidoris squeaked out, high and shrill. His eyes darted frantically around to the faces of the milling crew members. "What?!"

"Dori, relax." Ciaan glanced at the crew members too, noticed that some of them were starting to eye the two of them suspiciously. She leaned in and whispered, "Keep your damn voice down. I didn't agree to *anything* yet. I just told them that I'd talk to you about it."

"Talk to me about what? There's nothing to talk about! The answer's no, of course." He hiked his hands on his hips and implored, "The answer *is* no, isn't it, Ciaan?"

Ciaan hummed, noncommittal, in the back of her throat.

"Ciaan, this is bribery we're talking about here. And customs dodging. And willful deceit of a government official." He ticked off the charges on his fingers. "You're still on probation—do you *want* to go to a detention center? Because I know I don't."

Ciaan rolled her eyes. "Dori, they wouldn't send you to a detention center. If you got anything, it'd be community service…but knowing your dad, you'd probably get off with a warning and I'd take the fall."

"Why're you talking about this so—so *casually*?!" Tidoris grabbed Ciaan's shoulders, hard enough that his blunt nails pinched through her uniform and into her skin.

She looked up at him, startled—his eyes were shiny

with panic and something else. Something like the concern she always tried to forget in her second mother's eyes. Something fierce and overwhelming and it was too much; she had to look away.

"This isn't a joke, Ciaan, or a game. This is your life and mine too, and I don't want to see either of them thrown away on something so stupid." His tone, iced with pleading but stone-firm below, made her flinch. He let go of her fast like she was cracked—like she was some fragile thing and he was afraid that he'd already broken her—and that thought made her clench her teeth until her jaw hurt.

"Then what're we supposed to do? Authorize them to fly damaged and take the hit for it? Bring the case to AH and have them docked here indefinitely?" Ciaan got up in his face, stared him down and dared him to answer.

Tidoris chewed on his thick lower lip but stayed quiet.

She pushed on, just a little further. "The sooner we take care of this and get all the filework uploaded, the sooner they'll be off Toi and out of our hair. And if we don't accept any, um, *gifts* from them then what's the worst we could be charged with? Disregarding standard protocol? AH would probably just send us to a disciplinary lecture and take away decomp for a few days."

Tidoris squirmed, pulled at his fingers like he wasn't fully convinced. "You're not gonna accept any bribes?"

Ciaan huffed out a rough laugh; if anyone other than Tidoris had asked that, she would've been insulted.

"No, I'm not. Despite what you and my second mother think, I'm not actually all that interested in seeing what the inside of a detention center is like firsthand."

Tidoris bit at the tip of his thumb. "I'm not even sure I could fix a stabilization system. I've never worked on anything but a simulation ship before."

Ciaan shrugged. "That's what I told them, but they seemed to think it wouldn't be a problem. It's all just wires and fuses, right?"

"Hardly." Tidoris scoffed but somehow still managed to make it sound polite. "I'll see what I can do anyway."

"Great!" Ciaan exhaled like a punch through the chest. "And if you can't fix it, then we'll go to AH and request an official repair. Fair?"

Tidoris held out a thin hand and Ciaan shook it.

"Fair."

"Everything's all settled here, then?" Mael popped up, sudden and loud. Ciaan wondered how long he'd been lurking around and if that was a common habit of Earth humans.

"Yes," Tidoris answered, rigid and sour.

Mael pouted. "Now you're not gonna be pissy about my little *theatrics* before, are you? Tidoris—may I call you Tidoris?"

Tidoris opened his mouth, but Mael didn't give him a chance to object.

"Tidoris, Ciaan and I already patched things up and I think it'd be practical for you and me to do the same. We got off on the wrong foot, don't you agree?" He extended a hand marked with some scars that Ciaan hadn't noticed before.

Tidoris didn't acknowledge the hand or the gesture. "I don't think you have another foot, Captain Moon. And no, you may not call me Tidoris."

Mael drew his hand back. "As you wish, TA von Ulger, but that's just extra syllables that could be spent saying something important."

"Anyway," Ciaan jumped in. She wasn't particularly interested in defending Mael, but she was even less interested in sitting through another passive-aggressive fight. "We've come to an agreement. Tidoris and I will do our best to help repair your ship and you'll do your best not to get us arrested or entangled in any prohibited activities. I've still got several months before I'm up for parole."

At that last sentence, Mael raised an intrigued eyebrow.

"No." She glared at him. "I'm not going to elaborate."

His mouth split into a vicious grin.

"And I still want my bribe." Ciaan ground out, avoiding Tidoris and the shocked disappointment she knew was soaking onto his face.

Mael dusted a streak of dirt off his jacket sleeve. "Name your price."

"The Artificial's name. Her real name." Ciaan didn't know why it mattered so much to her, but it did.

"Not one for traditional bribes, are you?" Mael's eyes flashed. "Well, I'm afraid I still can't give that to you. But I know someone who can."

Ciaan tapped the toe of her boot impatiently.

"She's in her quarters, writing up your filework if I'm not mistaken." Mael winked at Tidoris. "And I'm not."

"I'll collect my payment later then." Ciaan nudged at Tidoris, who glowered back at her.

Looking between the two men, Ciaan sent up a small plea to anything that might be out there—singular, plural, sentient being or omnipotent power or cosmic vibrations or *whatever*—for them to not kill each other before this whole thing was over.

[SIX]

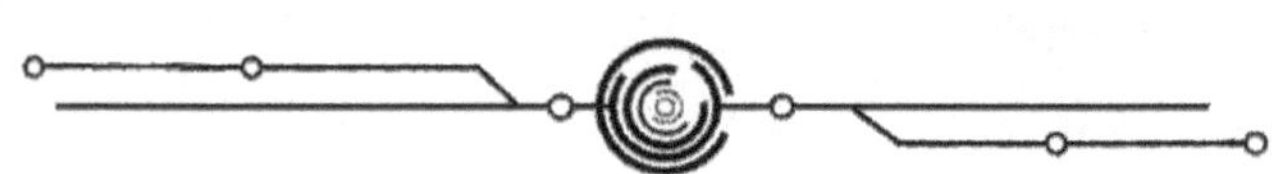

CIAAN PICKED AT THE FRINGE of her braids while her second mother flattened and smoothed the collar on her vest. A flurry of civilian colors that Ciaan hadn't realized she'd missed on the base whirled past them as they sat on a bench outside Probationary Review Courtroom number 7.

Once every six months she was allowed one day's supervised leave for her court check-in; she sped off base that morning to spend her leave day with her second mother acting as her probation guardian.

"I wish you'd worn your white jacket. It would've been more…" Her second mother's knees shook, and she picked at the corner of her thumbnail.

"Innocent?" Ciaan stared at the matte wall across

from them.

"Fresh," her second mother countered. "You know judges like to critique the defendant's appearance for signs of rehabilitation. Or relapse."

Her second mother reached out towards Ciaan, but she shifted away from it.

"I don't think the judge looked at me once for the whole thirty seconds that he came on screen. Besides, my white jacket has a stain from when I got into that disagreement with that building lacquerer."

A shadow flitted over her second mother's face. "When you got into that fistfight with a sector maintenance contractor, you mean."

Ciaan looked down at the slick-shined floor. "Whatever."

Her second mother sighed and tried to brush the wrinkles out of her old grey skirt.

When had their whole family started to look shabby? Maybe Ciaan had been too busy fist fighting anyone who looked at her the wrong way to realize that they'd slipped into the lower classes.

This wouldn't have happened with my first mother, Ciaan thought darkly then felt the guilt prickle up behind it. *It also probably wouldn't have happened if my father and second mother didn't have to keep bailing me out and paying off my legal fees.*

Ciaan didn't like guilt, whether she deserved it or not, so she pushed it down as far as it would go.

"The judge seemed pleased with your conduct record at least." Her second mother reached out again, dropped a tentative hand on Ciaan's leg. Ciaan knew that it'd probably be a while before her second mother would get another chance to do that, so this time she let it stay.

"We're proud of you, your father and me. I know things haven't always been the easiest for you and this is your first time living away from the apartment—honestly, we were worried. But the independence seems to be good for you."

Ciaan squirmed; she didn't know how to take compliments from the woman she'd spent most of her life—sometimes unintentionally, sometimes not—trying to break.

"There isn't exactly a lot of independence in the reserve ranks."

"Well, there's something there that's working. Something that we never could figure out for you." Her second mother's mouth twisted sad and a little bitter. "If things keep up like this, I think the judge might grant you an early release. You could look into applying for a skills academy, and maybe Briette could help you find some housing…"

She trailed off, an optimistic smile lighting up her face.

Ciaan swallowed against the lump rising in her throat, prodding her to confess about Mael and his ship and the whole probation-breaking scheme. Her second mother squeezed her thigh, misunderstanding her conflicted silence.

"Not that you wouldn't be welcome back at home. You know you'll always have a place with your father and sisters and brother and me. It's just that—maybe you're ready to move on. We don't want to keep you from growing and have you acting out because of it."

Ciaan snorted, wondered if her second mother had been reading those Guides to Self-Management that she always heard wives and mothers touting on the Information Channels.

During the hollowest nights in the reserve barracks, Ciaan missed these moments of earnest kindness from her second mother. But she'd never, ever admit it and had nothing else to say, so the space between them went quiet.

Ciaan scanned the crowds as they waited for the check-in filework to go through, pretending that she wasn't just a criminal out on a day trip. It was easy to tell the probationees from the guardians: the former looked like they couldn't care less while the latter looked like, if they tried to care more, they'd burst. She thought she might've known a few of the disgruntled (alleged) criminals—former friends or former friends-of-friends, maybe. She chuckled to herself about their badly-tailored suits and over-slicked hair, like p-kids playing at being important Earth humans.

At least she'd kept her own outfit—silky pants and a button-up vest—simple and solid-colored.

She was enjoying one particularly hideous multi-print dress—probably suggested by another well-meaning second-mother—when a face slipped by that she was sure she recognized. It was just a flash in the crowd; a crisp official uniform and a dull, pale face against the dark blur of p-skin. She got up and followed it before she could stop herself.

"Ciaan?" Her second mother called after her.

Ciaan started running through the crowd and didn't look back, keeping her eyes fixed on the back of the Artificial. The crowd was almost entirely p-people; it should've been easy to track her but—caught in a throng of other humans—the Artificial didn't seem as different as Ciaan'd once thought.

Maybe the difference is hidden at a distance; maybe it's only up close that they expose their strangeness. The idea flitted through Ciaan's mind—in and out between her heavy, breathless pants.

Luckily, the Probation Courts were all housed in one compact building annexed from the massive Central

Courts. If her second mother and she had been there, Ciaan wasn't sure that she would've been able to spot the Artificial in the churning, mixed masses.

Ciaan elbowed her way down the stairs and across the lobby. Everyone there seemed to be milling slow and aimless, so Ciaan didn't feel all that bad about cutting in front and around them. She would've preferred *not* having to shove an old man out of her way, but he bumbled into her path at the last second and it was either shove him or barrel straight through him.

At the security gate for the Parolee Meeting Rooms, Ciaan finally caught her.

"Aaniin!" She sputtered loud; it echoed off the rotunda ceiling. The soles of her shoes squealed as she skidded to a stop and doubled over.

The Artificial froze, rigid and angular, like she'd been hit with a stun laser. Behind them, Ciaan could make out the patter of her second mother's low heels getting closer. After a few seconds, they died down and a warm, soothing hand started rubbing at Ciaan's back. Once she'd gotten her breathing back to normal, Ciaan straightened. Aaniin was staring at her warily, a dangerous edge to the cut of her jaw.

"Aaniin." Ciaan repeated and it rung silly in her ears. She realized suddenly that she had nothing to say to the Artificial. Either that or she had so many things to say that they'd all crashed together in a garbled, incoherent jumble.

Aaniin pursed her lips—seemed to consider the situation—then folded her hands loosely in front of her. "It would be best, I think, if you didn't refer to me so informally in such an official and public forum."

Ciaan nodded but didn't correct herself; she wasn't sure what rank Aaniin held now. They stood in silence as a puffy p-man passed by and gave Aaniin a slight bow.

"Major General 2719. Nice to see you again. Day off?" He glanced at Ciaan, managed to somehow make it feel both appraising and dismissive.

"No, I'm afraid not, Official Miens. I'm scheduled for testimony at fourteen hundred hours." She gave a cursory nod to the digital clock mounted high on the lobby wall.

The man hummed, mumbled something that Ciaan couldn't quite hear.

"I'll be seeing you at the next conference, yes?" he continued. There was a gleam in his small, beady eyes like what he said and what he meant were two totally different things.

Or maybe I'm just paranoid, Ciaan considered. But not very seriously.

The faint color in Aaniin's cheeks seemed to drain out, but her expression didn't change. "Certainly, sir.

Give High Official Yeager my regards."

Yeager—Ciaan remembered that name, and the way Tidoris had gone sheet-white talking abou him. If this bulbous man was associated with Yeager, that was another thing to dislike about both of them.

After another minute or two of inane small talk, the official finally puttered away. Aaniin maneuvered them out of the thick of the crowd; once they were wedged behind one of the ceiling support columns, Ciaan set her hands on her hips.

"You told me you'd come and see me again." Her voice was rung out with young, childish hurt and she hated it.

Aaniin closed her wide wet-dark eyes, pinched the bridge of her nose. "I said I would try."

Then she turned away briskly—cut Ciaan off from challenging her—to greet her second mother. "Hello, I am Major General 2719 of the Artificial Human Forces. Ciaan and I met…a long time ago. I met her on a night when she fought for her life and won."

She and Ciaan shared a swift, secret smile.

"I believe you're Illonde Tohannson, Ciaan's second mother."

Ciaan glanced at her second mother, hoping she wasn't completely lost with all of this.

The person standing there—face flat and cold, eyes

flinty with thick-slab rage, eyebrows knotted together in a hard line—was someone Ciaan didn't know, a stranger to her. For the first time in her life, Ciaan was frightened of her second mother.

She also felt a shock of sudden respect for her.

The polite smile dropped from Aaniin's lips. "Have I said something to offend you?"

"Your whole being offends me." Her second mother seethed, hushed and vicious.

Ciaan's jaw dropped; she couldn't believe that the woman who'd spent the past decade or so cooing reassurances to her was capable of such hatred. Aaniin blinked in shock, opened her mouth to defend herself, but Ciaan's second mother had already grabbed Ciaan's wrist and jerked her away towards the main exit.

Ciaan twisted against the tight grip. "What're you doing? What were you talking about? Do you know Aaniin?"

She stumbled, tripping over her feet as her second mother dragged her to the doors.

"Illonde!" she shouted. Her voice reverberated off the bright metal corners tiled with expensive Earth ceramic.

After their first year as a new family—their adjustment year, her father had called it—Ciaan had promised him that she wouldn't call her second mother by her first name anymore. That was one promise she'd kept, more or less, but she told herself that breaking it was justified here. It must've worked, too, because her second mother stopped short of the security checkpoints.

"No, I don't know her." Her second mother gritted out, kept her back to Ciaan. "But I know Artificials, and the people who control them. Don't trust them, Ciaan. No matter what compelling lies they tell you."

Ciaan thought about her first mother, about the way Aaniin had talked about her. That green patch—the budding hope that'd been crushed in that patrol cruiser and drilled over with cold metal all those years ago—crept into the space behind Ciaan's ears. She shook it away, sharp and furious, and wanted to rip her second mother apart for bringing this all back up again.

"You sound like those p-pride groups." Ciaan sneered, let the nasty insinuations soak in.

Her second mother bristled but still didn't let go of her hand. She closed her eyes and sighed.

"You're so young, Ciaan, and you only know a small part of this universe and how it works. You see the big picture from here, but you have no idea what it's like on the ground."

Ciaan huffed, insulted that her second mother was trying to lecture *her* about the brutalities of life.

"Like you've seen anything else! You've never been off Toi—you probably haven't even seen as much of it as

I have!" Ciaan pulled her arm back hard and her second mother let her go.

Then her second mother reached up to the high collar of her blouse.

"Haven't I?"

Everything—her body, her voice, her anger—deflated.

She pulled the neck of her blouse as far back as it could go, almost to her armpit. Faded marking—a series of numbers and symbols that Ciaan didn't recognize—were seared into the skin just below her collarbone.

Corrections sectors (on p-planets at least) didn't brand their prisoners; Ciaan had no idea who could've done that—or why.

Her second mother answered one of the unasked questions.

"Earth."

A beat, then she straightened her collar and smoothed her blouse like nothing had happened. Like she wasn't anyone more than Illonde Tohannson, second mother to the currently-reforming delinquent Ciaan Gennett. Same as she'd always been.

Ciaan blinked once, twice, three times, trying to keep up.

"You've been to Earth?" It was a stupid question—Ciaan resented sounding stupid to this new version of her second mother—but it was out before she could think of a better one.

Her second mother smiled like a hot poker to flesh, and a chill tickled up the base of Ciaan's spine.

"I've done things that'd shock the rebelliousness right out of you." Her second mother's expression darkened. "Why do you think I've been so adamant about keeping you out of the detention centers?"

Ciaan tensed, skin prickling.

"Aaniin—that Major General—said she knew my mother. She told me that she died." Ciaan didn't know if she'd wanted to share all that or not, but the lead weight that'd been hanging from her soul did feel a little lighter now.

The corners of her second mother's mouth turned down, like she was disgusted by every part of this situation.

"I wouldn't doubt that—the first part, at least." She hesitated and Ciaan held her breath. "As for the second part, it's most likely true. In this very particular case, the word of an Artificial is probably the closest you—*we*—will ever get to the truth."

At that confirmation, Ciaan's hope sank with a metallic clang.

She had questions—even more than she'd had on that bloodied, bruised night seven years ago—and she knew her second mother had more to tell. Looked at her and knew she had more that she wasn't gonna tell. At least not today.

So she swallowed down her desperation and kept her mouth shut.

"It's not my place, Ciaan." Her second mother's gaze dropped. "You know more than your father does now."

Ciaan hadn't expected that; her stomach lurched with shame and pity.

"Someday, when you're ready to accept it, you'll learn the truth about your first mother." Her second mother reached out and squeezed her arm, quick and fleeting. "All of it."

Without really listening, Ciaan nodded.

Her second mother turned and walked through the checkpoint without taking Ciaan's hand. Ciaan found herself trailing after like a dog, following the steady beat of her second mother's heels down the court steps. When they stopped at the street crossing—watching the slick government cruisers sped past—her second mother finally glanced at her, but didn't smile.

For the first time since her first mother had disappeared, Ciaan thought that maybe she didn't want to know the whole truth after all.

Back at the CPZ base, Ciaan was greeted by a shrill, wild-eyed Tidoris.

"—that he won't let me open to inspect (he says it's a private delivery off Toi and I have no reason to go snooping around in his stuff)—Ciaan, I'm *sure* it's a forbidden item—maybe *drugs* or *weapons*—I told you this wasn't a good idea and that we'd all end up in the DCs, but no, *someone* wouldn't listen and now look where it's gotten—"

Ciaan cut him off with a sharp: "Tidoris!"

At the sound of his name, his ranting cut off like it'd been hacked with a cleaver.

At least—she chuckled to herself—*some things are still the same.*

"What are you talking about, Dori? Give me the one-sentence summary."

Tidoris took a moment to collect himself, like he was afraid of getting chopped again. "Mael has a large cargo container that was locked away in a secret compartment and he won't let me open it for inspection."

Ciaan's eyebrow quirked up. "Mael?"

"Captain Moon is too many syllables." Tidoris waved his hand impatiently. "*Anyway*, this is a problem, Ciaan. If he's transporting forbidden items and we let him leave here without a thorough inspection, we're the one who'll be screwed."

Ciaan rubbed the sides of her forehead; it'd already been a long, draining day. "Well, then, let's go and use all the authority we have to make him open it. And when that doesn't work, let's threaten to tell on him to the people who have real authority."

Tidoris let out one short, staticky laugh.

They marched over to the port, only to find Mael already waiting outside, his arms crossed petulantly.

"Good. You're back." He spoke only to Ciaan. "I'd like to file a report against TA von Ulger for attempted destruction of private property, emotional intimidation, and attempted physical intimidation. What files do I need to upload?"

Ciaan looked between the two of them in disbelief.

Tidoris gaped. "You—I—how *dare* you! And after I risk my job *and* my freedom to help you and your dumb heap of junk metal! I oughta…"

He made a threatening motion, though it wasn't all that effective coming from him.

Mael raised his hands in exaggerated defense. "You see? You see?! I have witnesses!"

They glared at each other and Ciaan rolled her eyes, so hard that it hurt.

She shoved Tidoris back and jabbed a warning finger at him. Then she grabbed Mael by his jacket lapel and tossed him a few feet away; he stumbled, stared at her in surprise as he fixed a few popped buttons.

"I'm done with this," she growled at Mael. "If we can't trust you to keep up your end of the deal, then I'll go to AH right now. At this point you'll get a much harsher punishment than we will. And please, stop acting like Tidoris could do anything to you. It's embarrassing."

Mael clenched his fists then flexed them out, giving up on his victim act.

"Where's the Artificial?" Ciaan spat; the word suddenly tasted bitter.

Mael dusted at an old smear of dirt on his sleeve. "Inside, guarding the container from nosy Technical Advisors."

Tidoris muttered something under his breath; Ciaan chose to ignore it.

"Well, her services are no longer needed."

She pushed them both towards the main deck hatch and motioned to Mael.

"After you."

He opened it begrudgingly and they all piled into the narrow deckway; the space fit one comfortably and two snugly, but three was definitely pushing it. They followed Mael—three sets of boots clinking against the grated floors—towards the bridge but turned before it, snaking down to where Ciaan assumed the captain's and first officer's quarters were. Eventually, they reached an old, rusted door with the words RESTRICTED ACCESS etched into it.

It screeched as Mael opened it, almost like the movement was painful.

Inside, 1119 was standing next to a container—larger than the ones Ciaan had seen being unloaded, but not by much. It came up to the Artificial's waist, though it probably would've hit the bottom of Ciaan's ribcage. The small, dim room was empty except for it and when Ciaan stepped forward tentatively, 1119 made no move to stop her.

Ciaan scanned around for the digital barcode. She stretched behind the container and saw frayed wires sticking out; someone had short fused it.

She addressed 1119: "First Officer, as the docking supervisor for this ship, I demand that you provide me with this cargo container's registration and statistics. If you are unwilling or unable to do so, it's my duty to use any means necessary to open it and determine its contents for myself."

1119 gave a small nod and stepped aside, like she'd never planned on challenging the order at all. Ciaan hadn't anticipated her bluff working so easily; now that it had, she wasn't sure what exactly to do next.

Tidoris shuffled behind her. "I've got a laser knife. I

think that should be able to get it open."

Once again, Ciaan was grateful that he was there to fill in the gaps for her. She stepped away from the container. "I'll leave it to you then."

Tidoris pulled an old rag out from one of his uniform pockets and wrapped it around his face and neck, leaving only his eyes visible, peering out behind his glasses. He switched the knife on.

The smell of melting plastic—chemical and putrid—filled the cramped space. Ciaan covered her nose and mouth; Mael did the same but it couldn't mask the anger and, Ciaan thought, fear that clouded his face. 1119 didn't move her hands from where they were folded behind her back, but she did cough softly once or twice. And although Ciaan was sure that Tidoris was still fuming, she noticed that he was trying not to cut through the lock and bolt mechanisms completely, which would've rendered the container unusable.

Finally, the knife buzzed off and one side of the container cracked open.

The air immediately filled with the stench of artificial oxygen, and something stronger and more pungent too. The smell stung like a slap and Tidoris—the closest one to the box—reeled back, shielding his eyes. Mael lurched forward to help him pry the cut section off. They heaved and sputtered for a few minutes, switching angles and trying different maneuvers and arguing over who was supposed to hold and who was supposed to pull. 1119 tossed Ciaan what looked like a smirk—though Ciaan supposed that it could've just been the light playing tricks on her—and they both walked over to join in the operation.

Eight hands curled around the sticky-warm plastic and pulled.

A large chunk broke off about three-fourths of the way down, leaving a jagged section still attached at the bottom. The force of it threw the four of them back hard; the boys tumbled and Ciaan and 1119 hit the metal wall. They groaned and shook their heads, struggled to get back on their feet.

The first gasp came from Tidoris.

Ciaan followed his stunned gaze; when she saw it, she stumbled and fell down again with a muffled thud.

Mael whispered a shocked, "*Oh, my God.*"

1119 didn't do or say anything—she just swayed like a burst of wind had suddenly rushed through the vents.

In the blackness of the cargo container, two figures sat huddled around each other. They were filthy, whimpering, young—and one of them was very, very pregnant.

[SEVEN]

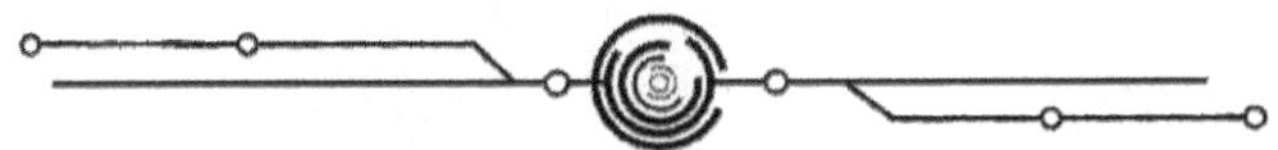

FOR A FEW SECONDS, there was nothing but the suck of silence stuffing its way into Ciaan's ears and down her throat; she felt like she was choking on it. It'd been just two or three minutes since they'd marched into this cargo hold but the world had changed, knocked off its axis and they were slipping off the edge or floating loose without their center of gravity to ground them. She tried to calm her heartbeat—stutter-skipping like it wanted to crack through her ribcage—and shut her eyes, willing the box to be empty when she opened them again.

Better yet, maybe it'd seal up on its own and this goddamned ship would whizz out of the docking channel and Ciaan and Tidoris could go back to their tedious, regimented lives.

She'd probably be getting a pretty irate lecture from him once all this was over.

Mael started pacing, hand clamped over his mouth. He looked back and forth between the sunken faces staring out of the cargo container and the toes of his boots, like he couldn't decide which was harder to see. 1119 kept swaying—anchored to the floor like her soles were soldered to it—and Ciaan fought the urge to go over and smack her hard across her pale cheek.

It was Tidoris, finally, who made the move. He crawled forward and the figures burrowed further into the box, clawed at the plastic like they wanted to dig themselves into it. He crouched on his knees in front of the exposed hole but didn't force his way in.

"Can you tell me your names?" Tidoris spoke soft and gentle, careful to keep his hands tucked under his knees.

No response, no movement or sound, reached out from the shadows.

He tried again. "What's your name? Where are you from? Why are you here?"

He knocked against the plastic panel; the figures jumped and held each other tighter.

"Maybe they're from a non-standardized region and don't speak Global." Mael scratched at the back of his neck. He sounded flustered and confused—more than Ciaan thought the captain of a ship transporting human cargo should in this situation. Almost like he knew as little about this as the rest of them.

"*Jiào? Ismee?*" Tidoris twisted his tongue around the unfamiliar words. "*Zovet? Nombre?*"

That impressed Ciaan; she couldn't even remember what she'd done instead of paying attention in Non-Standards. Technically, all humans—Earth humans, Artificials, and p-people alike—were required to pass basic Global levels, so the figures should've recognized *name* no matter where they were from.

But they didn't—or if they did, they were damn good fakers.

Maybe they're bluffing. Or stalling. Ciaan tried to catalogue all the reasons why someone would lock themselves in an interplanetary cargo container. *Maybe they're stowaways or criminals trying to buy some sympathy now that they've been caught. Maybe they're dangerous, maybe they killed the last jerkass captain and unwitting companions who found them.*

Ciaan tried to decide who she'd have to sacrifice first in order to save herself; she wished Dori would get away from that container already.

"If they can't—or won't—tell us who they are, we should search them for identification chips." 1119's voice was steady but she fumbled with her regulation scanner, almost dropping it.

Tidoris half-nodded and groped for his own Right Hand, muttering, "I think I have the latest updates for the translation program. Hopefully, they don't speak some really obscure sub-language—whoops…"

He accidentally hit a button and a high whirl spun out of the machine—before he could shut it off, one of the figures lunged out of the box, feral and fast. Tidoris yelped and scrambled back as the Right Hand fell, shattering. Mael and 1119 pulled out their stunners and Ciaan grabbed the fractured device from the floor; its screen glow flickered against the rusted metal walls.

"Shit!" Tidoris shouted, shaky with fear and adrenaline.

Mael advanced on the container, much more aggressively than Tidoris had. He pointed his stunner at the non-pregnant, lunging figure—seething and growling near the hole—and kicked the plastic corner with his thick boot.

"Up! Out! Now!" he barked. "Hands up! Both of you! Hands up!"

Ciaan could see now that the lunger was male, with scruffs of hair growing across his face and long, dirty fingernails balled into fists.

Mael steadied his shot. "If you don't put your hands

up, I will stun you at the maximum setting! Don't think I won't!"

The male crouched low and predatory; without another warning, Mael pulled the trigger.

The male went tense and then shook apart, like he'd lost control of his bones. He fell back into the box with a shudder and a weak cough, which sounded more like a gurgle. When he hit the ground, the pregnant female screamed.

It wasn't like anything Ciaan had heard before—the sound was terrifying, primal, anguished. The female began lashing out, beating her arms and head against the inside of the container, and 1119 reached in to lock her body around the girl before she could do any serious damage—to them or herself.

"Get a tranquilizing booster!" 1119's voice faltered and broke as she held on desperately to the thrashing girl.

Mael ran to the door, but Tidoris caught him by the ankle before he could get there.

"I have one!" Tidoris tore apart different compartments of his TA pack, littered the floor with pieces of wire and damaged circuit boards. Finally, he pulled out a thin, liquid-filled capsule and tossed it to Mael.

1119 braced the female's shoulders with one arm and her head with the other; one long leg wrapped around the female's small, bucking knees. The Artificial propped her back against the sloped cabin wall, using her other leg for leverage. The girl's nails—black and jagged like the boy's—ripped at 1119's uniform and skin, wherever she could get to it.

No hint of pain crossed the Artificial's dark eyes, even as thin lines of blood bubbled up along her hands and wrists.

In the middle of the chaos, everyone leapt into action except Ciaan—she just sat there feeling useless, *being* useless. This wasn't some scrappy back-alley brawl or one of the situational drills they'd run during training; she had no instincts—no mandates—for this.

The base manual's mantra looped in her brain: *If you can't be useful, stay back and try not to cause any unnecessary complications.* Beneath it, the voice that'd goaded her into every confrontation and turn-tail chase after the fact whispered: *Better them than you.*

She slid against the wall, out of everyone else's way. A delinquent halfie wasn't gonna be the hero, wasn't gonna save anyone's life anyway.

Mael inched towards 1119, slowly approaching from the side; the girl's eyes were wild and reeling.

1119 twisted them both and shouted, "Get her in the arm!"

Mael dove and jabbed the booster into the girl's bare

bicep. She flailed and squealed, twitching against 1119's firm grip. After ten seconds or so, her breathing evened out and she went limp, eyes rolling back and shut. When 1119 let go, she slid onto the floor.

"Medical bay." Mael said it first, to no one and everyone. He wiped the sweat from his forehead with his sleeve. 1119 stepped closer to him—over the tranquilized female—and they looked at each other for a long moment. Then Mael nodded and turned to Tidoris.

"Help me with him." Mael pointed to the boy, still lying crumbled in the container.

Ciaan wondered how long the effects of stunning lasted, hoped it'd be long enough to move them without another ambush. Tidoris shoved the loose contents back into his TA pack and shuffled towards Mael.

"You two take her," Mael continued, already reaching into the container to pull out the boy. "We need to get this cargo out of here."

Ciaan glanced at 1119, who was standing over the female. The Artificial's features were cold-set, betraying something in their severity that Ciaan thought she should recognize but didn't. Her own throat was dry, stale from artificial oxygen and thick slabs of silence. When she swallowed, it hurt.

After a couple failed tries, they managed to hoist the two slack bodies up and headed out into the bowels of the ship. They maneuvered up stairs and around corners as carefully as they could, watching for jutting ledges or pipes. Near the main deck hatch—but before the dining and crew living quarters—they turned into a cramped little room. The ceiling slanted up and then down, kept people ducking so they didn't smack their heads, and there seemed to be too many corners for such a small space. It looked clean only because the walls had been lacquered over in white; even so, there were still clusters of cracks and chips and dirty discolorations.

Jutting out from the middle of the far wall were two narrow cots with no partitions between them, so short that—if he'd needed to use them—Ciaan guessed Tidoris's feet would've hung right off. There were no sheets or pillows, only plastic liners that looked more yellow than white. Five straps hung off the side of each cot; Mael and Tidoris dropped the boy onto the closest one with a casual thump.

1119 led them over to the other cot and ordered, "Don't drop her."

Ciaan let the female down more gently than she probably needed to.

Mael strapped the two of them down, careful to work around the girl's pregnant belly. 1119 went to the supply cabinets and sprayed some antiseptic on her hand wounds. Ciaan and Tidoris stepped away from the beds and closer to each other.

They're so small. Ciaan gazed down at them; in the harsh light of the medical bay, all the ominous shadows lurking in the cargo room were washed off their faces. She suddenly thought about Helona's tinkling laughter and Eerick's mock-stern expressions when he lectured his older sisters with his little hands on his hips.

She clenched and unclenched her fists against her thighs.

The girl looked so pregnant, her belly swollen and etched in veins. The stubby crewman Ciaan had encountered (what seemed like years ago) had just been dirty, but these two were filthy in a way Ciaan had never seen—not even among the poorest p-people. Their coarse clothes—a long shirt and regulation knee-length pants each—hung on their bodies like parachutes wrapped around a piles of straws, but even under all that, Ciaan could still see their pink skin and stringy light hair.

It was, Ciaan realized with a prick of revulsion, the same color as hers.

These two were unmistakably Earth humans.

"We should get someone to examine them." Tidoris

sounded detached, like he was running on autopilot. "Where're your medical officers?"

"You're looking at them," Mael replied with a weak smile.

Tidoris scrunched his forehead, narrowed his eyes. "You mean you don't have a trained medical officer on this ship? As registered ships of all classifications are required to have?"

Mael shrugged. "It's not in our budget."

"Well, then, you are once again unbelievably and—honestly—unfairly lucky." Tidoris swung his pack down on a free cot. "I happen to have very *basic* medical training, but it should be enough for a preliminary exam."

He rooted around in his pack and finally brought out a small silver case, similar to the one he kept his more fragile TA equipment in. 1119 handed him the antiseptic bottle and he rinsed his hands and each tool, one by one. Ciaan didn't recognize any of them except the thin, flat, expandable bar that was used to scan bodies for implanted electronic chips and devices. Tidoris used that first, swept it over the male then the female.

It didn't beep.

"No identity chips, though if they come from a non-standardized region, that's not really surprising." He paused and wiped away the grime on both their left shoulders.

"They were tagged, though—but the tags were removed. I don't know if that was an authorized surgery or not." He pointed to an ugly, raised scar under the girl's collarbone. "You can still see the mark here, and on him too."

Mael glanced at the boy's shoulder and nodded.

"Why would they have been tagged?" Ciaan only knew a little about tagging—mainly that it was frowned upon by the Beings' Rights groups.

From what she'd heard, a sensor was injected under the skin to monitor movement, habits, consumption, and general vital statistics. Tracking had been developed to supervise inmates but was eventually discontinued after claims of privacy invasion were made public. That'd been before Ciaan was born, and now she only heard rumors of shady fringe groups—traffickers, slavery rings, and other fantastical creations of late-night sensationalist Information Channel hosts—using them.

Tidoris chewed at his lip. "I don't know. Maybe they were being held in some off-the-map detention center? Not everyone follows the rules."

He felt for the girl's pulse, like he needed to convince himself that she was still alive. Then he lifted both their eyelids and pulled down the boy's chin to check inside his mouth.

"*Goddamn it,*" he swore, low and ground out.

Ciaan wondered if all the cargo's—*no identification so that's what they are for now*, she rationalized to herself—teeth had rotted out.

"I know why he wouldn't answer our questions." Tidoris gritted out. "His tongue's been disintegrated."

"What?!" Mael shouted, a note of panic pitching it.

Tidoris folded his arms stiff across his chest. "His tongue's been disintegrated."

Ciaan didn't know how it was possible, but it sounded even worse the second time he said it.

Suddenly, Tidoris rushed over to the girl's cot, opened her mouth and exhaled.

"She's fine—or at least her tongue is."

They all eyed her swollen stomach warily.

Tidoris picked up a long plastic coil with a lens on one end; he worked it slowly between the girl's lips and let it snake itself further in.

He peered through the viewfinder. "I can't see any irregularities in her throat, though her tongue muscles don't seem to be that developed."

Tidoris pushed a button and the coil retracted; Ciaan choked back a dry heave. He lifted the girl's eyelids again and shined a small light—hooked at the end of the coil—into her pupils. After he was done with that, he wiped down the coil with antiseptic and stuck it up her nose and then in her ears, where he paused.

"What is it?" 1119 hovered on the other side of the girl's bed.

Tidoris shook his head distractedly without looking up from the viewfinder.

"I don't know. Something." He pressed another button.

"It looks like there's some damage to her inner ear." He moved to the other side of the cot. "This side too."

When he was done with the girl, he walked over to the boy and checked his ears.

"His ears aren't damaged." Tidoris hummed, rubbing his fingers along his jaw.

"Well, what does that mean?" Mael pressed, like he knew the answer was there, but he just couldn't grab it.

Tidoris frowned. "It means that we have two Earth humans—*who seem to have gotten aboard your ship without your knowing it*—who can't communicate verbally with us. He can't speak and she, I'm guessing, can't hear."

"How did this happen?" Ciaan flinched, spoke before she could tell herself to shut up.

"With her, I can't be sure. Maybe disease or trauma, or maybe she was born with it." Tidoris opened the boy's mouth again and pushed the coil inside. "As for his tongue, that's not something someone's born with. It looks like the kind of amputation I've seen performed with new nano-medical technology, only far less clean and… necessary. Maybe it was some kind of punishment?"

"Or torture." 1119 added, and her jaw ticked with it.

"But they can still communicate, right?" Mael ran a shaky hand through his hair. "I mean, they can read and write, can't they?"

Tidoris shook his head. "Maybe, if they aren't from any of the far non-standardized regions. And if we can figure out what language they would've even learned there—which is difficult without any identification."

He looked coldly at Mael. "Where did you pick up that container?"

Mael hedged. "We make a lot of stops. Things get loaded and unloaded; how am I supposed to keep track of every piece of cargo that goes through this hull?"

"Because," Tidoris seethed, biting out the words, "you are the *captain*. That is your *job*."

"All right! *Shibal!*" Mael threw up his arms. "Sometimes I let on boxes as favors to loyal customers or bargains for generous merchants, and they don't always make it on my official inventories. Go upload a report about it, why don't you?"

He huffed, petulant, and the lines on Tidoris's forehead dug in deeper.

"I believe that container was loaded at a stop in the

West Asian Union, near a sea." 1119 offered, ignoring Mael's betrayed glare. "I can't remember the port's name, but I know it wasn't a major city because we didn't stop at one. You'd probably be able to find the coordinates in the ship's navigation logs."

Tidoris turned to 1119. "So you had knowledge of this unauthorized cargo and you failed to inform your captain about it? Is that what you're saying?"

1119 pursed her lips, jutted her chin out defiantly.

Ciaan tried not to scoff as Tidoris played at High Official.

"I don't think I need to tell you that the penalty for insubordination within the Artificial Human Forces is far more severe than the penalty for non-Artificial civilians." A familiar glint—flashing and cruel like his brother—sparked in Tidoris's eye; it was familiar to Ciaan, but not from him.

That glint and the flat menace of his voice made Ciaan's stomach churn.

There was an icy beat and then Mael interrupted, stepping between 1119 and Tidoris.

"It was from one of my most reliable traders. He said that if I got it safely off Earth, he'd make sure all my competition's business funneled to me. Do you have any idea what kind of profits that would mean?" He sneered at Tidoris. "Of course you don't, little prince von Ulger, heir to the wallets and ballots of the High Assembly."

Tidoris stiffened, and Mael kept twisting the knife.

"You think I didn't recognize your name? I'm not an idiot. Whose company do you think buys off the officials at immigration posts? Vouches for falsified customs checks? Outsources their most dangerous illicit imports and exports to private traders and third-class cargo ship captains? I've got family too, and they sure as hell aren't eating with any illegally-mined silver dining sets."

It was a low blow; then again, Ciaan had pretty much the same thoughts on Tidoris's family.

Tidoris stood there, brittle and shuddering. Then— before anyone could stop him—he hurled himself at Mael and crashed them both onto the floor.

He pummeled Mael with sloppy, inexperienced punches, missing more than he landed. Mael shielded his head with his forearms, even though Tidoris wasn't hitting above the shoulders.

Ciaan moved to separate them—or at least keep Tidoris from getting seriously hurt—then hesitated. *They need to settle this now,* she thought, *before things get really out of hand between them.*

Even she and Melean had been on better terms after they'd almost beaten each other to death.

Mael waited until Tidoris had worn himself out a little, then curled a leg around the back of Tidoris's ankle and spun him off balance. Tidoris's back hit the metal floor with a crack, but Mael caught him by the collar before his head could snap down hard too.

Tidoris blinked up at him, stunned like he didn't understand how their positions had reversed so quickly.

Now Ciaan was a little worried; Mael obviously had a lot more training and far better fighting instincts. He straddled Tidoris just below the waist and—no matter how hard he kicked—Tidoris couldn't knock him off.

Mael caught his wrists and pinned them down against his stomach with one hand. His other hand, still full of Tidoris's uniform collar, lowered Tidoris's head to the ground.

"I'm not gonna hit you." Mael leaned in a little too close, even for a fight.

Their chests rose and fell off-rhythm and Tidoris's legs stilled. 1119 cleared her throat loudly.

"Truce?" Mael pulled back, just a little.

"Truce." Tidoris hadn't screamed once during the fight, but his voice still came out raspy.

Behind them, one of the Earth humans shifted on their cot. The restraint straps creaked, cutting through the lingering strangeness in the room.

[EIGHT]

"**Y**OU WANT TO DO WHAT?" Tidoris croaked, rustling behind the makeshift partition they'd set up between the two cots in case they needed to separate the cargo.

The unregistereds, Ciaan corrected herself, staring down at the sedated girl sprawled out under the restraints.

They looked like they hadn't been cared for in years, these Earth humans—worse than restricted animals smuggled onto Toi, fifty to a cage, and left to die. The four of them had drawn straws (or, rather, Tidoris's spare cuts of wire) for bathing duty and Ciaan'd pulled short; she'd put it off until Tidoris was between shifts and roped him into helping her.

"I want to have dinner with your family." Ciaan scrubbed a cloth across the distended stomach.

The girl's eyelids fluttered; Tidoris had given them both short-term tranquilizer shots—though he'd been hesitant about her, worried that she might overdose. But since both her and the boy got violent whenever anyone tried touching them, and since they still hadn't figured out an effective way to communicate—Tidoris'd tried Global sign language and thought the girl might've understood a little, but just refused to answer—for now, it was tranquilizing boosters or no contact (medical, sanitary, or otherwise) at all.

"See—" Tidoris knocked his knuckles against the partition, "—that's what I thought you said."

Ciaan snorted, loosened the restraint strap across the girl's chest to get at the caked-on grime. The unregistereds were still too weak to move around on their own, so they spent their non-tranquilized time strapped in the cots.

It'd been almost a week since Ciaan, Tidoris, 1119, and Mael had pried open that storage container and—after a terse debate over what could happen to the unregistereds if they were turned in to the base commander versus what the four of them risked by not reporting them—they had decided that, for now, it was better not to bring AH into this.

Once that'd been settled, they worked out a rotating system for managing their new responsibilities. Mael and 1119 were on regular guard duty during the day, making sure that the unregistereds were kept secure and out of sight from the rest of the base workers and docked crews, with Mael volunteering to deflect attention as often (and obnoxiously) as needed. 1119 administered muscle repairing boosters (from the *Maelstrom*'s private stash) every other day, and Tidoris monitored their vital signs whenever he could sneak off for a visit—usually during meal breaks or decomp or after hours—recording everything in case the histories were demanded later. It was easier for Ciaan to stop by between shifts, since the *Maelstrom* was under her assignment for the duration of its docking at the CPZ.

They all took turns on wash duty, which meant cleaning off as much filth as they could with a hand towel and two bowls of water and antiseptic solution. This was Ciaan's third time and she still thought the girl looked like she needed a long, hot shower.

She squeezed the towel out over the dirty water bowl and wiped again under a breast.

"Dori, what's the big deal? They're coming on base anyway to see you. I know you can make the request to my supervising officer," she wheedled. "And it's not like there're any significant negative marks on my performance record that he can use to deny it."

"You mean, not yet there aren't." Tidoris laughed on the other side of the plastic wall, cold and humorless. "They're not gonna have negative marks strong enough for our records when we get caught. We're gonna *wish* for negative marks."

"Exactly," Ciaan said cheerfully. "All the more reason to live life to the fullest before we're executed for crimes against p-people."

Ciaan wedged her arm under the girl's back—it was hard to wash her thoroughly without help. When Tidoris popped his head over the partition, she instinctively covered the girl's naked body.

"Why?" he pressed, kept his eyes focused just above Ciaan's head.

For half a second, she thought about playing dumb—but then decided it'd just be a waste of time. Tidoris knew her too well for that.

"Because Mael was right." Ciaan gritted her teeth; the words tasted sour on her tongue. "You and I both know that your father's success has less to do with business savvy and more to do with finding loopholes and exploiting them."

Tidoris dropped back behind the partition, something dark itching across his face. He sounded stiff behind the plastic. "Why are we talking about this?"

Ciaan lowered her voice, glancing behind her. There wasn't anyone there.

"You know why."

"Yeah, I know." Tidoris muttered, paused. "It's a bad idea, Ciaan."

"Why? A halfie isn't good enough to bring over for dinner?" Ciaan tossed out the slur, going for effect.

Tidoris started up in protest. "Ciaan, please don't talk about yourself like—"

She cut him off.

"I'm not gonna accuse your father of anything—it's not like he put them in that container." Ciaan glanced down at the girl's blank, tranquilized face. "But your father knows people and things, more than any of us do, so it's a place to start. The only place I can think of, anyway."

Tidoris didn't answer for a while; when he finally did, his tone was guarded.

"I don't know, Ciaan. You know how my father can be—I don't think he'd take the bait. Besides, Melean and my mother will be there…"

"So we throw out some vague questions and see what he lets slip. That should at least give us an idea of the kind of shit we've stepped into." Ciaan threw the towel into the laundry receptacle with a wet splat and covered the girl up with a thin sheet. "Unless you have another plan?"

Tidoris mumbled, then reappeared from behind the partition. "And why do you have to come? Are you hoping that two spying heads will be better than one?"

Ciaan grinned. "Yeah, and also I don't think you'd do it by yourself."

Tidoris scoffed but didn't argue the point.

Ciaan fumbled with the zipper—from the base of her spine all the way up to the nape of her neck—on the long, sleek, silver dress. It was the only one she owned, much to her little sister's disappointment. Helona swore that dresses suited her figure, round and soft with wide curves instead of angles, and even Briette had said it looked good (the one time Ciaan had worn it). Her father had shipped it to the base—rush, just liked Ciaan asked him to—and it got there the morning of her debut dinner with the von Ulgers.

She looked at herself in the choppy, warped barracks mirror—noted how the seams caught on her pudge, how the elegance of the length was lost on her short body, how the bright color made her skin look darker by contrast. She ran her hands over the wrinkles and pinned back a few stray blonde hairs that poked out of her braids, then slipped on a pair of heeled dress boots and exhaled through her nose before heading to the barracks door. The tips of her fingers jittered and she tried to shake the nervousness out of them; it had to be gone before she met Tidoris's family.

Out in the dry chill of the base, Ciaan felt exposed, bare arms brushing against the smooth fabric.

I'm practically naked, she thought with a scowl.

Tidoris was waiting near a small crane, parked mid-lift, with a few metal scraps and disassembled parts scattered nearby. He waved Ciaan over, heel bouncing out an anxious rhythm on the tinny ground.

"You look more nervous than I feel." Ciaan called out loudly, trying to sound calmer than she was.

The closer she got, the better she could make out Tidoris's lanky frame and the outfit that hung on it. He was wearing a tightly-tailored, dark blue suit and sharp, black boots that he'd clearly tried to shine the scuffs off of. The jacket was buttoned high and straight with one collar folded open at the breastbone—similar to what Ciaan had seen among fashionable First-tier diplomats who commuted through the base—revealing a thin slice of Tidoris's dark skin. The buttons were big and shiny, though, which Ciaan guessed was a faux pas if the suits in the few fashion publications (skimmed from surplus shipments) that she kept jammed under her barracks cot were anything to go by.

His braids had a faint sheen to them too—like he'd put oil in them tonight—and a few beads of sweat pricked around his hairline, invisible unless someone was looking for them.

Ciaan coughed, cleared her sticky throat.

"I didn't know you owned a suit."

Tidoris pulled at his cuffs. "Everyone owns a suit—or dress clothes, at least."

He looked her up and down, quick like he was afraid of being caught.

"You look nice."

"I know." She blinked at the empty space just past Tidoris's ear. "Helona says I'm built for dresses."

Tidoris's heel stopped tapping. "She isn't wrong."

"I just wish it had a little more cover." Ciaan poked at her elbows, shifting the topic. "Feels like I'm painting a target on myself."

Tidoris chuckled and offered his arm; Ciaan raised a skeptical eyebrow.

"My father's a stickler for manners," he chewed around a smile and Ciaan wondered if he was laughing at her.

"Yeah," she countered, "but we still have to walk all the way to the private dining rooms before we see him."

Tidoris's smile dropped; he nodded stiffly and lowered his arm. Ciaan suddenly wanted to take it, wanted him to know that it wasn't a problem, but the moment had already passed. They walked in uncomfortable silence until they got to the Administrative complex—then Ciaan took his arm, even though he hadn't offered it again.

With their arms linked, Ciaan was abruptly aware of the strict distance between the rest of their bodies. She pushed it aside, focused on not tripping over the uneven hem of her dress.

She'd never been inside the Administrative complex—only the main building at the entrance, which was AH. Beyond that was where the base supervisors and stationed officials lived and socialized, away from the basics and low-level workers. Ciaan had always assumed that this area was much nicer than the barracks, but seeing the difference firsthand actually made her mad.

The buildings were larger and far better maintained than most of the civilian housing on Toi. There were no gaudy, lacquered colors; everything was coated in a crystal sheen that mimicked a perpetual fresh buff. She couldn't see any cracks or dents, and nothing was warped or mis-soldered. Embossed plaques hung above the wide doorways, stamped with names like *Dignitaries' Hotel* and *Leisure Hall* in a swirling script.

Ciaan thought about the hard bunk mattresses and punctured barrack windows that sucked in the frigid air at night. She hissed through her teeth.

"My original living quarters were in here, you know." Tidoris seemed less shocked; his gaze was passive, like it all was just what he'd expected. "I assume it was a combination of my last name and a DM from my father that got me into the officers' apartments."

"Oh really?" Ciaan dug her nails into his starchy sleeve. "Then why aren't you living there right now, Your Highness?"

"Because I rejected the offer and requested quarters outside the complex," he shrugged.

Ciaan loosened her grip.

"That's why Father had Melean take me to the base—I filed the request the night before I left so he wouldn't have time to try to personally change my mind. He did say that it made the whole family look bad—having me live in some tin can at a transit port—over breakfast, so that was something."

Ciaan held on a little tighter and smirked. "Melean couldn't persuade you?"

"I think the only people who find Melean persuasive are the ones who haven't known him very long." Tidoris snickered. "Besides, what kind of life would I have had cooped up behind these fancy walls with only limited access to you and your shenanigans? Why—my job would be safe, I wouldn't be facing a potential detention sentence, and there certainly wouldn't be any mysterious and potentially fugitive Earth humans needing to be nursed back to health. And the food would probably be a lot better too."

"Well, then, you're pretty dumb." Ciaan pinched him and he winced. "I wouldn't give up this kind of luxury just to slum it with you in the network tunnels."

Tidoris grinned, mouth full of white teeth, as they stopped at a building with flourishes etched around the oval windows. Its plaque read, *Grand Dining Chambers*.

"Here goes nothing." Tidoris took a deep breath and they started up the stairs, not quite in step with each other. At the top, his finger hovered over the door button for a moment; when he finally pressed it, a deep bell rang from somewhere inside.

They waited, and a few seconds later the door swung open, held fast by a black-suited recruit.

He didn't ask any questions or make any helpful gestures, just stood oddly-erect as they walked past. A digital board above what looked like an information desk flashed names and room numbers; *Von Ulger* blinked next to 1F7. A floorplan was projected below with red lights blinking in what had to be occupied rooms.

"This way." Tidoris pointed to their left and Ciaan

followed, stumbling a little over her feet as she went.

As they made their way through the halls, the nervous flutter kicked up again under Ciaan's skin. The dining room doors were either open or non-existent—there'd be no warning, no time to prepare herself for the wolves' den.

When they reached an open door at the end of a wide block of rooms, Tidoris leaned down and whispered, "Remember—you're here to get information, not to impress them."

But both would be nice; Ciaan winced and shook away that traitorous thought.

Soft light poured out of the doorway and, at first, Ciaan didn't see anyone inside—all she saw was the thick sweep of curtains, the curve of real wood in the chairs, how the clusters of chandelier crystals danced in the room's bronze-warm glow. She heard the clink of ceramic and metal—not shrill like their world, but heavy and melodic. Something smelled sweet, like syrup glazing the air.

That, she realized, *must be perfume.*

Someone cleared their throat, delicate but firm.

Tidoris folded down into a formal bow and Ciaan let him guide her; she'd never given more than a cursory one to anyone before, not even officers. She brought a hand up to her chest, grateful for the high cut of her neckline.

Once they came back up, Tidoris led them over to the circular table. Their empty chairs were sandwiched between Melean and High Citizen von Ulger—she'd never met anyone else with that title. Tidoris sat in the chair by his father; Ciaan dropped down rigidly next to Melean.

"Good evening, Father. Mother." Tidoris gave deferential nods to his parents, then glanced at Melean. "Brother."

"You're late," High Citizen von Ulger drawled, but there was a calculating edge to his tone. He cut into the air around him, not big so much as *encompassing*. Ciaan couldn't see a single loose thread on his suit or a black-grey hair out of place in his thinning braids.

"Sorry, Father. We were held up at the security checkpoint." Tidoris folded his napkin precisely over his lap.

"That's absurd. We left specific instructions with the guards for your clearance," Melean cut in haughtily, sawing through a tough cut of meat.

Then he turned and eyed Ciaan's bare, muscled arms. "Hello, Ciaan. You're looking very robust—the reserve exercise routines keeping you hardy?"

She bit the inside of her cheek and fought the urge to wrap her arms around herself and away from his lewd gaze.

"Yes, Melean, you did leave those instructions for me," Tidoris sniped at his brother. "Unfortunately, you didn't do the same for Ciaan, so we had to get her fully verified before we could get in."

Melean swished his fork dismissively.

"That's what you get for keeping this kind of company. I'm surprised they even let a green halfie like her inside." Melean had learned how to dress-up his hate, but still didn't bother disguising his contempt. "Father, you ought to speak with them about keeping track of the garbage around here. If they're not careful, this place will get *filthy*."

Ciaan dropped her knife with a clatter, tasted copper pooling on her tongue.

"That's enough, Melean." High Citizen von Ulger's wife was smaller than her husband, but the steel arc of her back somehow made her more imposing. Her features jutted out in fine lines that caught shadows between their angles and her voice was soft, almost frail, but when she spoke everyone listened.

The purple dye of her gown accented her dark complexion—Tidoris's rather than Melean's. Melean, like his father, was a shade or two lighter; Ciaan hoped that Melean would end up fat and balding like his father too. HC von Ulger didn't even wear a hairpiece to hide it—except, Tidoris had told her, at First-tier galas. She thought about her own father's loose braids, usually frayed at the ends with uneven tangles and clumps of hair sticking out.

Lady von Ulger was watching her, gaze penetrating and suspicious, and the room suddenly felt ten degrees colder.

"My sons tell me that you attended primary grades with them. I can't remember seeing you, though I think that—with such a distinctive attribute—I would remember if I did. And now you're serving a community service sentence at the base." The woman left no opening for confirmation or denial; Ciaan couldn't read her flatness but knew that she had to be beneath every one of Lady von Ulger's standards for social interactions.

"It's interesting." Lady von Ulger's eyes narrowed.

Ciaan brushed a pale wisp behind her ear. "My criminal history?"

"Your hair." Lady von Ulger's mouth pinched, like she was holding something else she wanted to say behind her lips. "It's natural, I suppose."

Ciaan hesitated, not sure if it was a question she was supposed to answer.

"Perhaps she would be willing to sell it, dearest." High Official von Ulger gestured smoothly to Ciaan. "How much would you want for your braids, girl? Cut to the scalp. Don't try to cheat us now."

"Excuse me?" Ciaan's skin pricked with a thousand invisible needles. The initial heat from embarrassment drained out of her.

"Father, she's not one of your Earth cattle waiting to be shorn. Her hair is not for sale." Tidoris set his fork down. "And her name is Ciaan."

There was a brief, tense staredown between Tidoris and his father, then—after ten or so seconds—the man scoffed and went back to his food.

The rest of them returned to their plates too.

Ciaan focused on a pile of multi-colored vegetables, unfamiliar and bitter to her. She ate them one-by-one, deciding that this might be her only chance to try them; when she finished the pile, she turned again to High Citizen von Ulger.

Now's as good a time as ever; she plastered an ingratiating smile on her face.

"So your trade is in materials and fabrics, High Citizen von Ulger?" She glanced admiringly at Lady von Ulger's gown. "I'm assuming, since your wife has such an eye for fashions."

The High Citizen swallowed a large mouthful then answered, "A little bit of everything really. You know, business comes down to who you know and what they can do for you. I always tell my sons: securing favors is the best trade deal you can make."

He stuffed another forkful of meat into his mouth.

"Mmm," Ciaan hummed. "And what about specific goods? Is anything particularly lucrative?"

High Citizen von Ulger sat back in his chair and assessed her, slow and deliberate.

"You've got a business mind, girl? You could go far with your half blood, contracting with both p-traders and Earth merchants." He glared at Tidoris. "Maybe you could even motivate my shiftless son to do something productive with his life."

Ciaan pushed on, trying to keep the conversation on track. "I *have* heard that trading can be dangerous if you get involved with the wrong kind of products."

"There are no wrong kinds of products. Everything has a market." He ticked off a list on his thick fingers. "Restricted items, Earth animals, gratification materials, uncontrolled substances, information—"

"People?" Ciaan threw it out and hoped it stuck to something.

High Citizen von Ulger cocked his head, leaned in and blocked almost everything else from view. He'd set a trap and she'd crashed right into it; Ciaan suddenly understood how he could be such an effective businessman.

"What do you mean, *people*?" Melean scoffed, oblivious to the tension between Ciaan and his father.

"You've been watching too many sensationalist reports, greenie—excuse me, *Ciaan*. There's no conspiracy of human traders and even if there was, you wouldn't need to worry; no one would want to buy you."

Ciaan held the High Citizen's gaze, didn't even acknowledge Melean's insult.

Finally, he blinked.

"Melean's right." High Citizen Von Ulger spoke carefully, sipping from his wine glass. "There is no black market trade in humans, at least not that I know of."

Ciaan pressed him, feeling reckless and on the cusp of something important. "Because it's too risky?"

"Because there's no market for it," he spat out roughly. "There's a device for almost everything—and if there isn't a device, it's probably not worth having another person around for anyway. No one's willing to spend the money and risk arrest on smuggled servants or sex workers when there are legal alternatives already so readily—and cheaply—available. What else would you need to buy a human for?"

Ciaan hesitated, considered his point. "But that's only on the p-planets, right? What about inter-Earth routes?"

High Citizen Von Ulger chuckled; it was condescending with something menacing at its core. "Someone put some foolish ideas into your head, girl. If we don't need to smuggle something onto the p-planets, then Earth humans *certainly* wouldn't need to smuggle it between Unions. If you're going to run a business then this is your first, and most important, lesson: there is only a one-way demand between the p-planets and Earth. No one exports anything from us; we have nothing Earth humans want or need, except our money. Once you understand that, the necessary choices become a lot easier to make."

Ciaan opened her mouth, had a dozen more questions to ask, but nothing came out. The meal continued on to politer, shallower topics until their desserts were cleared then ended with another stiff, formal goodbye. As she and Tidoris made their way back to the barracks, Ciaan tried to decide whether none—or all—of her questions had been answered.

[NINE]

FOUR DAYS AFTER THEIR DINNER with the von Ulgers, Ciaan popped open a false panel in the *Maelstrom*'s decompression room and found a bundle of old-tech hard disks tucked away inside.

She'd been looking for some old Information Channel files—ostensibly for research and not her own personal interest—that Mael said were saved on the decomp drive. While she was waiting for them to download, Ciaan had knocked around the walls until one spot echoed back hollowly; she'd pried the panel off, stomach sinking as she reached in and grabbed a handful of dusty, pressed plastic. Something was off, and not just because the disks had clearly been hidden in a secret compartment. No one had used hard disks for decades;

now they only held backups of backups of files and originals of data that wasn't meant to be seen. Most people didn't even know what disks looked like, much less how to read them.

Luckily, Ciaan was on good terms with the best Technical Advisor on the base.

"Why do you need to read disks?" Tidoris was crouched inside a hole in the metal ground, working on an exposed section of network tunnel. The tool in his hand sparked and sizzled.

"Just answer the question!" Ciaan shouted over the noise. "Do you have something that can read disks?"

"Of course I do! You don't get rid of a machine that can read obsolete technology—you never know when something might need to be accessed and no one else will have the right equipment." Tidoris poked his head out, dark goggles catching Ciaan's unimpressed reflection. "Roll your eyes all you want, but this just proves my point."

Ciaan sidestepped his argument. "So where's this machine? Is it on the base?"

He pushed the goggles up his forehead, wiped the sweat from under his eyes.

"Yes, it's on the base. Do you think I'd leave it at home for my father to confiscate or Melean to break?" He squinted at her. "*Why* do you need to read disks?"

Ciaan huffed and gave in; she wasn't sure why she hadn't just told him to begin with, but when she'd found the disks it'd felt like a mission, like something she was being entrusted with. Almost like she'd been chosen—like maybe she was special for more than just the color of her braids.

That, she now realized, was stupid.

"I found some disks in a false panel on the ship. I figured if they were hidden—"

Tidoris finished the thought for her. "There must be a good reason. How many?"

His eyes were bright and Ciaan bit back a grin; whether he'd admit it or not, Tidoris was starting to enjoy their (relatively minor, all things considered) intrigue.

"Three."

"Decomp starts in thirty minutes. Meet me at my quarters." Tidoris slid back into the tunnel and Ciaan wandered away, looking for something to keep her busy for no more than half an hour.

"Give me just one minute," Tidoris heaved, shifting stacks of partially deconstructed machines from one place to another—under the table, against the wall, on the part of the bed that Ciaan wasn't sitting on.

His quarters were nicer than the barracks, no question about that, but it was still cramped and a little shabby inside. The furniture was barebones: a narrow bed, one table, one dresser, and one bookshelf—all pushed against opposite walls. Ciaan assumed that the door on the far end of the room was the bathroom.

As for his actual stuff, it was mostly electronics in various stages of dissection and repair. Six or seven books sat piled on the top shelf of his bookcase and a tool kit lay open on his table. Other than that, the room was empty.

"Ah, okay, here it is." Tidoris held up a hunk of metal and exposed wires triumphantly. "Now I've just gotta connect it to my Right Hand…"

He tinkered at it with a tiny screwdriver.

"Okay, give me the disks."

Ciaan reached into her bag and took them out in a stack; Tidoris gaped, snatching them away from her.

"Don't hold them like that! You'll ruin them! These are antique electronics—we have to treat them with respect." He wiped each one gently with a soft square of fabric, then snapped them into a protective case.

"I'll respect them later, Dori." Ciaan bounced on the mattress lightly, then froze when the tower of dismembered machines next to her lurched. "We need to see whatever's on them—fast. Decomp ends in twenty."

Tidoris grumbled and slipped the first disk into the machine. He typed out long strings of code, one after the other, hunched over his Right Hand's screen. After a minute he stopped, leaning back in his chair.

"That was surprisingly easy." He almost sounded disappointed. The Right Hand beeped and buzzed on the table, churning with effort. "There's only one file—I think it's a video file—but it's compressed. I'm extracting it now to see if it's uncorrupted. That was one of the big problems with disks; they were too sensitive. Too much data was lost."

The Right Hand stilled; Tidoris typed in a few more commands.

"It looks like the file's okay. Let me just expand the display…"

A grainy image materialized in front of them—it was an Earth woman standing against a colorless background. Her clothes were crisp, professional but outdated; double folded lapels hadn't been worn since Ciaan's first mother was in university. She still remembered the creased, faded school photos her first mother had kept in a scrapbook, along with Earth transit tickets and the few awkward love letters Ciaan's father had written to her.

The woman began speaking in choppy, throaty

words that Ciaan couldn't understand.

Tidoris leaned down and said into the built-in microphone, "Translate to Global."

A ting-y, robotic voice fed over the original language:

"—the crisis has reached what officials are calling an epidemic stage, particularly in the most developed standardized regions. New studies are reporting a 27% increase in female infertility levels over the past year, with the majority of patients ranging in age from 18 to 35. The same studies found a lower—though still alarming—14% increase in male sterility Earth-wide. There has also been a dramatic rise in late-term miscarriages and still-births; full-term live-births, however, appear to have no heightened risk for infant mortality. Although research now suggests that 1 in 11 Earth women are or will become sterile in their lifetimes, along with 1 in 25 Earth men, doctors are cautioning against the many marketed 'miracle cures.' They emphasize that there is no conclusive evidence supporting any of these cures and add that there have been several cases of these so-called 'wonder drugs' causing further damage to the reproductive organs and occasionally leading to life-threatening complications. Still, couples and single women desperate to conceive have started seeking out more drastic, and costly, options. Scientists are still unsure of what could be causing this crisis but are concerned by the rising number of women and men reporting symptoms and seeking out pre-emptive fertility testing. If these rates remain constant, 50% of Earth women may be unable to become pregnant within the next forty years, due to either their or their partner's sterility. In the face of this global emergency, the question now becomes: What can we do to stop this new generation from being Earth's final one?"

The image stuttered and flickered out; for a heavy minute, Tidoris and Ciaan stared at the empty air where it'd been.

"That…" Ciaan started, not quite sure where she was going. "That was some kind of joke, wasn't it? Somebody's overactive imagination on a boring cargo run, right?"

The list of percentages and statistics rang in her ears—and something else too, a memory she couldn't pull up all the way.

Tidoris had already switched out disks.

"Let's see if we can get some clarification." His fingers tapped out, frantic and hard. The screen shook with the pressure. "No video files on this one, just some images. Expand."

What looked like old-fashioned news articles popped up; Tidoris flipped through them while Ciaan scanned the titles.

'Infertility Crisis a Potential Global Threat'

*'Union Leaders Urge Unilateral Action to
Develop Infertility Cure'*

*'Baby Steps; Scientists Successfully Grow
First 'Test Tube Girl'' 'Research Still
Unclear on Sterility Origins'*

*''Devastating Blow'–Artificial Females Lack
Viable Eggs'*

*'Precious Cargo; Government-Funded Facilities
Monitor and Protect Earth's Pregnancies'*

'Global Sterility Rates Reach 44%'

*'GDPs and Standards of Living Suffer Without
Babies'*

*'Health Organizations Focus on Environmental
Factors in the Search for Sterility Causes'*

*'Orbit of Hope; Researchers Are Looking to the
P-planets for Possible Infertility Answers'*

Something pulsed in Ciaan, ached like a boot to the sternum.

*'Sterility Rates Reach Five-Year Low–
Geneticists Laud Experimental Procedures as
'Success''*

'Rights Groups' Calls for Inquests into Fertility 'Units' and Alleged Atrocities Largely Dismissed'

''The Extinction Paradox'—Politicians and Scientists Defend Their Response to the Crisis'

'Survivors Speak Out: 'The Crisis Took Our Fertility but the Units Took Our Humanity''

The last article stayed up on the screen; Ciaan reread its title slowly.

"These reports are over 40 years old." Tidoris magnified the publication dates, turning to Ciaan with wide, panicked eyes. "Earth had an infertility crisis 40 years ago—why did we never hear about it? Why wasn't it mentioned on the Information Channels or in government alerts? Something like this couldn't just happen without the p-planets knowing about it..."

Ciaan ran through the Information Channels in her mind, cataloguing all the inane reports they transmitted—it was either advice on what to buy, how to dress, what to change about yourself, or trashy gossip about prominent Earth humans and p-people (peppered with outlandish rumors and hints of nasty scandals). No one bothered watching the current event reports; they were usually just live feeds transmitted from some boring committee session or stock messages lauding the pleasant, comfortable lifestyles that Earth humans were enjoying.

Even her first mother hadn't really watched those reports; she'd only turned them on when Ciaan asked her to. Ciaan remembered their game—mimicking the funny accents—and how her first mother's laughter danced in her ears during many lonely, sleepless nights.

Now those memories spun more sinister—what would she and her first mother have heard if they'd been listening with the translations on?

Everything Ciaan knew about Earth had come from those transmissions; it was all prosperity, happiness, growth and re-growth. Not just living people, but a living world.

Lies, Ciaan realized, swallowing back the bile.

No wonder the p-planets had no idea what was really going on down there.

Tidoris jammed in the third disk, glancing at his old jerry-rigged digital clock. They had three minutes before decomp ended.

"Just one file." His jaw ticked as he brought it up. "Text."

It was a list of names and numbers; Ciaan assumed they were census codes or whatever the Earth equivalent was. There were two sets next to each name, then a bold **S** or **F**. Tidoris scrolled down and Ciaan tried to skim each name, but only caught a dozen or so. There was page after page of them—*thousands*, Ciaan thought—and even in the blur of letters she could see that the Ss clearly outnumbered the Fs.

"Ciaan?" Tidoris sounded strange, distant and strained, like he was being strangled in a dream. "Your first mother's name was Gytha, wasn't it?"

"Yeah…" Ciaan choked it out, didn't ask why.

The scroll stopped and an entry highlighted itself on the display:

Janot, Gytha. [ALIAS Gennett] 0000301631 241806 F

Ciaan stared at it, blinked once, twice, three times, but nothing—not a single letter—changed.

Back on their own metal planet, something was ringing.

"That's the afternoon shift signal." Tidoris moved closer to Ciaan—reached for her hand but she shook it off; he pulled back. "Do you want me to put in an overexertion exemption request for you?"

"What I want you to do is get a new recruit to cover my inventory detail and keep it off the base commander's radar," she snapped, trying to stop her body from shaking. "Captain Moon and I need to have a long, *private* talk."

It hit Ciaan as she punched in the port door code, like a crack to the jaw.

Those words: *precious cargo*.

Marching past 1119, who was doing some minor seam repairs on the hull, Ciaan climbed aboard the ship and ran fast along the deckways. She didn't bother knocking when she got to the bridge—just burst in, ready for a confrontation, but the room was empty. After kicking the back of the captain's chair and leaving a scuffed boot print behind, she decided that the medical bay was the next best bet.

She found Mael standing near the tranquilized boy's cot, hands shoved in his jacket pockets.

"I heard you coming." He didn't turn around. "*These two* probably heard you coming, what with all the stomping."

Ciaan wanted to wreck him. She wanted to sneak up from behind and blitz him—show him how p-kids really fought. She wanted to demand answers and then smash his face in before he could give them. She wanted—

But she couldn't move, couldn't speak, couldn't do anything except suck the stale ship air into her lungs and push it out again.

"You found the disks." It wasn't a question.

Mael scoffed. "You think the captain doesn't know

the false panels in his ship?"

"And what else does the captain know?" Ciaan seethed, fury crawling up from the bottom of her throat. "How much of what you told us wasn't a lie?"

"Technically, I didn't lie—you just never asked about it." Mael shrugged, slumped a little like he was suddenly exhausted. "What do p-people care anyway? Earth is just a myth to you; it might as well be a billion light years away for all you really know about it."

"And them?" Ciaan pointed to the unregistereds, the *cargo*—Earth humans like him.

He flinched.

"I honestly didn't know I was transporting anything like this. But..." Mael paused, then continued bitterly, "I didn't make any effort to know, either. I have a no-questions-asked policy; obviously it's not always failsafe."

Ciaan ground her back teeth. "Obviously."

Mael finally turned to face her—crossed his arms and tucked his fists tightly under them. He looked serious, seemed older than she'd thought he was before.

"I can't deliver this cargo, not now that I've actually seen what it is."

Ciaan hooked one eyebrow up. "So now you remember the details for this particular shipment?"

"Yes." The smug, confident glint in Mael's eyes was gone. "1119 was telling the truth when she said that we'd picked it up in the West Asian Union. One of my most reliable traders—he usually deals in restricted animals and refashioned herbs from the non-standardized regions—asked me to get it to the Capital Port Zone on Wakan Tanka, said it'd be taken care of from there."

His voice cracked. "I thought it was just some exotic pets for the First-tiers."

Ciaan studied his odd Earth face—the slope of his nose, the flutter of his short eyelashes, the grim downturn of his mouth.

"So why didn't you just go to Wakan Tanka? Why stop here?"

"There was a tip that customs officials were increasing Capital Port security for interplanetary transports ahead of the One Worlds Gala. Of course, because we all bend over backwards for Earth First-tiers but when it comes to these kinds of humans"—he nodded viciously towards the cots—"we couldn't care less."

"Then why didn't you say something to us before?" Ciaan stepped closer, got in his space. "Why do you keep lying to protect people who clearly don't give a shit about anyone?!"

"Because saying something about it on the p-planets is treason!" Mael shouted, red-cheeked and panting. "Because, unlike illicit traders, people who break the

Information Sharing regulations actually get whisked away in tinted government crafts—every day—and they don't come back."

Ciaan closed her eyes, saw her second mother's brand seared into the back of her eyelids.

"And because I'm a coward." Mael deflated—stared at her, eyes glassy and flat. "You don't know what it's like on Earth."

Ciaan's throat went dry, gaze settling on the girl's bulging stomach. A needle-prick chill tiptoed up her back.

No, I don't know, she shivered. *But I have an idea.*

[TEN]

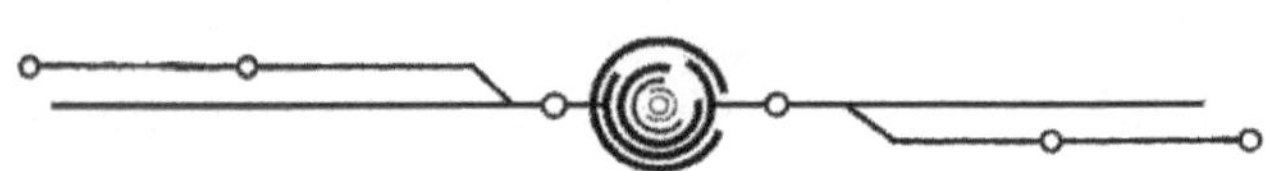

A PLACID, FULL DARKNESS—the kind that only comes in the absence of the sky hologram—blanketed the barracks.

To regulate weather-related physical and psychological disorders, the artificial atmospheres of the p-planets were coated in a hazy mimicry of the skies on Earth, with the real Earth looming big like the shadow of a giant behind it. Sometimes the hologram displayed rain and snow, but without any actual water vapor or clouds to produce storms it was just a visual effect.

The only areas it didn't cover were the ports, for obvious visibility and security reasons. The first few nights of Ciaan's reserve term had been sleepless; she couldn't relax in the absolute blackness. But now she fell asleep as soon as her head hit the bricky mattress, sometimes sooner.

She'd started to forget what the sky looked like without its dark vastness.

Ciaan had fallen asleep faster than usual tonight; her reserve unit had gotten several filework violations over the past few weeks, so the commander assigned them to double cleaning duty for the day. She'd skipped dinner for a nap but was still bone-tired when the lights-out signal rang.

These days it wasn't the darkness that kept her tossing in her blankets—it was the frigid port air. She woke up to toes stiff like icicles under the sheets and decided that she needed to get a thicker pair of night socks. When she begrudgingly opened her eyes, the first thing she saw was a shock of whiteness hovering above the cot, blinking down at her.

She took a deep breath, ready to scream, but a hand was on her mouth fast and firm before the sound could well up in her throat.

"I'll remove my hand, but only if you promise not to make any loud demands." 1119 whispered. Her face still glowed, even without any light to reflect.

Ciaan nodded and bit her lips shut.

"What are you doing here?" Ciaan rasped against the night cold.

"There's a problem. Your assistance, as our docking supervisor, is required." 1119 stood up, waiting for Ciaan to follow. Her eyes weren't bloodshot and she didn't have dark circles under them—Ciaan thought sulkily that maybe Artificials didn't need as much sleep as humans; maybe they didn't need any sleep at all.

Ciaan zipped up her thermal jacket and reached for her boots. 1119 stopped her, glancing around at the rows of sleeping recruits.

"Carry them outside."

Ciaan picked them up obediently and shuffled to the barracks door. Outside in the dull glow of the few base night lights, Ciaan struggled to wedge her freezing feet into them.

"What time is it?"

1119 answered mechanically, like a Right Hand. "3:15 Night Time, approximately."

Ciaan groaned, stamping a heel on. "What about Tidoris?"

"The captain went to get him." 1119 looked at Ciaan's long night dress, pouring out from under her jacket, with a ghost of a smile. "Under the circumstances, we felt it was the only appropriate way."

"Yeah, yeah." Ciaan was walking ahead of her now, trying not to trip over any stray mooring straps or ground hatch handles.

The ports were dark except for a single stream of light pouring out of the *Maelstrom*; Ciaan didn't have to ask where the problem was. As she and 1119 boarded the ship, an anguished howl tumbled down the deckways.

She looked back at 1119—the Artificial's face was blank—and raced towards the medical bay. Mael and Tidoris were already there, perched over the wailing girl and the thrashing boy.

Mael braced the boy's restraints, yelling, "Relax! Relax!" He was wearing his pants and boots but his jacket was off, leaving just a sleeveless undershirt stretched tight over his straining muscles.

Tidoris held the girl's chest down, clutching an imposing medical tool in his free hand. He'd clearly had less time to get ready; his faded, striped pajamas ended at slippered feet and his thermal jacket hung open. His braids were frizzled, and Ciaan realized that hers were loose too, pattering against the nape of her neck.

Under him, the girl was shaking her head wildly— eyes huge and wet—and a stream of malformed sounds and shrieks surged out of her.

"Dori, what are you doing?!" Ciaan reeled, not understanding anything she was seeing.

Tidoris looked up, eyes flashing with urgency and real, deep fear.

"They're sick—probably picked up a nasty bacteria

or virus somewhere in transit. The girl's condition is more serious, though, and the fetus might be in danger. I have to examine her before I can figure out how to treat it." He sounded broken, pleading, like he needed someone to forgive him for what he was doing.

He turned back to the girl, signing his words to her.

"I'm sorry, I'm sorry…"

Her arms clattered against the straps.

"Tidoris." Ciaan watched the girl's fingers twist into distinct shapes. "Take off her arm restraints."

"Are you insane?!" Mael shouted, pressing his body weight across the boy's abdomen.

Ciaan pointed at the girl's hands. "She's trying to sign—look!"

They all froze; the boy grunted frantically at them, nodding in agreement. Tidoris glanced at Mael and hesitated, then bent over to release the clasps. As soon as she was free, the girl's arms shot up—everyone jumped at the movement—and her fingers began stamping out patterns.

Tidoris watched her intensely.

"What's she saying?" Mael lifted himself up off the boy, who'd gone still on his cot.

"I'm not totally sure. I never got formal signing communication training…" Tidoris started; Mael coughed and Tidoris shot him an irritated glare. "And I think she's mixing in a lot of her own regional slang. But she does keep saying, *why?*"

"Why what?" Ciaan asked; no one answered.

"Ask if she can give us her identifying information." 1119 stood back near the wall, like she was afraid of catching some of the human mortality.

Tidoris made a brief sign, then repeated it out loud. "Name?"

She signed back and his face wrinkled.

"She spelled out *Y-O-U* and *M-E*." He tried again. "Home?"

She signed a series of characters and Tidoris nodded.

"I don't know the first part—I'm guessing it's the name of her hometown in the local dialect—but she's from the West Asian Union."

He paused, searching for signs he knew.

"Uh…sick. Disease. Baby will die."

The girl sat up in alarm, signing rapidly.

Tidoris corrected himself. "Maybe! Baby will die, *maybe*. Examination—check? We want to help you."

Her eyes roved around the room, sweeping over each one of them. She pointed at Tidoris and signed.

He wavered—shifted guiltily—then shook his head. "No, I'm not a doctor."

The girl narrowed her eyes and signed something emphatic.

Tidoris cocked his head, eyed her more carefully. "Yes, I'm really not a doctor."

A beat—then she nodded, satisfied, and laid back down.

Ciaan cringed as she watched Tidoris delicately examine the girl. He was trying to act clinically detached and professional, but without any real medical training Ciaan knew he was one wrong move away from a mid-exam breakdown. She was actually pretty proud of him—considering the circumstances—but that didn't stop her from winching as he pried the stiff, unflinching unregistered open.

Everything was hushed, like the room itself was holding its breath. Mael stayed near the boy, looking just as uncomfortable as Ciaan felt. 1119's expression was still smooth and unreadable—but Ciaan noticed that she wouldn't look directly at the exam table.

The boy, however, wouldn't look away; he focused on every mutter and prod. Ciaan hoped Tidoris remembered that the other unregistered could still hear.

When it was finally over, Tidoris peeled off the used medical gloves and dropped them into the waste compartment, pausing with his back to the rest of them.

His shoulders shuddered softly.

Ciaan wanted to pull him into a hug; instead, she offered an awkward, "Good job."

He turned and smiled at her, weak and shaky.

"Well?" Mael tapped his foot without any rhythm and Ciaan noticed the sunken circles under his eyes.

Tidoris scratched at his elbow. "I think it's an intestinal parasite, probably food or waste-borne."

Mael's lips curled. "Lovely."

Tidoris ignored him. "It's already taken a lot of nutrients away from her and the fetus, but if we can get our hands on some strong anti-parasitics, we might be able to get rid of it before her condition goes critical."

1119 cleared her throat and motioned towards the cots. Tidoris walked back over to where the girl was signing again and squeezed her hand reassuringly.

"Baby is okay. We will get medicine." His eyebrows knotted together; he pointed to the boy. "Who?"

The girl repeated a sign phrase and Tidoris muttered under his breath.

"She keeps saying that the boy is *You* and she is *Me*." He asked again. "Him—*You*—husband?"

Her fingers fluttered like she was erasing what she'd said before. She paused, then signed a new word.

Tidoris exhaled. "Brother."

The rest of them exchanged startled glances.

Tidoris opened his mouth and pulled out his tongue, pointed to it and then at the boy. He slurred, "Brother, tongue cut how? Prison?"

The girl shook her head and signed out defiantly.

Tidoris gaped. "Doctors."

Someone gasped, small and punched-out. Ciaan couldn't say if it was her or not.

Tidoris pressed three fingertips to the top of the girl's swollen belly. "How pregnant?"

Her jaw clenched; she signed the word again.

"Doctors." Tidoris signed back steady now, voice hard. "You escape here?"

He frowned at her answer.

"More slang?" Mael asked quietly.

"No, it's a word with multiple meanings." Tidoris blinked at him. "It can mean trade or sale—or transfer."

Mael stared at the two humans like he was seeing them for the first time. "Transfer of what?"

"The child, probably." 1119 stood by the door, fists balled at her sides.

After a sticky stretch of silence between them, Ciaan bit out, "Well…shit."

By the time they'd stabilized the unregistereds and hushed them into an untranquilized sleep, it was less than an hour before first call. They'd all scattered to change into their day clothes and Ciaan—zipping her thermal up over her jumpsuit—got back to the dock first. The wide plates of metal and plexiglass seemed to shiver around her; she sat down on a discarded container and let the cold quiet wash over her tired body.

All of a sudden, there was someone next to her; Ciaan looked up in surprise and saw 1119's pale profile cut out against the shimmering sky. There hadn't been any warning—no footsteps, no heavy thud against the rickety plastic box. She was just there, where she hadn't been before, like she'd rewired the atoms around both of them.

"Is it better to know?" 1119 folded her hands in her lap, sounded tarnished and hollow-out.

"To know what?" Ciaan stared out past the port gate at the span of forever, trying to focus on the farthest star she could see.

1119 followed her gaze. "Everything. The truth."

"I don't know everything." As Ciaan watched it, the star blurred—seemed to flicker and burn out, then flare to life again. "I actually feel like I know even less now. At least before, I had a full story to go on…it was mostly lies, sure, but it made sense to us. Before, I could understand the Earth. Now that—that whole world, it's gone."

The thick space between them stretched into that

twinkling ever-night.

"You know why we were created, right? Artificials, I mean," 1119 asked, cracking out her knuckles. "We were meant to be surrogates for infertile Earth woman. I guess we were human enough for that, but not human enough to be mothers—or anything else, really—on our own. The Earth pundits and politicians thought that we lacked the emotional capacity for it…for our—our humanity. They told us, over and over: *emotions don't grow in test tubes*—how could we feel anything about anything, if we had nothing to feel with at all?"

1119 dropped her elbows to her knees, snapping the rigid lines of her posture.

"In the end it didn't matter; the geneticists never could quite get the recipe right and they wouldn't admit it until the third generation—after thousands of Artificials had already been created. We were purposeless then, at least in the eyes of the Union governments, and without our viable surrogacy we were no longer considered human—not in the ways that mattered, anyway."

The pain, vivid and brutal, that pulsed out of 1119 hit Ciaan in the pit of her empty stomach.

"So why didn't the governments stop creating them and just let the first generations die out?" Ciaan flinched; analyzing the lives and deaths of Artificials suddenly felt disgusting.

"Because,"—1119 gazed ahead, calm and clear—"they realized that they'd inadvertently discovered the perfect resource. We are expendable human labor; we die and are immediately replaced with the next one in line. We cannot create life, but we can sacrifice our own to defend it—what better use for us than enlistment in the security forces?"

1119 shifted, buttoned the top clasps on her collar.

"We're raised in group facilities by senior Artificials to follow orders and mandates. We swear to protect our planets and their people no matter what. We are needed. This is our duty—the purpose the first generation of Artificials built for us. It's our part in the worlds." Her voice faltered, losing its precise core. "What else could there be for us?"

Ciaan blinked and the stars seemed to multiply, skipping across the universe. "Do you want to be a mother?"

1119 pushed her short hair behind her ears.

"I don't know. I don't even know if I want to be—if I *am*—a woman."

"Maybe you don't have to be," Ciaan offered.

"You mean, I don't have to be a human." 1119 scoffed. "I can just continue as a machine—an *it*."

"I mean"—Ciaan reached out for the Artificial's

hand, running on strange instinct—"maybe you (not every Artificial, but *you*) are more than a woman, or a man. Not *it*, but maybe…*they?*"

"*They,*" 1119 echoed, trying out the shape of the word.

Ciaan nodded.

After a delicate minute, 1119 turned towards the *Maelstrom*; it seemed to emanate a life force all its own, rumbling from deep within its rusted hull. Without looking back at her, 1119 squeezed Ciaan's fingers and didn't let go.

[ELEVEN]

THEIR RESERVE UNIT WAS in the middle of running spot checks on the baggage checkpoints when Ciaan's Right Hand—which she was technically, *technically* not supposed to have on her person during duty hours—buzzed urgently in her hip pocket for the fifth time in one hour. The other recruits eyed her as she tried to check the screen discreetly, before groaning and hitting the defer button again.

"You fighting with that TA boyfriend of yours?" One of the recruits—overly-muscled with a lumpy, small head—leered at her. "Or is that just a really aggressive stalker?"

A few of the other recruits glanced between them, chuckling nervously. Private Boote was big and nasty, but Ciaan had a (proven) reputation too.

She didn't bother looking up from the stack of busted craft engines she was sifting through. "TA von Ulger isn't my boyfriend."

"Oh yeah?" he taunted. "Then who've you been sneaking off to see in the middle of the night? That midget space captain? Or maybe his Artificial whore…"

The laughs got louder—more recruits started to cluster around them—and harsher, like all the humor had been vacuum-sucked right out of it.

Ciaan tossed one of the salvageable engines into a pile behind her.

"Yes, Boote, you're right." Something coppery settled in her throat, like blood at the back of the tongue. "Why else wouldn't I be fucking you?"

The laughter stopped, died down abruptly, and a few recruits muttered to themselves.

"Exactly!" Boote boomed, soaked in bravado and puffy like the birds they'd learned about in Sciences. He stomped towards her. "You'd be begging for it, like the mutt you are!"

Ciaan was on her feet and ready for him before he realized he'd stumbled into a fight. Boote was half a head taller than her so she knew she couldn't play fair; her only option was to get him before he knew what was coming.

She reached out with both hands, grabbed his ring

fingers and bent them away from his palms. The bones and tendons resisted—so she twisted harder. Boote's knees buckled and he crumpled to the ground, whimpering pitifully.

A judge might've ruled for instigated assault, but the unspoken rule of the reserves (and the p-planets themselves) was *better safe than sorry*—and, if they could, p-people would always make you sorry.

The other recruits backed up, giving them a wide circle, and the scrawniest ones scattered away.

Ciaan had the upper hand; she had to keep it. Had to finish this once and for all—make her point crystal clear for Boote and every other recruit holding their breath around them. No hesitation, no mercy.

She'd learned that lesson a long time ago.

"No, Private Boote." Ciaan leaned down, whispering against the buzz of his sideburns, and forced all her weight onto his straining joints until they popped. "I wouldn't."

When she let go, he curled up and cradled his mangled hands against his chest.

One or two recruits moved cautiously forward to help him as Ciaan walked away, nails digging into her palms until they stung.

The urgent messages and calls were from Ciaan's second mother, with one noticeably less urgent DM from Briette.

Ciaan had briefly thought—after recording a sleepy message full of vague questions about pregnancy medications and prenatal care facilities before first call— that she'd regret sending it to her second mother.

Huddled behind the port public restrooms, Ciaan muttered to her Right Hand, "Play all messages, and expand display."

Illonde's image flickered—still in pajamas, with a scarf wrapped around her braids—and spoke in a slow, careful tone:

"Ciaan, good morning, honey. Why're you asking about these things? If you have something you need to tell us, you know you can just say it—your father and I would take care of you, and anything…else. We'd understand if something happened…although we always hoped that you girls, and Eerick too, would find someone dependable before—but that's not important. Ciaan, sweetie, I can't help you unless you tell me everything. Please call me when you have a shift break. We love you."

Her second mother disappeared into white noise and Ciaan grumbled, "Delete."

A second later, Illonde reappeared—still in pajamas and a scarf—looking less groggy and more concerned.

"Ciaan, honey, I want you to be careful who you talk to about this. Don't go to the medical unit on the base— can you get leave? Even just a day? I'll come and get you and we'll deal with this privately. Don't tell any of the other officers or reserve workers…and see if Tidoris can get the day off too. He should be a part of this. Now baby, don't worry, I gave birth to all my children here on Toi without any problems and—"

Ciaan rolled her eyes. "Delete."

A fully dressed Illonde materialized, fast like there was no delay in the recording.

"Ciaan, please call me. I haven't said anything to anyone about this, but if you don't call me soon I'm going to have to tell your father. Please, *please* call m—"

"Delete!" Ciaan checked the display time; it was only 10:07 MT. She should've known that her second mother would misunderstand and blow this all out of proportion.

"View call log."

The Right Hand chimed in, stilted and monotonous, as the screen changed. "3 missed calls from Second Mother at 8:41 Morning Time, 9:28 Morning Time, and 9:50 Morning Time. One unviewed direct message, sent at 9:19 Morning Time from Briette. Do you wish to continue viewing your direct messages?"

"Yes." Ciaan watched the slender, attractive figure of her older half-sister appear. Her box braids were bound together in one thick strand; the few decorative gold beads wound in it complemented her dark, smooth skin.

Briette was beautiful; Ciaan had always thought so.

"So, I just got off the phone with Mom. She says you're knocked up," she started.

Beautiful, Ciaan sulked, *but overwhelming.*

"Congratulations, if it's true, on finding a completely new way to screw up your life. But I actually hope it isn't true because being pregnant while having parasites is no joke. Unless you were just asking about anti-parasitics out of curiosity? Either way, I can get a hold of some, but I don't know how I'm supposed to get them to you on the Zone base. Mom says you can receive packages—do you just want me to mail them and hope nobody scans it along the way? Let me know soon; you'll want to kill those parasites before you get too far into your first term." Briette wavered, and for a moment Ciaan thought it was just the display. "Take care of yourself."

The image faded away.

"Store or delete?" the Right Hand droned, scraping into Ciaan's fuzzy thoughts.

"Store," she murmured. "For now."

"She really thought you were *pregnant*?" Tidoris giggled, tried but didn't succeed in hiding it behind a cough. "And that *I* was the father? Why?!"

Ciaan punched him, only half-hard, in the shoulder.

"I guess because you're the only person I hang out with who could get me pregnant—that she knows about, anyway." Ciaan snorted. "And she thought I was pregnant because of a poorly-worded DM I may or may not have sent to try and see if she knew about this whole infertility thing. But don't worry Dori, I clarified the situation for her."

Tidoris cleared the last few laughs out of his throat. "So does she know what's really going on?"

"Not that she's telling—and it's kinda difficult to pump your parents for information while they're lecturing you about safe sex." Ciaan scoffed, "Like they have anything to tell me that I don't already know."

Tidoris's eyebrows shot up, but she didn't offer any more details.

"Well," Tidoris said after a beat. "Do you think she knows anything?"

Ciaan sighed, rubbed the bridge of her nose. "She's been to Earth, so she's gotta know something. She won't talk about it, though, and I have no idea how long she was there—or why."

The smell of burned flesh flooded Ciaan's nose; just a memory from some on-base accident, but she still gagged at it.

"I don't think it was a positive experience."

Tidoris didn't press her.

"Anyway," she continued. "It's all straightened out. Briette said she'd ship the anti-parasitics tomorrow—if the package is marked personal, it probably won't get scanned, right?"

Tidoris shrugged. "Let's hope so. What'd you tell her?"

"That they were for me. That I'd probably picked something up from badly-refrigerated food cargo and didn't want the base medical officers poking around down…anywhere…if I could avoid it." Ciaan winced. "Not too hard to believe."

"Mmm." Tidoris played with the buttons on his chest pocket. "So why'd you break Private Boote's fingers?"

Ciaan's throat tightened, like it was trying to choke her.

"Because he asked for it."

She stared at him—waited for the disappointment and disapproval—but he just nodded, pulling at a loose seam thread and unraveling it.

"And I only dislocated them." she offered, not sure how to read Tidoris's silence. "He's such a baby."

None of the supervising officers registered a disciplinary complaint for the fight, and by the next evening, Ciaan had more or less stopped worrying about getting her probation revoked over two dislocated fingers. Boote was probably too humiliated to upload the filework anyway; either that, or his hands were too swollen to type it up.

She was washing dinner trays and utensils, chatting with some recruits from another unit, when 1119 found her.

"You need to come with me," 1119 ordered across the cleaning trough, grim-faced.

Ciaan dropped the fork she was holding; it clattered against the metal basin. The other recruits eyed the Artificial warily.

1119 relaxed her—their—stance, trying to look more casual. "Captain Moon has some questions about the stern hull repairs. He doesn't feel they were done correctly and needs you to assess if further work is warranted."

Ciaan muttered low and rolled her eyes—made the expected fuss about port work after dinner—while 1119 waited off to the side. After a minute or two, the rest of the washers turned back to the trough.

When they were out of earshot Ciaan whispered, "What's going on?"

1119 leaned in, fear etched into the faint lines around their mouth. "The girl's getting sicker; TA von Ulger isn't sure if she'll make it through the night. I—we—thought you should know."

Ciaan's stomach lurched, threatened to throw up what little food she'd had that day.

"When're those anti-parasitics arriving?" 1119 asked as they left the mess hall.

"Briette sent them rush today so—as long as they don't get held up at any scanners along the way—they should be here tomorrow morning." Ciaan imagined the box, small and unassuming, crushed under a pile of discardables that the mail inspection officials were too lazy to go through.

She raced towards the *Maelstrom*, running to match 1119's long strides.

The atmosphere inside the dock was tacky and smothering—it stuffed itself down Ciaan's throat. The ship's windows were dark; inside, they only had the dull glow of safety lights to guide them. A single light was on in the medical bay—casting deep shadows and caving out sharp, neon lines—like it was already time for last rites.

The boy (*You*, his sister kept insisting) shuddered under a blanket, staring blankly at the ceiling. Every once in a while, he looked over at his sister—*Me*—like he thought he knew her, but wasn't totally sure.

The girl was stretched out still on her cot—eyes closed and skin clammy—and if it wasn't for the soft rise and fall of her belly, Ciaan wouldn't have known if she was alive or dead.

Tidoris stood over *Me*, helpless, dabbing at her forehead with a wet towel.

"If she dies, what'll happen to the baby?" Ciaan crouched next to *Me*, held her limp hand.

It wasn't much to do, but it wasn't nothing either.

No one answered Ciaan except *You*, who raised his arms (Mael must've unstrapped him) and signed something weakly.

They turned to Tidoris for the translation; he stared at the air where the sign had been.

"Gibberish," he said, wiping *Me*'s cheek tenderly. "He's probably delirious from the fever."

You repeated the sign with a little more strength, then slumped back onto the cot, eyes finally fluttering shut.

[TWELVE]

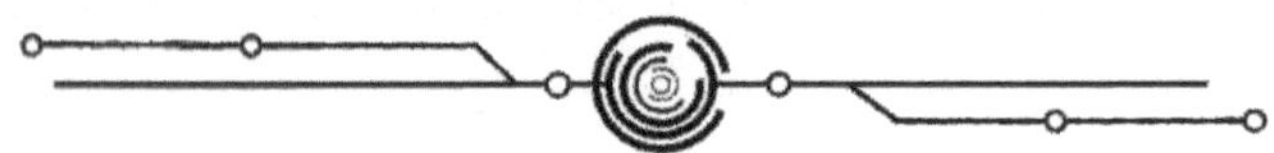

CIAAN BLINKED AWAKE, muscles stiff and cramping from being curled up on the unforgiving metal floor. Her boots poked out from under a thermal blanket; something warm and lightly snoring pressed up against her side.

At some point during the crisis watch, they must've fallen asleep in the medical bay.

Mael sat propped against some cabinets on the opposite wall—legs stretched out with Tidoris's head nestled in his lap. Another thermal blanket was thrown over them; Tidoris huddled greedily under most of it.

Ciaan opened her mouth, was about to say something loud and incredulous, when Mael caught her gaze and raised a finger to his lips.

Her mouth clicked shut.

She tried to shift gently—rearranged herself so her joints wouldn't hate her as much in the morning—and found 1119 wedged along her back, one arm slung loose over Ciaan's waist. In the darkness they sniffed and wheezed and, for a brief moment, looked just like any other human.

"Did you sleep at all?" Ciaan grunted at Mael, voice scratching against her throat.

He shook his head. "I gotta lot of things keeping me up these days."

His fingertips brushed over Tidoris's braids; Tidoris huffed and twisted his head away.

Ciaan glanced between the two of them, squinting through the sleep-grit in her eyes. "How'd *that* happen?"

Mael shrugged.

"He was exhausted and trying to stay up all night with them. Look at him—he probably hasn't gotten a decent night's sleep since we met." He smiled, small and bitter. "After you and 1119 passed out, there wasn't anywhere else for him to go. This ain't exactly a luxury freighter I got here. Nothing happened, though—if you were worried about that."

Ciaan's neck flushed hot.

"I'm sure he wouldn't have taken me up on my offer for shared body warmth if he hadn't been completely desperate and probably a little delirious too." Mael continued, deflated, "He's put all the responsibility for the unregistereds' lives…or deaths…on himself, and it's gonna break him."

He was right, but Ciaan didn't let him know that.

The docks were less insulated—and therefore much colder—than the barracks (which were already pretty frigid at night) so she guessed the rest of it checked out.

She nodded curious at 1119.

Mael stretched one of his arms out over his head. "1119 valiantly volunteered to keep you from going hypothermic."

Ciaan hummed. "I thought Artificials didn't sleep."

"I don't know about other Artificials, but this one does." Mael chuckled, fond and soft. "She's beautiful when she sleeps, isn't she?"

"Yeah"—Ciaan turned, burrowed into 1119's chest—"they are."

She must've dozed off again, because the next time Ciaan opened her eyes someone else was drawling out into the icy air.

"What'll we do if they die?" Tidoris's voice shook,

frayed at the edges.

"What'll we do if they live?" Mael whispered. It came out in a rush, like he'd been holding the question in. "What're we gonna do with two sick humans and a newborn baby?"

"Aren't there facilities on Earth that can take care of them?" Tidoris asked.

Blood started pounding in Ciaan's ears.

"No," Mael bit out—and there it was, blunt and honest. "None that we can afford, anyway, and none that'd take them without official documentation and a damn good explanation for why we had them in the first place. Any place that says otherwise is just a front for baby traffickers."

The thermal blanket crackled around her; Ciaan tried to keep still.

"You don't know what some Earth humans were—*are*—willing to do for a child. The threat of mass sterility's gone now, but the fear…what if things go back to how they were? What if it's worse this time? They never did figure out what really caused it the last time…something like that—it changes people. It changes the world." Mael's tone went thin and brittle. "Even my mother—and she got pregnant with me when the pandemic had already started to recede—was herded off to one of their Fertility Research and Care facilities. She and I both made it out of there alive, which was more than others—especially infertile women—got."

He paused. "My father also got taken in for testing; he wasn't as lucky as my mom and me, though. Came back when I was 3 and jumped off the roof of our apartment complex when I was 6. She still won't talk about that—or the *place*—and I figure there's gotta be a good fucking reason why."

The room went frosty, like someone had poured liquid nitrogen down Ciaan's jumpsuit; she squeezed her eyes shut.

Mael couldn't be that much older than her and Tidoris, which meant those facilities were running at capacity two or so decades ago. She thought about her second mother—marked with a brand the detention centers didn't use—and her first mother, shuttling to Earth and never coming back.

She thought about *Me*, crated up and smuggled across planetary borders, and choked on the rising bile.

"You're from the Eastern Asian Union, aren't you?" Tidoris sounded shy all of the sudden, timid in a way he usually wasn't.

"Yes," Mael hedged, clipped and cautious.

"It's your features," Tidoris explained. "I couldn't place them when I first saw you, so I did some research. We mostly get American or European Union humans up here. And your swear words too—they're Korean regional dialect."

"Yeah, that's right. I mean, it's not like it's some big secret—I just usually don't go around announcing it to my docking supervisors." Mael laughed hoarsely. "EAUs who go into trade or transport are usually the butt of everyone's jokes, at least on Earth. We're all supposed to be shrewd businesspeople and efficient, deferential workers—not space bums. That's what my family always told me, anyway, when they were reminding me of how much I shame them with my bad life choices."

"Believe me, shaming your family isn't specific to EAUs," Tidoris muttered, sly and acidic. "But then again, you know who my father is. Rather than disowning me right away, he's waiting for me to fail at this and come crawling back to him, begging for a spot at his company."

Mael scoffed.

"We don't have a family business; but if we did, I'm sure I would've been barred from it after the fourth or fifth arrest. That's how I got 1119; she was my parole escort—before I seduced her into black market fetus trading." The joke fell heavy and awkward; he coughed around it. "If anyone asks now, my family just says that I died."

The quiet turned uneasy, choppy like navigating

through a debris field. Ciaan chewed at the inside of her cheek to keep from cutting into it.

"My real name's Jongmal Mun; I changed it to help them out with that particular lie." Mael cleared his throat. "And besides, M-o-o-n sound a lot more galactic than M-u-n. That's a real space captain's name, right?"

Ciaan rolled her eyes, lips twitching up at the corners.

"You know, you remind me a lot of Ciaan." Tidoris sounded faded, washed out. Tired but not angry. "You've both got arm-long arrest records, major problems with rules and authority, poor decision-making skills…and you're both running away from something. From a lot of things, probably."

"Like that illusion of Earth—green and fertile and attainable, if you just reach hard enough for it—that all you p-people have? Ciaan and I know better." Mael spoke sure, but Ciaan couldn't feel any answers running through her veins.

If she had, she would've sliced them open and read their secrets already.

"Maybe that's why you can't hate me—even though you want to," Mael challenged. "Because you love her and all her failings and I've got some of those same failings inside me."

Tidoris snorted. "I'm not delirious enough to be

seduced by you. Yet."

"*Shi—bal*, Tidoris…" Mael crooned.

Tidoris giggled at him, like bubbles pricked and popping, and it crept under Ciaan's skin—settling there and buzzing just below the surface.

The anti-parasitics arrived unconfiscated the next morning and Tidoris requested personal time off to administer the medication and monitor its effects. By lunchtime, he'd sent out a DM claiming to be cautiously optimistic; at least, he said, the unregistereds were no longer in critical condition.

He also reported that the ship's stabilization system check passed as fully operational, though they'd need to do some test runs before interplanetary flight could be reauthorized.

Mael passed out a few small bars of (possibly-restricted) Earth chocolate—darker and bitterer than what was sold on Toi—in celebration. He and 1119 took the afternoon medical bay shift and Ciaan promised to check in before night call.

When she came back after dinner, Ciaan immediately noticed the new mood aboard the ship; the smothering tension of the past couple days was gone, evaporated out through the pores of the port dock.

You and *Me* were lying in their cots, unrestrained, resting peacefully. 1119 lounged in one of the medical officers' chairs, particularly slouching. They greeted Ciaan with a small nod.

"How're the patients this evening?" Ciaan grinned, giddy from the change in atmosphere.

"Still weak and fighting off the parasites, but they've been resting well and even ate a little dinner." 1119 smiled. "TA von Ulger says the fetus shows no signs of damage from the infection, so that's also good news."

Mael's voice from last night rang in her ears: *What're we gonna do if they live?*

She shook it out of her head and leaned back against the wall.

"Have you and Ma—Captain Moon decided on your next plans, now that the ship's repaired and the unregistereds' conditions are improving?"

The soft spark in 1119's eyes hardened, went dim and sour. "I'm not sure what choices we have. If we bring the girl to a hospital for the delivery without official documentation, the baby will probably end up with traffickers again. But none of us—not even, I think, our capable Technical Advisor—have experience with neonatal care. And once—*if*—the baby is born alive, what are our options? House this family aboard our ship? Leave them with some charitable organization that may or may not be legitimate? Turn them over to the officials?"

They wavered; Ciaan realized it was the first time she'd seen 1119 in doubt.

"I worry that the baby's fate might already be set. Maybe it'd be better if these two did die; at least then we could be sure that they wouldn't be mistreated anymore."

Ciaan shuddered, wished she hadn't asked.

The conversation fizzled; they stayed there without talking for a few more minutes until a very excited Tidoris and Mael burst into the room.

"Hey!" Mael boomed.

You jerked under his sheets and Mael hushed himself.

"Hey, our little—er, big—genius Dori here has cleared the stabilization system for a full run."

Ciaan bristled at her nickname for Tidoris coming out of someone else's mouth. She eyed the hand Mael had clasped on her best friend's shoulder; Tidoris's ears blushed pink under the scrutiny.

Mael didn't notice—or didn't care. Or both.

"Who wants to go for a ride?"

Ciaan gaped at him. "Departures aren't allowed after dinner. Port patrols would be all over us."

"Not if the designated docking supervisor enters an override code." Mael winked at her. "And besides, it's not like we'd actually be departing. Just a quick flight out of the docking channels, a short hover above Toi, and then re-landing. Nothing to get worked up about."

Ciaan waited for Tidoris to interrupt, back her up on the regulations and risks, but he didn't. When she glanced at him he was blinking, fast and eager, and Ciaan wondered if maybe he had a rebellious streak in him after all.

"I can only override the codes for ten minutes," Ciaan conceded. "So we gotta be back at the dock with engines off by then. Deal?"

Mael took her hand and kissed it. "Deal."

She made an instinctive move to punch him, but stopped short. Instead, she wiped her hand off on the side of her uniform while he clapped once in victory.

They all piled onto the bridge, tripping over each other on their way up the crowded steps. Ciaan catalogued the controls and wires lining the walls, stacked one on top of another; it was so much messier and more ragtag than the company cargo ships. Mael pointed at a central screen, already connected to the CPZ base's digital network and ready for the override codes.

She typed in a series she'd copied from one of the more seasoned recruits' Right Hand, left out in the open during chores. The screen flashed—ACCESS GRANTED—and the ship lurched suddenly as the docking mechanisms released.

Ciaan screamed a little at the motion; she'd never actually been on a flying ship before.

1119 reached out and held her firm by the biceps; Ciaan almost relaxed into the strong grip before realizing that she was being moved out of the way. The first officer took the seat next to Mael at the control panel. Tidoris and Ciaan stood nervously behind them, watching the base rotate out of view, replaced by the illuminated docking channel and beyond that—space.

"Easy now." Mael pressed a few buttons and grasped the faded, scuffed steering handle; 1119 took the second, smaller handle.

"Be nice to her," said Mael. "She hasn't run healthy in a long time."

They glided forward slowly and Ciaan felt like she'd been strapped into a full-immersion hologram— everything seemed so real, but couldn't possibly be. She held her breath when they started drifting uncomfortably close to the channel barrier; next to her, Tidoris was gripping Mael's headrest, knuckles white and shaking.

When they were spit out at the end of the channel, they finally saw it—nothing and everything stretched out before them, blocked only by Earth. It loomed there, swallowing the entire bridge window, half of it covered in swirls of green and blue and white and the other half shrouded in darkness.

Floating there in front of her, Ciaan thought that she'd never been both so close and so far from Earth. From her first mother.

From the rotted-out green parts of herself.

"Perfect," the captain murmured, low and reverent.

Ciaan didn't know if he meant the ship or his home planet.

The control panel alarm beeped five minutes; Mael sighed and turned the steering handle.

Earth slipped away and Toi came into sharp focus; Ciaan'd never seen it like this before. Bright against the void of space, fighting for its light in the blackness. It shined fierce and defiant and Ciaan felt something—like pride, or sympathy—for its struggle. It had no green, but it was alive nonetheless.

From within a vacuum its metal heart kept on beating.

"Perfect," Mael whispered again.

Then he lowered the steering handle and guided the ship back into the docking channel.

[THIRTEEN]

CIAAN SAT CROSS-CHECKING the *Maelstrom's* unloaded cargo file against various pickup receipts, trying to figure out how many cargo containers were still unclaimed and technically under her jurisdiction (as docking supervisor) in the port warehouses, when she heard footsteps approaching. She glanced up—not in the mood for anything that was gonna make her inventory check longer than it already was—only to find Melean standing there, hands tucked behind his back, flanked by two expressionless sub-officials.

"Surprise inspection," he announced. "I expect that you're prepared for review of your long-term docking supervision ship, Private Gennett, where you are in no way concealing prohibited items or conducting restricted activities in the hope of being overlooked amidst this port's heavy transit traffic by your otherwise-occupied superiors."

Ciaan snorted; she would've been worried if she thought he actually had even an inkling of what was really going on at Gate 13.

"You're free to browse through all my properly uploaded filework, Official von Ulger." She held her Right Hand up so he could see the screen. "I'm just going through the unclaimed cargo lists now; I'd be more than happy to get you a copy of those too, as soon as I'm done."

"I've already seen all your filework which, as you said, is impeccably filled out. Almost like a lazy *halfie* had foisted it off on some more diligent colleague…or overly-accommodating Technical Advisor," Melean snapped out.

Ciaan raised an eyebrow but didn't look up, didn't stop typing.

"I'd think that a clerk—sorry, *underclerk*—would have something better to do with his mornings than hang around port bases insulting basic recruits. That just seems like a waste of both our times." She bit the snide, nasty edge off the tip of her tongue; her world was bigger now than pissing contests with Melean von Ulger. "I need to get back to the ship."

"Good,"—Melean grinned, exposing the bleached white of his teeth—"then you won't mind me accompanying you. I've requested a full ship inspection, with sentient inspectors."

Ciaan nodded curtly, didn't trust herself to answer, and clenched her jaw as she led them silently to the dock.

She spun back on them at the port gate, just before entering the door code. "May I ask why I was submitted for an inspection?"

"Random." Melean shrugged, full of insincerity. "Nothing personal."

Yeah, Ciaan seethed as she pounded at the keypad. *I bet.*

The door slid open and she scanned the area for any items that looked even remotely suspicious. Behind her, Melean was ticking off orders to his henchmen.

"Start with the main deck and work your way down. Make sure to open all hatches and demand key codes for any locked doors. Knock on all panels to ensure they aren't hollow and use the infrared scanner on surfaces. Note temperature irregularities, instrument misreadings, and any interplanetary transit vessel code violations."

Ciaan looked over her shoulder at the sub-officials. They swayed, staring vacantly; sentient may have been a stretch.

"Don't I have the right to an inspection performed

by my peers? And shouldn't there be a commanding port official overseeing this whole charad…" Ciaan stopped herself. "Thing?"

"I already have the necessary official signatures." Melean shuffled through several tiny-print forms on his Right Hand, not pausing to give Ciaan more than a blur of black and red.

"And I'll have you know that these two"—he stretched up to pat the sub-officials' shoulders, then pulled his manicured hands back—"are the most decorated inspectors in their field."

Ciaan very seriously doubted that.

She crossed her arms, planted herself between him and the ship. "And what field is that?"

Melean's nostrils flared and Ciaan felt a current in the air, like a dream or déjà vu or a joke that kept repeating itself even though it hadn't really been funny in the first place.

He leaned in. "A field that an uneducated, Third-tier, little *greenie* who takes night flights with her new space trash friends wouldn't know anything about. Now are we going to be allowed to complete this inspection, or will I need to upload a report for insubordination?"

A cool, refined venom dripped from his lips; Ciaan wanted to rip them off his face.

"No," she drawled. "I wouldn't want your daddy

having to grease any more wheels to settle your petty grievances."

Melean cocked his head, took one step closer to her.

Ciaan wasn't that much shorter than him now, so she stood firm—inside her sweaty boots, her toes curled and uncurled.

"I am, however, invoking my right to accompany you during all parts of your inspection."

A short, predatory beat before Melean slipped his hands into the pockets of his long overcoat—lined with what Ciaan knew were restricted Earth hides. "After you, Private."

She climbed the ladder to the main deck hatch, knocked three times in what she hoped was sufficient warning, and opened it.

One by one, they all ducked in.

If Melean's face was anything to go by, the inspection was—so far—a bust.

Ciaan didn't know what exactly they were looking for, but whatever it was, they hadn't found it. Not yet, anyway.

The bridge was clean; so were the crew quarters, the

decompression room, the sanitary facilities, the general cargo hold *and* its adjacent overflow rooms (which were all—thankfully—empty). Mael must've gotten rid of what was left of the unregistereds' container.

The engine rooms got an automatic pass because none of the so-called inspectors had been willing to go down there and risk ruining their expensive suits. The captain's quarters were ransacked and Melean eyed a few items skeptically, but in the end nothing had been conclusive enough to document. That left the few shelves and cabinets that lined the deckways, which were being wrenched open as they went, and the medical bay.

Its lights were on; as they approached, Ciaan hands started shaking. Excuses bubbled up her throat, rejected one after the other for being too stupid or unbelievable.

She decided to go with *extremely lifelike holograms* as they turned into the doorway.

1119 stood in the middle of the room, folding plastic sheets, with two patient-less cots behind them.

"Officer 1119, this is Official von Ulger and his associates. They're just finishing up their inspection of the *Maelstrom*." Ciaan did her best to swallow down the shock and relief.

Melean circled past her, stopped domineeringly in front of 1119. He displayed his blur of authorization papers again.

"As acting inspection supervisor, I demand that you state your name and purpose aboard this ship, Artificial."

Plastic crinkled softly as 1119 dropped one sheet onto the stack; they looked at Melean—looked through him—like he wasn't even there.

"Kwe EU 11198706, First Officer aboard the *Maelstrom*."

"Artificials aren't sanctioned for transit duty," Melean sneered. "Are you aware that your *alleged* captain is under probationary watch, with several frozen warrants that will be reinstated should evidence of his participation in further illegal activities be discovered?"

Ciaan gnawed at the inside of her cheek; she sometimes forgot that Melean had become an actual voice of authority in their world.

"Of course I am aware of all of this," 1119 said, impassive. "I was assigned as his probationary watch supervisor, which is why I'm cleared for transit duty. You may check my records, and the captain's as well, for confirmation."

"Oh, I will." Melean scoured the room, grasping for something to accuse someone of.

"What are you doing there with those sheets?"

"Folding them," 1119 answered without a hint of sarcasm or condescension. "I'm taking inventory of our medical supplies to make sure that we're well-stocked for our next flight. We've had some unfortunate incidents in the past involving gaping wounds and what can only be accurately described as pools of blood, with not enough gauze and bandaging pads for—"

"Enough!" Melean barked.

The two sub-officials exchanged wary glances.

He stood sputtering for a second—then whirled around, shoved hard past Ciaan, and stomped out the door. The two others followed quickly after him, with one tripping over a floor seam on the way out.

Ciaan marched out after them, catching Melean at the port door as he slammed his palm against the uncooperative keys.

A calm, robotic voice repeated, "Please enter the correct pass code."

She pulled up short behind them, just a little out of breath. "I take it the inspection's over? Just so I'm clear on our timeline and everything."

Melean wheeled on her, lunged forward and Ciaan thought he was finally going to show his real self—the one she knew lurked under that imported braid oil and bureaucratic sniveling.

He was close enough for Ciaan to smell his sickly sweet breath, hot over her cheeks.

"Don't let them fool you with their little flying tricks," he whispered. "You'd never fit in there, even more than you don't fit in here. You know why?"

He smacked her across the face, sharp enough to sting but not bruise.

She smacked him back, harder.

He touched his cheek and smirked. "Because you hit back, twice as hard. That's what'll always make you more *us* than *them*."

"Maybe"—Ciaan went stiff, rusted at the joints—"but I'm not a p-kid anymore, Melean."

She reached over and entered the door code, moved aside to let him go.

"And I am done with your games."

Once she was sure that Melean and his cronies had left the base, Ciaan stormed over to the TA living quarters and pounded on the door until it creaked open and Tidoris hesitantly peeked out.

She burst past him, ready to rail—against his brother, his family, and the whole goddamn p-society— before she noticed a large, human-shaped lump shivering under his bed sheets. She pointed, opened her mouth but Tidoris leapt forward and shushed her.

It shifted and Ciaan torn the blankets off without

thinking; she just hoped it wasn't aggressive—or naked.

Huddled together in the middle of the bed were Mael, *You*, and *Me*—docile and thankfully all still clothed. Ciaan blinked down at them, then turned slowly back to Tidoris.

"How'd you get them here?"

"I borrowed a few reserve jumpsuits from the laundry." Tidoris picked his blankets up off the dusty rug, waving her surprise away. "They couldn't exactly be on the ship for the inspection, could they?"

"No." Ciaan's forehead wrinkled. "But how did you know about the inspection?"

"We were tipped off," Mael interrupted, nodding towards Tidoris.

Tidoris cleared his throat.

"Melean told me he'd gotten orders for it, though I think he might've traded some favors for this particular assignment. Anyway, he warned me not to be around when things went down." Confusion—and something stronger—clouded his eyes. "I don't know what kind of game he thinks he's playing."

"I don't either," Ciaan conceded. "But I think I'm his main opponent."

Tidoris murmured, "You always are."

Ciaan peered at him, but didn't push for more. "Why was 1119 in the medical bay?"

"To distract from any evidence of recent patients." Mael stood up and held out his arm to support *You*. "Besides, it would've looked really strange if a ship was docked without any crew members around. The inspectors probably would've made you locate the captain and then I'd have to explain why I was in a Technical Advisor's private quarters in the middle of the day…"

He trailed off. "A hassle."

Tidoris threw a stray pillow at him, then looked anxiously at Ciaan.

"Did it work?" he asked. "Did Melean cause any major problems?"

Ciaan touched her cheek lightly, unconsciously.

"No," she said, flat like tempered steel.

Tidoris's eyes narrowed—he stretched his fingers out and, for a wild moment, Ciaan thought he was going to hit her too. She stumbled back and caught *Me*'s strange, penetrating gaze from where she was still tangled in Tidoris's sheets.

For the first time, Ciaan felt like the girl was aware of what was going on around her.

"We're being monitored." Mael jumped in casually, like an afterthought. "Today was just a ripple in the pond. I don't know who knows or how much they know, but they know something."

He steadied *Me* against her brother. "They know *enough*. We need a new plan."

"You mean, a plan other than sitting around at a space port waiting to get caught?" Ciaan sniped, trying to shake the feel of Melean off on her skin.

Mael muttered something snide under his breath. "Yes, that's exactly what I mean. Do you have any amazing ideas that you've been keeping from the group?"

Ciaan went serious, considering. She remembered a rush of people, the tick of digital clocks, the sudden and fierce grip of her second mother. She remembered a face in the crowd that she'd first seen on a cold, tinny night.

"You know," she started. "I just might."

[FOURTEEN]

AFTER MORNING CALL THE NEXT DAY, the four of them met up in an extra cargo room and locked the door behind them. They clustered in tight, didn't want anyone—especially not *You* and *Me*—listening in.

"This is crazy." Tidoris jittered, eyes wide and frantic. "I mean, how would it even work? I'm not cleared for interplanetary travel. Ciaan is restricted to the base for her community service."

"That's why it'd be a *rogue* mission." Mael rolled his eyes, talked to Tidoris like he was a jumpy little kid. "You wouldn't be alerting your superiors to it or uploading any official requests for leave."

"Right," Tidoris snapped back. "And no one would

notice when Ciaan and I didn't report for daily checks."

Mael's confidence wavered, just for a moment.

"Fair enough. Then I'll put in an urgent request for assistance on a minor run. I'll say that I have to deliver some sensitive cargo to the capital p-planet and you two need to come along to…to monitor any system malfunctions, since we haven't been cleared for fully operational flight yet." He looked pointedly at Tidoris, who shook his head.

"Where would this conveniently sensitive cargo come from? We've already submitted the inventories and Melean has seen what I *hope* was an empty cargo hold. And not only have you not been cleared for fully operational fight, you haven't been cleared for *any* flight," Tidoris huffed. "It was probably thanks to your little late-night blast-off that we got hit with an inspection in the first place."

Mael shrugged, waggling his eyebrows. "From what I hear, you know more about this base's digital network than anyone. We still have some unclaimed cargo in the warehouses; who's to say that one of those can't register as an urgent delivery tomorrow? And who's to say that this ship can't end up on the *Cleared with Discretion* list? I'm sure there's at least one lonely, frumpy clerk at the Requests Station who hasn't heard about our little rule-bendings yet—if the cargo and ship statuses were to *somehow* sort themselves out, I think I'd be able to take care of the administrative clearance."

He leaned back on his heels, clearly trying not to look too smug.

Tidoris turned seriously to Ciaan. "Are you sure this commander is stationed on Wakan Tanka? And that she'll be able to help us?"

"Yes. I mean, probably. I know she's on Wakan Tanka and…" Ciaan hesitated, hedging. "She knew about my mother, so she's gotta know about Earth. And she saved my life."

The others shifted, not totally persuaded.

She gritted her teeth. "Do we have another choice?"

After a stiff second, 1119 spoke up. "I can't say that I agree with seeking help from an Artificial, especially a high-ranking one. Not all of us are as *permissive* as I am, and we generally aren't loyal to anyone but our commanders; this is a not-insubstantial gamble. But Private—Ciaan is right: at this point, there is no other choice."

That settled it then; it wasn't a perfect one, or even a great one, but at least now they had an actual plan.

"I cannot *believe* I did that!" Tidoris paced back and forth outside the reserve barracks, overnight pack in hand, waiting for Ciaan to finalize her clearance filework.

He flailed, waved his arms at everything. "I cannot believe I'm doing *this*!"

"Yeah,"—Ciaan deleted a typo—"you keep saying that."

She scanned the last paragraph for errors and found three more.

"If you don't pull it together, Dori, people are gonna start wondering what exactly you did and/or are still doing."

"They'll probably just assume we had sex," he grumbled.

Ciaan sputtered; her fingers slipped and she accidentally cleared an entire section in the report. She almost hurled her Right Hand at Tidoris for that—but stopped short, not wanting to deal with the replacement filework. Instead, she punched him just under his ribcage.

He blushed fire-red, winced more from shock than pain.

"It was a joke!"

"You've been hanging around Mael too much." She scoffed, then leaned in, lowering her voice and typing in shorthand. "No one's gonna know that you hacked the filework because no one knows this system like you do. And we'll be back before anyone has time to suspect anything, so just relax. Nothing tips off a nosy official like fear—there."

She hit the *upload* button triumphantly.

"Done. Now let's get out of here before you change your mind." Ciaan hoisted her travel sack over her shoulder, jabbing Tidoris in the chest before heading off towards the docks.

When they passed through the port door, someone shouted out cheerfully from behind a wing.

"Good morning, you two—and what a good one it is! Flight traffic is light, we've got clearance, and listen to her…" Mael rubbed a seam of bolts lovingly. "Isn't she just singing?"

"Yeah, yeah, it's like listening to a damn opera," Ciaan yelled over the engines. "When're we getting out of here?"

"Just as soon as 1119 gets her warmed up." Mael bounded across the wing and swung over to the main deck hatch ladder. "Last call for the crew of the *Maelstrom*!"

He disappeared inside; Ciaan and Tidoris exchanged bewildered looks.

Tidoris held out his hand. "After you."

Ciaan snorted as they both followed Mael into the

ship.

They tripped over each other a little in the deckway trying to maneuver their way onto the bridge. When they got there, Mael and 1119 were already harnessed into their seats, concentrating intently on pulling levers and pressing buttons.

Everything felt so much more official than it had on Ciaan's first flight.

"Port to Captain Mael Moon of EAU registered cargo ship *Maelstrom*. This is the control room; please confirm that you have successfully completed preflight check for interplanetary travel." A scratchy voice buzzed over the intercom.

1119 unhooked a microphone set from the wall and secured it behind her ears. "*Maelstrom* to Port control room. Preflight check has been completed. We are initiating our hovering boosters now."

They pushed a faded yellow button and the whole ship lurched; Ciaan staggered behind them.

Mael craned his neck to wink at them. "Sorry, kids, there are only seats for the parents up here. You'll have to stay back in the crew quarters until we land."

"But we got to be up here before!" Tidoris sulked, childish in a way Ciaan almost never got to see. He jutted out his chin defiantly and even 1119 glanced back at him.

Mael chuckled, more fond than mocking.

"That wasn't a real flight—it was barely a hover—and even then you *technically* shouldn't have been up here. I let it slide because I figured you might not get a chance to do something like that again." He turned back to the steering handle. "But this is an actual run and I can't have you two in here distracting me while I'm trying to do my job."

Ciaan choked. "All you've done since docking is distract us while we were trying to do *our* jobs!"

"True,"—Mael didn't even try to deny it—"but your jobs can't get us stranded in space or exploded in a combustion fireball or sucked out into an oxygen-less atmosphere."

Ciaan crossed her arms. "They could if I shoved you into the airlock disposals."

1119 laughed, sudden and choppy, like a pane of plexiglass shattering. It hit Ciaan in the gut, lodged something gummy in the back of her throat.

"I swear," Mael sounded different now, like a big brother, affectionate but authoritative. He put his palm over his heart. "It's for your own safety. And there's a large rear window—much bigger than this one—so you'll still have a decent view."

Ciaan and Tidoris begrudgingly trudged back to the bow and tossed their bags onto opposite bunks. The

Maelstrom had already rotated in the channel so all they could see was the base—units stacked upon units, molded out of the same rusted metal as the ground and the rest of the planet.

Seen through one cramped ship window, the CPZ port seemed lackluster—bland compared to the things that passed through its space gates. It started to slide away as they drifted out of the channel; eventually, it blended into the rest of Toi's surface. The stars chased behind their little world, unmoved by its tiny people and their tiny concerns.

Orbiting beyond Toi were Nuwa and Noah—the twins—built the most recently and sparkling fresh in the black space. Enkai orbited far too, bigger and streaked with dark lacquers. As Toi faded, Manco Capac came into view—its surface coated in a bronze sheen, dotted with tall buildings that stabbed like knives up against the bubble of its artificial atmosphere. They caught sight of Aether last, circling close and slow; it was really more of a satellite to the capital than its own p-planet, though its population had grown enough in recent years to warrant the distinction.

As always, Earth hovered just on the edge of sight— both a shadow and a sun to its metal children. Ciaan gazed at the living, glowing ridge of humanity and wondered what the view looked like from down there.

The ship began to turn, swinging around Aether and coming up behind a looming giant, blacked-out against the vast green-blue of Earth. Ciaan'd heard that Wakan Tanka was huge, but until now she hadn't had the scale for it. It had to be at least five times bigger than Toi—though, swimming in the space beneath, it felt much larger than that.

Next to her, Tidoris exhaled in awe, "Wow."

Their speed slowed and the capital planet slipped away. It was replaced by a dark, starlit infinity and then Earth, wide and stretching across the whole window space. A few more ships began to pull up behind them; a line was starting to form.

"The *One Worlds' Gala*," Tidoris said hazily. "It's this weekend."

Ciaan had completely forgotten, not that galas were something she normally had to remember. She'd only heard about this one in passing—mostly in complaints from Tidoris about his parents' yearly preparations for it—but hadn't bothered remembering any details.

She stared out at the rope of vessels and wondered if this was gonna be a problem.

"Won't there be heightened security?" Ciaan bounced her heel against the floor.

"Sure, for free agents and ships without filework. But we have an interplanetary port clearance so there shouldn't be any problems for us." He sounded smooth and sure—it suited him. "If anyone gives us trouble, I'll handle it. I know someone in customs here—and besides, my name has to be good for something. Something more than bullying and intimidation, anyway."

Ciaan's chest swelled—full of pride and tenderness for Tidoris that always sloshed around inside her. She smiled soft and reached out, covering his cold hand with hers.

The Wakan Tanka CPZ base seemed surprisingly similar to the Toi CPZ base, though Ciaan guessed that made sense. Capital or not, it was still a p-planet, and built from the same designs and specifications.

As soon as they disembarked, Tidoris strode off with a purpose, leaving the rest of them to be harassed by an overly self-important docking official. He demanded ages, names, ranks, purpose, ship weight, port of departure, intended length of stay, records of insurance, itemized lists of inoculations they'd gotten within the past six months, declarations of exposure to any potentially infectious pathogens, and a number of other tedious and (Ciaan knew) non-required pieces of information. Small, hapless recruits plodded around in ugly uniform sets, unable to answer anything other than the most basic questions.

By the time Tidoris returned, Mael was in the middle of explaining a small rash on his elbow.

"Who are you?" The docking official looked Tidoris up and down, perching one spindly arm on his hip. "No crew members are allowed to leave the docking port until they've submitted the required personal information."

He thrust his Right Hand ominously towards Tidoris.

"I would check your uploaded filework," said Tidoris. "This ship has pre-clearance from the Interplanetary Trade Commission."

The official clicked through the files cramming his screen, then paused to scan one in particular.

He muttered out loud as he read: "…departed from the CPZ base on Toi…sensitive transport mission…interplanetary crew…under the supervision of Technical Advisor Tidoris von Ulger."

He stopped and reread the section silently; when he glanced back up, his face had lost its color.

"Technical Officer von Ulger, welcome to Wakan Tanka. If you and your crew"—Mael balked at the officer's phrasing, but Ciaan elbowed him in the ribs before he could say anything—"require any assistance during your visit, please do not hesitate to contact our Administrative Headquarters directly."

Tidoris cracked a half-smile. "I can't contact you?"

"I…well…" The docking official stammered, tried pathetically to shield his name patch. "I think you will find the AH far more knowledgeable and able to serve you more *promptly* than me."

Then he snapped his fingers, gathered his scattered recruit assistants and marched off, giving a final bow to Tidoris only.

"Well, what d'you know, Technical *Official*." Ciaan gathered up both their bags and strutted ahead of Tidoris. "It looks like your name's only good for intimidation after all."

Tidoris flushed—mumbled something lost in the sounds of the base—and dove for his pack when she tossed it back to him.

[FIFTEEN]

THE GOLDEN STREETS OF WAKAN Tanka ran luxuriously wide, freshly polished and—when they started getting closer to the central city sector—coated in black lacquer. Almost all the central city buildings were lacquered and some were even coated in Earth ceramic tiles or woodgrain fiberglass paneling. Ciaan suspected that the windows were paned with real glass—something she'd never seen before—rather than the acrylic used on Toi.

(She didn't throw anything at them to test that theory—but the thought did cross her mind.)

Ciaan and Tidoris gaped at everything and everyone, tried to keep their mouths from hanging open as they craned up to trace the tops of buildings and spun around whenever a huge, modified hovercraft whizzed by. They even snuck a few particularly impressive, pathetically unsubtle photos on their Right Hands; something to brag about back at the barracks.

1119 walked between them, back stiff and eyes forward.

"So much for blending in." Mael trailed behind like he was trying to distance himself from the embarrassment.

"We need to find the Interplanetary Headquarters for the Artificial Human Forces," 1119 reminded them, tone clipped. "Renting a hovercraft would be faster."

"And miss all this extravagance?" Ciaan grinned at the Artificial, ears buzzing with excitement. "No way."

1119 frowned.

Ciaan waved it off into the artificially bright skies, which radiated a prickly sort of sunlight here. "Don't worry. Dori knows where we're going."

Tidoris offered a hesitant thumbs-up, reassuring nobody.

As they walked, Tidoris pointed out landmarks from the expanded surface map on his Right Hand. A museum lined with pillars, a theater whose marquee was taller than most of the buildings in Ciaan's home sector, a zoo, a park—words Ciaan'd had no visual reference for before now.

It was like the Earth she'd always pictured, only skinned alive and draped over a metal skeleton; so well done that you almost didn't notice, except for that slight ting every time a shoe hit the ground.

They stopped in front of the park—Ciaan and Tidoris stood at its edge, not letting their thick work boots touch the green carpet.

"It looks so *real*." Tidoris squinted at the lush patches of shallowly rooted plants and bushes; a row of small trees lined the single, straight path in. "I wonder what kind of imaging system they're using?"

"None." Mael tapped his foot, sounded impatient. "It's all imported from Earth."

Tidoris gasped—like he'd surprised himself—and took a second, more careful look.

Beside him, Ciaan squatted and wiped a hand against her shabby pants. She brushed her fingers along the tips of a hundred grass blades, so much more fragile than she'd thought they'd be. On impulse, she pinched a single blade between her fingertips and wrenched it up— the green stalk snapped with a strange, wet sound and dangled from her fingers, suddenly lifeless and limp.

Ciaan stared at its jagged edge—frayed and unable to be seamed up again—and let it drop. It fluttered down, landed without a sound; she stood up and walked away from the others, back onto the sidewalk, not looking at anything anymore.

This place, she suddenly felt, had lost its appeal.

The AHF Headquarters were located in the diplomatic sector, a sub-street lined with consulates for the other p-planets and the Earth embassy (surrounded by pots of gaudy Earth flowers) at the broad dead end. Loose clusters of people were milling around the street, dressed in vibrantly colored fabrics and glimmering jewels. The cuts of their clothing were against p-planet regulations—pants that reached the tops of shiny boots, gowns without sleeves or support straps, animal hide wraps, shoes with thin-spiked heels—and their skin ranged from pale to dark, with varying shades of hair and eye colors.

This street had more Earth humans on it right now than Ciaan'd collectively seen in her life; there'd been pairs and threes strolling together through the central city earlier, but it hadn't been like this. These Earth humans laughed loud and chattered continuously, effervescent and overwhelming.

The rush of roaring, unfamiliar noise gave Ciaan a headache.

"They're probably diplomats or socialites here for the

gala." Mael answered the question before she could ask it, while 1119 went to present their identification to the AHF guard.

He glared at a group across the way, crowding onto the steps of the embassy. "These types of Earth humans prefer places that cater to them and the company of other Earth human expats. You're not gonna see them out and about, exploring the local culture."

1119 returned from the guard post with a handful of badges.

"All right, you have clearance, but you need to stay with me at all times. We'll have to go to the directory first so we can locate this Artificial." They handed out the guest IDs, saving Ciaan's for last. "You'll be able to recall her name, yes?"

Ciaan grabbed the card.

"I can't remember her full number—but I know her title, union, and real name."

1119 nodded. "That should be sufficient enough to track her."

They all clipped on the IDs and started making their way to the security gate.

"Let's just hope that she's still alive and preferably stationed either here or on Toi." 1119 pressed their palm against the sensor; the electrified door slid up.

One by one, they stepped inside.

If the embassy was the personification of Earth humanity's excesses, the AHF Headquarters was the abstraction of Artificiality— tepid, unadorned, overlooked, and rigidly functional. Every surface— interior and exterior walls, floors, ceilings, doors—was lacquered in a thin beige sheen, making it feel both inoffensive and vaguely ominous.

Every soldier greeted them with a reflexive nod; no one raced or rushed or bustled. The whole complex was well-paced, efficient, and civil—like a precisely-regulated machine.

They weaved through scuff-less hallways until they hit a door labeled *Directory*; inside, an older Artificial stood behind the main desk, glancing up when they walked in. A few others sat in the three rows of waiting chairs, shuffling through loose papers and uploaded filework on their Right Hands.

"Sit down," 1119 ordered, but caught Ciaan by the elbow.

"Not you."

The boys complied; Ciaan followed 1119 to the desk.

"Good morning,"—1119 saluted the other officer— "I am Kwe EU 11198706. I'd like to request assignment data for a commander."

The older Artificial's eyes were placid, and her skin

was slightly sallow. She shifted towards a churning old computer.

"Registered name and number." Her spidery fingers arched above the keyboard.

"We don't have the full registered number, but…" 1119 prompted Ciaan.

"Major General 2719, NAU," Ciaan hesitated. "Her real name is Aaniin."

The fingers twitched, then started typing.

"Kwe NAU 27198607. Current status is Retired."

"Retired?" The word tumbled out before Ciaan could stop it.

1119 grabbed her wrist and squeezed. Ciaan balled her fists, dug her fingernails into her palms so she wouldn't blurt anything else out.

"How long has the Major General been retired?" 1119 dropped her wrist.

The older Artificial checked the screen. "11 months, 17 days."

Ciaan's nails bit hard into her skin.

"Can you tell me her designed office address?" 1119 took out her Right Hand, but the worker shook her head.

"No office address. She requested assignment to a gratification complex on Wakan Tanka. Would you like that address?"

Ciaan watched 1119 out of the corner of her eye—their face was a mask, a blank stretch of nothing. The only slip was the squeak of their boots against the polished floor.

"Yes," 1119 said. "Thank you."

As soon as they got outside the AHF Headquarters, 1119's mask tore apart at the seams. They immediately hailed a taxicraft, refusing to explain anything until everyone was inside, and uploaded the address they'd gotten from the *Directory* to the driver before shutting the partition between the front and back seats.

"Are you *sure* this Artificial had Major General rank?" They wheeled wild-eyed on Ciaan.

"That's what she told me when I saw her at the courts few weeks ago." Ciaan swallowed against a dry throat. "And wouldn't that officer have corrected us if the title was wrong?"

"Wait, you saw her a few weeks ago?" Tidoris chirped. "But she's been retired for a year."

1119 waved a hand dismissively. "Retired Artificials retain their last-held rank; it's common practice to introduce yourself by it even after you're off active duty."

They fidgeted in the padded seat; Mael put a hand on one of their jittering knees.

He gazed at his first officer seriously. "What's wrong?"

1119 took a deep breath.

"An Artificial's duty is to fill the gaps in society—that's the code the first-generations established in defiance of being labeled as purposeless."

The speech sounded rehearsed, a practiced regurgitation.

"For young, healthy Artificials, their duty is keeping order—and sometimes repurposing themselves as weapons, soldiers willing to sacrifice themselves for the greater victory. But old bodies don't make very effective soldiers, so retired Artificials are usually designated to administrative positions. Those with higher ranks, like Major Generals, are given an office at Headquarters and a desk job. And those who didn't rise high enough in the ranks are assigned to outposts and training facilities—a less comfortable retirement."

"So why wasn't Aaniin at the AHF?" Ciaan cut in.

She paused, considered the phrase *gratification complex*—it sounded fairly self-explanatory, but maybe it wasn't.

"Gratification complexes are mostly run by local governments with the AHF acting as hands-off maintainers on the p-planets. You have to apply to work there, just like any other job, and it's mainly regulated Earth and p-humans. Standards are strictly enforced." 1119's jaw tensed. "Given our…*complicated*…history with sexual autonomy, designation to the gratification complexes is one of the strongest punishments available for Artificials. To be sent there, an Artificial would have to be convicted of regiment desertion or insubordination that resulted in death or some equally serious crime. I suppose it could be an elected designation, but I've never heard of an Artificial—much less a *Major General*—requesting assignment to one of those places."

Ciaan tried to tie up all these new implications. "But why would Artificials be sent to gratification complexes instead of detention centers?"

"I think it's presented as redemptive." 1119 slumped back into the shadows. "We can still fill some gaps, so to speak, in society at there. We'd be purposeless as detainees."

It wasn't cold in the taxicraft, but Ciaan shuddered.

"What exactly *is* a gratification complex?" Tidoris leaned forward awkwardly, glanced around to see if he was the only one who didn't know. "I've never heard that term before."

"Have you heard of pleasure ports?" Mael spat the slang out like it tasted bitter in his mouth.

Tidoris froze and murmured, "Oh."

Nobody said anything for the rest of the ride.

They sped past the central city spacescrapers, past the sprawl of boutique shops and cafes, past the enormous apartment complexes with scattered playgrounds and small storefronts. Then the taxi veered left and continued on for a while, to where the buildings were shorter and more crunched together with their gold sheen dulled off.

This, Ciaan thought, *is the p-planet.*

In the middle of a narrow street lined with over-crammed buildings, the taxicraft skidded to a stop. 1119 paid and they all piled out; the familiar smell of steel and desperation hit Ciaan like a punch in the nose.

Mael rang the intercom bell.

"What?" A thick-raspy voice came over the line.

Mael hesitated and 1119 pushed him aside.

"We're here to see 2719. Aaniin."

The voice replied, brusque, "No groups for walk-ins. You need an appointment."

1119 flashed their identification card at the tiny camera installed above the speaker. "We're here for a post-designation interview, but we could make it a full conditions inspection, if you want."

The line buzzed static for a few seconds, then the voice barked back, "You can only interview her until her next appointment."

The intercom went dead and the door clicked open with a shrill beep.

Inside, the building was just as creaky; the owners tried to hide it with elaborate decorations, but Ciaan could still see the seam cracks and warped corners. A matted red carpet ran along the main corridor, with cheap black-and-red striped wallpaper curling up the walls. Lamps were welded at shoulder-height—fitted with red gauze shades and black lace trim that washed everything in a dim orange glow, like the last light of a dying fire.

A staircase jutted up on their right; on the opposite wall, a digital board like the one in the Toi CPZ Grand Dining Chambers flashed, with names followed by two digit room numbers lit either green or red.

Lumbering footsteps echoed down the upstairs hallway—a short, solid woman appeared wrapped in a shiny robe and low heels, greasy hair hanging around her heavily painted face. She stopped halfway down the stairs and glared at them through cakey eye makeup.

"Aaniin's got an appointment in 35 minutes—you'd better be outta this sector by then." She crossed her bulbous arms, then turned and started back up the stairs.

The four of them scurried to follow her.

The second floor was just as garish as the first, only tinted more pink than red. They walked down the corridor in lockstep, pressed together to avoid knocking into any of the rickety side tables or plaster stands. A few stray pants and groans floated out from behind sealed doors and Ciaan tried to ignore them, focused on an ugly ceramic statue at the end of the hall—a naked baby with a heart-shaped bow and arrow.

"You can't get me on *anything*." The big woman, who had to be the owner, toddled and wheezed. "I run clean. Got all my filework updated and my license straight from the Headquarters. Only regulated workers, no abusive clients. Everyone gets monthly disease screenings and I fire anyone who comes back positive. *Clean.*"

When they got to a door with a gold *43* painted on it, the woman pressed the bell key with a fat finger.

"Visitors with no appointment!" she pounded against the door, then—not waiting for it to open—shoved past them and headed back towards the stairs. She shouted over her shoulder, "Thirty-two minutes!"

After the owner disappeared, the door cracked opened and a face peered out—one that Ciaan both instantly recognized and almost didn't know.

Gloss tinted her pale lips dark, and powder and rouge dimmed her naturally luminous skin, smudging the shine off it. Wide eyes stared out behind sticky black lashes—gaze dulled, like her skin, but not hollowed out.

Ciaan saw the same alertness in them that she'd seen at the courts—and years earlier—like headlights in a dark alleyway.

Aaniin assessed each of them, lingering only momentarily on Ciaan, before stepping back to let them in.

It was a small space—not really built to accommodate more than two people at once—and sparsely decorated, without much in the way of personal touches. Against one wall was a narrow, neatly-made bed and an oval table with two low chairs; a sink and an old electric range with a few cabinets perched above it lined the other wall. A closet was built into the far corner, while a sliding panel (with two pairs of plastic slippers sitting outside) was wedged next to the front door— Ciaan guessed that was whatever passed for a sanitary room here. The single window was boxy and scratched, a little too high for a decent view.

Aaniin stood with her back to the window, gestured at nowhere in particular. "Sit."

1119 and Ciaan took the chairs; the boys sat gingerly on the edge of the bed.

A sliver of sunlight smeared into the room; Ciaan squinted at it, eyes already adjusted to the weak lighting in this place. It striped across Aaniin's long grey slip, so thin that it would've revealed all her curves if she had them. She wore dark regulation socks and the jacket of an old uniform, covering bare shoulders and a low-cut neckline. Her hair was still mousy and chopped off at the jaw, but wasn't slicked back tight anymore. Ciaan noticed a few more uniforms, pressed crisp, hanging neatly in the closet.

"I thought I might see you again, Ciaan." The corners of Aaniin's lips turned up, but it wasn't a smile. "Although I hoped that it wouldn't be under these circumstances."

"Why are you here?" It was 1119 who spoke first, always a bit more prepared than the rest of them. "You retired as a Major General—you could've been designated a respectable bureaucratic position. Why request placement at an interplanetary whorehouse?"

Aaniin gazed at them coolly, squaring her shoulders.

1119 dropped their eyes, mumbling, "Sir."

"Don't do something if you're unwilling to face the consequences." Aaniin smiled now, but it looked painful. "I spent many years outrunning what I did, then many more years trying to make up for it somehow. I can't say that I was successful in either venture."

She smoothed down a few stray hairs.

"I would've been monitored too closely at Headquarters, even more so because of what I knew from my time on Earth." Her eyes flicked to Ciaan but didn't stay. "I couldn't have gotten any information out to…non-governmental entities…from AHF. All things considered, this was the safest place for me."

She hesitated. "Besides, you never know what useful things a client might mention during a session."

1119 grimaced.

"We found a pregnant Earth female and an Earth male with a disintegrated tongue in our latest cargo shipment." They spoke slowly, focusing on their superior's kneecaps.

Aaniin flinched, went stock-still and didn't correct 1119's informal address.

She closed her eyes. "Since we first met that grim night on Toi, I'd always selfishly hoped that I wouldn't see you again, that you'd be able to live without the whole truth—but I also knew you'd demand it, eventually. And now there's not really another choice."

She blinked—finally looked at Ciaan—and sighed.

"I still can't say it…for years I practiced what I was going to—what I *should*—tell you, but I never could get it right. So in the end I decided that, if you came looking for answers, I would give you this."

Aaniin bent down and pulled back an edge of the frayed carpet; a large file envelope lay sandwiched between the lining and the metal floor, sealed and unmarked. She handed it to Ciaan.

"What is it?" Ciaan stared at the envelope dumbly.

"It's your mother—your first one." Aaniin smiled again, and this time she just looked old.

"I want you to know that…I loved her from the beginning to the end, in spite of what she became. And even then…I loved her for who she was. She did what she did because she believed it was the best solution, and I believed in her." She gritted her teeth. "But I should've stopped her, not abandoned her. I owed her that much."

Aaniin finally let go of the envelope. "You should find out your own story, Ciaan, without being told someone else's version of it."

She flattened the carpet down, walked over to the closet and rummaged through her uniform pockets, then turned to 1119.

"This is the backup." Aaniin handed a small disk to them. "It contains a list of names and files that I keep in code: trust the odd names, don't trust the even ones. Politicians, officials, citizens, p-people, Artificials, Earth humans—these are all the ones I've been able to personally confirm through my networks. There are others on both sides, obviously, and many who have no idea about any of this. But until you confirm someone, don't take any chances. I check in with my contacts as frequently as I can—and I get their updates as well—but I don't want to risk sending transmissions to you and having them tracked. So for right now, this is the best I can do for you."

1119 shot up abruptly, their chair clattering to the ground. On the bed, Tidoris and Mael jumped.

"You can't do this." 1119 stood fiercely at attention. "*Sir.*"

Aaniin placed a hand on their shoulder.

"I am not afraid of death—I deserve it." She paused, looked hard at each of them. "I'm only afraid of dying knowing that, in the end, I could've made the right choices but instead I made the easy ones."

She squeezed 1119's shoulder.

"Everything catches up with you. Even this"—she motioned at the room, at them—"you coming here today, it will catch up with you."

A chill seeped out of the walls and into their bones. Mael and Tidoris shifted awkwardly; Ciaan shivered, clutching the envelope tight against her chest.

Aaniin's eyes softened. "This is not necessarily a bad thing."

She started, like maybe she had more to say, but then a red bulb began blinking above the bed. It reminded Ciaan of sector emergency lights, or the critical systems lights at the Port.

"Appointment," Aaniin said flatly. "I'm afraid you'll have to leave."

They shambled out, Mael and Tidoris first with a reluctant 1119 behind them. Aaniin caught Ciaan by the wrist before she could follow, leaning down to unclasp something around her bare ankle. She came up with a silver chain of charms.

"Your mother gave this to me during our first years together on Earth. Take it." She held out her hand, but Ciaan hesitated. Aaniin pressed it into her palm. "Remember that, at the end, everything your mother did was for herself."

Ciaan nodded but didn't understand; it didn't matter anyway, because Aaniin was guiding her to the door. She shoved the chain into her pocket—the charms tinkled against each other—and waited until the last possible second to murmur, "Goodbye."

Then the door closed and, without an answer, Aaniin was gone.

[SIXTEEN]

STAYING OVERNIGHT ON THE *Maelstrom* was safer; there was less chance of being spied on or harassed on the ship than at a local hostel. They couldn't take *You* and *Me* off-board anyway, so someone would've had to come back and check on them regardless. Of course it was cheaper that way too, and Ciaan suspected that was probably the main reason why Mael suggested it.

In any case, it was a clean bed not surrounded by strangers—which already made it better than the barracks—and it was private, which was what they needed to debrief the disconcerting events of the day. They ate quick and quiet in the base's guest dining hall, then headed for the dock with Aaniin's mysterious envelope tucked carefully inside Tidoris's pack.

Once onboard, they automatically headed to the extra cargo hold; somewhere along the line, it'd become their inadvertently agreed-upon safe room.

Tidoris handed the envelope to 1119 and left the bag outside, unasked, in case they'd picked up any bugs or trackers since their pre-trip check. Mael closed the door and locked the latch behind him.

They all circled in the middle of the room; Ciaan clutched the envelope, held it away from her like it needed to be quarantined.

"You have to open it," Tidoris urged gently. More than anyone else, he knew what this envelope was—what it represented. "You have to know."

Ciaan nodded, tried to force her fingers to break open the seal, but they wouldn't budge.

Finally, she held the envelope out to Mael. "Open it."

He did, tearing off the sticky sealing tape in one swift movement, then passed it back to her without looking inside.

Ciaan could see reams of papers, clipped together and crinkled, in several different sizes and colors. She reached in and pulled out the top sheet—a press release printed on thick paper, embossed with the header: *Earth Unilateral Commission for Fertility Research*. A small picture accompanied the text; the young woman in it could've been related—distantly—to the first mother Ciaan'd locked in her memories.

She read aloud:

EUCFR is proud to announce the winner of this year's prestigious *Lifesource Award* presented for Excellence in Fertility Research.

Dr. Gytha Janot joined the Commission only two years ago and has since risen rapidly to the top of the field through her work with isolating the effects of potential sterility-causing environmental factors in humans. Her development of successful, minimally-invasive pre- and post-conception treatment methods have begun being implemented at Fertility Research and Care facilities all over the world.

Motivated by an early-term miscarriage as a teen and a subsequent high-risk diagnosis for sterility, Dr. Janot has displayed both personal and professional courage in her dedication to the cause of finding a cure. It is EUCFR's great privilege to honor one of their brightest stars this year and celebrate the advancements in progress – through Dr. Janot's work – towards tackling the global infertility crisis.

Ciaan paused and reread the paragraphs, not sure what to make of them yet. She handed the press release to Tidoris and reached in the envelope again, pulling out a thick report:

'Mismanagement and Abuse in Global Fertility Centers'

Since their creation, the Fertility Research and Care facilities have been plagued by accusations of mistreatment and secrecy. Now with newly-mandated examinations for all sexually mature, pre-menopausal humans – along with required long-term treatments for those with 'advanced cases' of sterility – reports of forced imprisonment, widespread corruption, research doctoring, and patient abuse and exploitation have risen dramatically, with calls for investigations into these allegations and trans-Union reform bills coming from all parts of the political spectrum.

Here, through analyzing available public statistics and reviewing gathered personal testimonials from affected humans, we will strive to uncover potential answers to one of today's most controversial social and ethical dilemmas...

The paragraph went on, disintegrating into scientific jargon—Ciaan hadn't realized that, halfway through, she'd stopped reading it aloud.

The next packet was a group of internal government memos stamped as CLASSIFIED. They were stapled together neatly and had no redactions; the first subject line blared:

RE: The Secretary of the Department of Population Management, North American Union

'Undercover agents report criminal cruelty, abuse, deaths at fertility care facilities'

She read on silently.

Undercover agents placed in various FRC facilities as part of a yearlong multi-Union investigation are reporting a systemic pattern of abuse and lack of accountability, with charges ranging from bureaucratic corruption and record tampering to cover-ups of human experimentation, sexual assaults, and deaths. These actions have allegedly been committed by certain administrators, staff, and researchers, and defended as 'necessary evils' inherent in the work of finding a lasting cure.

All sexually mature Earth humans are

required by unilateral law to report for yearly examinations – including blood, urine, and tissue sampling, as well as a pelvic exam. But agents reported that some conditions (particularly in less regulated FRC facilities) are worse than detention centers, where doctors are given permission by administrators – with corporate and private backers turning a blind eye – to perform any procedures they deem subjectively essential. Allegations of these procedures include:

- *nonconsensual chemical and radiation treatment*
- *forced insemination*
- *electroshock therapies*
- *exposure to extreme temperatures and environments*
- *injections of viral and bacterial strands*
- *psychologically violent experiments*

The DoPM strongly recommends the implementation of a task force to further investigate the FRC procedures and facilities and to take appropriate action towards substantiating and prosecuting such abuses.

Ciaan flipped to the next memo.

RE: Department of Inter-Union Relations

'Responses to EUCFR task force and allegations'

Beings rights organizations are demanding an end to the EUCFR program and the immediate closure of all FRC facilities, Earth-wide. Petitions to designate these as crimes against humanity as well as release the names of alleged perpetrators have already begun circulating on open-source networks. Union representatives, prominent scientists and EUCFR members, doctors, and military personnel – both Earth and Artificial Human Forces – have been accused of direct and/or indirect involvement in the FRC abuses case. The petitionees claim that many global leaders should also be held accountable for either their failure to notice and address the crimes or for their silent complicity in the system.

International spokespersons for the Fertility Research and Care facilities have declined to comment on the specific charges.

The EUCFR did release a statement reiterating that, "We as a scientific organization would never condone unethical practices within our ranks. The EUCFR firmly believes that everything done at these facilities was done for a larger purpose.

Fighting a crisis is never simple or easy, but the alternative – giving up – is unacceptable. The sacrifices we all made, and continue to make, must be framed in the context of working towards a cure."

The World Health Organization reports that, as of January this year, an estimated 5 billion Earth humans have been treated in some capacity at these Fertility centers.

That number—*5 billion*—burned behind Ciaan's eyes.

She scanned the rest of the memos for names, but there were none—only grainy photos of things that looked like they might be horrific, but she couldn't be sure.

The last memo was shorter, brusquer in tone; it was dated almost three years after the first—still a few years before Ciaan'd been born.

RE: EUCFR Multi-Union Task Force

*'Resource allocations, concerns over EUCFR
tribunal'*

As you've probably heard, government spending is being cut this year in hopes of stabilizing the global economy and preemptively avoiding a financial crash. Early reviews of this year's budget indicate that resources for the EUCFR task force will need to be reduced by at least 53%.

The task force's report on rogue fertility clinics and the undocumented baby trade is being heavily circulated among Union representatives. However, due to current strained diplomatic relations between Unions and the jurisdictional issues surrounding the non-standardized regions, extensive and coordinated action cannot be committed to at this time. Be assured that Union and Project Planet leaders have been made aware of the task force's concerns.

The Department of Union Security is also looking into the allegations that private contractors bribed certain Project Planet officials with trade materials in order to open trafficking routes between Earth and the Planets, although it expresses concerns about the feasibility of prosecution.

Ciaan glanced at Tidoris—caught the reflection of herself in his glasses—as the specter of his father and brother and their snide, insistent whispers hooked its claws into the back of her mind.

Underneath the stack of Aaniin's fine-printed list of trust-or-not names, the only things left in the envelope were two yellowed articles, so thin that Ciaan worried they might disintegrate if she touched them. She started with the smaller one, squinted at the faded print.

'Justice, Closure Eludes Fertility Center Victims'

With global pressure for a formal trial of and convictions for accused humanity criminals stalling, and in the wake of faltering economies and a breakdown in control over the non- standardized regions, government leaders are urging citizens to look to the future of fertility treatment – not the past.

Ciaan skimmed through the article, heart pounding against her ribcage.

One of the most serious issues with this case, critics claim, is the pattern of complicit aid from some non-accused officials in protecting the alleged criminals – often helping them get new identity papers and census numbers so they can escape and remake their lives in secret. Rumors persist of these humanity criminals fleeing to the Project Planets, where strict Information Sharing regulations are enforced and most people aren't even aware of Earth's recent crises.

With fertility rates once again on the

rise, Union leaders hope to keep news of this so-called 'Earth problem' away from the P-planets. P-people have shown no signs of fertility issues thus far and Earth governments fear that releasing information could incite mass panic and destabilize the p-planet governments.

However, rumors of an interplanetary black-market baby trade and resistance movements continue to crop up...

Keys started fitting into locks; Ciaan could almost see the whole picture in front of her now. There was just a piece or two still missing, one or two more clicks to get it into focus.

She picked up the last article and the first thing she saw was the photo, that same half-relative of her first mother, bracketed between bolded words:

'Long-Missing Fertility Scientist and Accused Humanity Criminal Dead; Found as a Patient at One of Her Own Centers'

The date was about seven months after her first mother had left Toi; Ciaan felt like she was going to vomit.

Dr. Gytha Janot, the celebrated EUCFR

researcher named alongside several colleagues as a supervisor of and occasional direct participant in Fertility Research and Care facilities' human experiments, was confirmed dead on Thursday.

Her body, apparently filed as unidentified, had been sitting in a free agent fertility center morgue for days after dying from what was listed as 'treatment complications.' A Government-sanctioned autopsy was performed and concluded that Dr. Janot had died from severe and prolonged internal trauma, most likely from a series of poorly-skilled invasive procedures. It also noted that she had given birth in the past, substantiating long-held suspicions that she had also experimented upon herself. Whether or not the baby survived is unknown.

All the heat in Ciaan's body drained—from the roots of her braids to her toenails—as she trembled, the charms in her pocket jangling.

Janot's whereabouts for the last seven years are also in doubt; anonymous tips have come in over the years with sightings across the Unions, as well as on Interplanetary Transits and even on a few of the Project Planets. The fertility center where she died refused to disclose records, so how long Dr.

Janot was there and where she had come from before that remains unclear. Many speculate that she may have been living inconspicuously in one of the vast non-standardized regions.

Dr. Janot was once considered the herald of the fertility cure through her work with successfully mapping an environmental factor the EUCFR claimed indicated a susceptibility to sterility. Subsequent reports revealed that the EUCFR's research was riddled with unethical and abusive methods and – though she only had direct contact in a few cases – Janot's status as a leading experiment designer, along with her refusal to admit to any wrongdoing during preliminary investigations into the facilities, led to her being widely vilified. Her subsequent disappearance months before the EUCFR scandal broke publically saw her become one of the most sought-after criminals in recent history.

In initial interview transcripts, when asked whether what she did at the FRC facilities was criminal, Janot famously replied: "Every experiment I build and oversee is one that I would be a willing participant in. As a classified infertile woman myself, I can't imagine anything I wouldn't do to have a child."

Alongside her alleged crimes against humanity, many also felt that she exploited certain Artificial humans – who were assigned to the centers as private security officers — into forcing patients to comply with administrative and researcher demands. These claims echoed similar ones brought up against other defendants during the multi-Union tribunal a few years ago, which prompted the Artificial Human Forces Headquarters to issue a statement strongly condemning any Artificial who participated in the atrocities and promising to conduct its own internal review.

Although we cannot be sure why Dr. Janot chose to reappear now — if she had a choice at all — government officials say they found filework on her with data on numerous still-missing criminals, including aliases, addresses, new census numbers, and a brief description of any altered physical characteristics. It is unclear if she compiled the data herself or if it was planted on the body postmortem.

News of her death has reignited public anger, with the designated tracking committees of Beings Rights organizations demanding that her lists — and any other previously-withheld relevant information — be released to the public. The government vowed Friday to hand over all new evidence to the EUCFR Task Force and summarily arrest as many of the remaining criminals as they can locate.

Meanwhile, amidst calls for it to be buried in an unmarked grave or destroyed, Janot's

body has allegedly been cremated and its ashes
spread in space; a stark ending for her
complex legacy.

The ink print stopped at the bottom of the page;
Ciaan flipped it over, trying to find the rest of the story.
This—a handful of paragraphs written as dispassionate
summaries—wasn't anything, wasn't *enough*. A thousand
articles, an encyclopedic series wouldn't be enough, not
for Ciaan. Not for any of this (her world, her first
mother, herself) to truly make sense again.

It felt like a stranger—answering to her first mother's
name and dressed in her first mother's skin—had stolen
her first mother's life and desecrated it. She smiled too
wide, too glossy, at Ciaan—mocking her for ever wanting
to know what really happened all those years ago.

The rest of them stood, close but not too close,
waiting for a cue. When the letters on the page started to
twist, rearranging themselves into cyphers that she
couldn't read anymore, Ciaan poured the envelope and
all its contents into their arms. They weren't ready; most
of it fluttered to the floor.

As they squatted down to collect the scattered sheets,
Ciaan turned and walked to the wall. She rested her
forehead against the cool metal; rust flakes ground
against her skin. She blinked against the tears searing in
the corners of her eyes.

Once, twice, three times. And again, and again.

Eventually, someone dropped a light hand on her shoulder. She thought it was Tidoris and shoved it away—but then it settled back again and squeezed.

"She'll be decommissioned for this," 1119 murmured. "The Major General, I mean. Aaniin. The illegal transfer of secure official documents is treason against the AHF."

"So she'll end up at a detention center instead of a gratification complex," Ciaan bit out, copper and tangy. "Who cares."

She blocked out the echo of Aaniin's sorrow and regret—stripped the memory of feeling, like how everyone thought Artificials were. How they should be.

1119 let go. "No, she'll be killed. A nanomite bullet to the base of the brain; I've heard it just tickles a little bit."

Ciaan spun on them, reeling. "What?! When?!"

"When Headquarters finds out. It could be years if she's careful and we aren't foolish." 1119 said it like they were itemizing a shipment's taxes, not estimating a death sentence.

Ciaan gulped, cold and sour, as 1119 continued.

"Or it could be much sooner. It depends on how good her contacts—and her enemies—are at tracking her interactions."

It was all so rational and precise, this Artificial

philosophy of life and death; Ciaan suddenly wanted to fit her fingers around pale necks and choke the lab-made life out of all of them.

"Why didn't you tell us?!" She was in 1119's face, screaming loud and accusing. "Why didn't you stop her?!"

Tidoris and Mael jumped up—ready to pull apart a fight—but 1119 waved them off.

"The Major General did what she thought was right—for you." 1119 sighed, lowered their eyes. "…and I guess I wanted to know what was in the envelope too."

Ciaan gnawed at her bottom lip. She wanted more—excuses, explanations, apologies, *whatever*—but something told her that there wasn't anything else to get. She started to deflate; after a minute, she and 1119 joined the boys again.

Mael and Tidoris sat poring over the backup disk data on Tidoris's Right Hand, what looked like pages and pages of meticulously typed and organized personal information.

Tidoris scrolled through one file after another.

"I can't believe it. There must be hundreds of individual profiles here—all tracked over what looks like several years—and a lot of corresponding arrest reports." He paused at a sparse file and looked up at Ciaan, eyes bright.

"Look at the name."

Ciaan followed his finger down a line of jumbled code.

Illonde Tohannson, file #237.

Aaniin had said: *trust the odd ones.*

The tears rushed back, snuck up on her and she tried to smother the sobs welling in her throat but it was too late. Tidoris moved to get up but 1119 was already there, folding Ciaan into their arms.

Mael watched, pursing his lips, then nodded decisively. "Okay, so I say come morning, we get the hell out of here."

No one argued with that.

[SEVENTEEN]

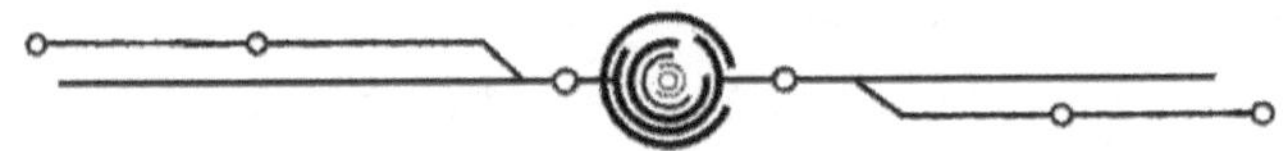

S SOON AS THE OFFICIAL work day started, 1119 put in a call to the AHF Headquarters.

The four of them sat in the ship's dining quarters; Ciaan, Tidoris, and Mael swallowed down their morning rations of protein bars and single-serving vitamin shakes—left over from the *Maelstrom*'s last run—while 1119 stayed patiently on hold through several transfers within the bureaucratic labyrinth.

"Hello, is this the AHF Directory?" they piped up after about 15 minutes. "I'd like to inquire about an Artificial's status: Major General, Kwe NAU 27198607. Yes, I know she's retired. I'd like to know…yes…yes, I see. And she's still registered with that gratification complex? No, I don't need to be transferred to her extension. Yes, thank you for your assistance."

1119 put the Right Hand down on the short tin table and picked up a half-eaten bar. "They haven't gotten her—at least, not yet."

They all chewed in silence for a few more minutes, then Tidoris started collecting the wrappers to dump in the waste compartment.

Mael drummed his fingers against the dented tabletop.

"I'm plan-less," he announced, then clarified.

"I mean, I'm plan-less for *You* and *Me*. I think the obvious overall plan is to get off this shellacked hunk of metal that's currently crawling with high officials and Earth dignitaries and get you two"—he jabbed a finger at Ciaan and Tidoris—"back to your little base as fast as we can. Finish the last of the ship repairs and get clearance ASAP, then we'll all be out of each other's hair. Forget all this conspiracy crap and go back to doing what we do. It's not like we can change any of it anyway."

Ciaan gaped at him.

"What, you got a better plan than that?" Mael scoffed. "One that doesn't end with us locked in solitary chambers at some fucking detention center, or with a nanomite bullet to the back of the head?"

Next to him, 1119 winced.

"No, I don't have a better plan." Ciaan admitted; she

wasn't afraid anymore. "But we can't do yours because it's shit."

His eyes narrowed, fingers stopped drumming. "You wanna be a hero? Be my guest—I'll send condolences to your family. But I've got better things to do with my life and freedom than get killed trying to help you sort out your mommy issues."

Ciaan stood up, abrupt, chain jingling at the bottom of her pocket.

"You were right—you *are* a coward."

Mael bared his teeth. "And you're the halfie daughter of a humanity criminal."

Tidoris whipped around, spilled the last of his vitamin shake on the floor and didn't even notice.

"Enough!" 1119 screamed and everyone snapped to attention. They took a deep breath and repeated, softer: "Enough."

They pointed to the doorway; *Me* stood there, leaning weakly against the wall. Ciaan walked over, cautiously, and offered an arm for support.

"What are you doing, walking?" Tidoris signing, hovering nearby but not touching her.

Me signed back nonchalantly with one hand.

Tidoris glanced at Mael. "She's hungry."

"Yeah, well, I'd be hungry too if I'd been impregnated and locked in a cargo container for god-knows-how-long and then almost died from a parasite." He rubbed his temples. "Get her something to eat."

Ciaan held *Me*'s bicep as she eased herself onto a bench; she could feel the girl's thin muscles shaking with the effort. Tidoris brought her a protein bar and vitamin shake—opened both of them just in case—and they all watched as the girl devoured everything.

Here now was a living, breathing, somewhat healthy human being who'd been entrusted to them—whether they wanted to accept that or not didn't change the fact that it was true.

"Let's focus on getting back to Toi first. It's safest there…" 1119 offered *Me* a napkin, eyes darting to Mael. "For all of us."

Mael clenched his teeth, glared at all of them then shouted, "*Shibal!*"

He jumped up, knees banging against the edge of the table, and stomped out of the room.

"I'll go upload the departure filework," Tidoris sighed. He got up and followed after Mael, leaving his Right Hand behind.

Their request for departure was cleared after lunch and

they were scheduled to leave, if traffic permitted, just before the afternoon shift change—but traffic didn't permit it, so they went to the base dining hall for a complimentary meal and then hung out by the scattered tethers and lifts that littered the dock ground underneath the ship.

They tossed around disjointed small talk—about the remaining repairs, the *Maelstrom's* next cargo route, when Ciaan might be eligible for early parole, Tidoris's planned upgrades for the base network system—and when they couldn't think of any other topics, the conversation sputtered out awkwardly. After a couple of quiet minutes, Mael cleared his throat.

"I may know a few people, Ex-Resistance Free Agents, who could help us." He spoke hazy and distant, eyes lingering on the curves of his ship. "If they're still alive."

"Ex-Resistance?" Ciaan told herself that, at this point, she should probably stop being surprised by anything.

Mael blinked at her, gaze sharpening again.

"Not any formal, unified resistance front. Just a sort of mishmash of people and groups who didn't agree with things the Unions were doing and wouldn't shut up about it. They all had different ideas about how to resist, which was probably why they never really worked well together." He kicked at a loose bundle of fuel cords. "They don't really organize open protests anymore since the crisis ended and the tribunal wrapped up—"

Ciaan cut in. "What happened with all that?"

"All what?" Mael stared at her flatly.

"The tribunal." Ciaan suddenly felt like she'd bathed in dirt and guilt. The hairs on her forearms pricked up. "Aaniin's files didn't mention the outcome."

Mael snorted. "It was all scientists and doctors who were tried, along with a few Artificials. Most were convicted and sentenced to the detention facilities—and a few were sentenced to death in absentia."

He scratched at his wrist and Ciaan ignored the spread of pity in his voice.

"But the trials were costing more than the governments could afford and, with the public demanding harsher sentences than what was being handed down, I guess the Union leaders felt like it was starting to make them look bad. They had other problems going on—especially in the non-standardized regions—so after the first round of convictions, the tribunal and task force went on a hiatus."

Tidoris edged into the conversation. "For how long?"

"I guess they'll let us know when they come back from it." Mael picked at the frayed ends of his boot laces. "Anyway, these days the Resistance is more of a network of disrupters, stirring up whatever irritations they can for the governments."

"Like illegal trading?" Tidoris poked, more teasing than scolding.

"Dubiously legal," Mael corrected with a slick-flashed smile. "It never hurts to have friends in all kinds of places."

Ciaan grunted noncommittally. "So these ex-Resistance people can help us?"

"Maybe, at least with our excess carg—er, them." Mael shrugged, looking grim. "If they can't, then I *really* won't know what to do."

A beat—an uneasy hiccup between them—and they all stared at their boots.

"Well." Tidoris shifted his weight on the edge of a container barrel. "In the interest of full disclosure, I think there's something you—all of you—should know before we leave our *cargo* with just anyone."

1119 and Ciaan looked up; Mael leaned in.

"You remember that night in the medical bay when *Me* was getting sicker a lot faster than we'd expected?" Tidoris coughed. "And *You* signed something that I said was gibberish?"

They all nodded, and a blush crept up the side of Mael's neck. Ciaan wondered if he was remembering sleepy bodies on a cold floor too.

She prompted, "Yes?"

"It wasn't gibberish." Tidoris's eyes dropped. "He signed *our baby*."

Mael, who'd been pretending to only half-listen, burst out. "What?! That's impossible!"

"Biologically speaking…" Tidoris murmured. "It's not."

"Then they were lying about being brother and sister." Mael crossed his arms, decided.

Tidoris shook his head. "Maybe, maybe not. It's about supply and demand, right? And desperate, awful measures."

"But that doesn't change our situation." Ciaan wanted to purge the lists of fertility center abuses—typed out in harsh black ink—and the unfamiliar picture of Dr. Gytha Janot that came with it from her mind, wanted to stop them from being the only things she could think about now. But it was too late; they'd already latched onto other memories and rooted themselves deep. "It doesn't matter if they're brother and sister or not."

"Except, I'd imagine"—1119 glanced fleetingly out at the ridge of Earth—"to them."

They continued on before the silence could seep back in.

"If we're telling secrets here, then I have one as well.

As an Artificial, I was—I believe—raised to accept my predetermined duties (and the greater duties of Artificial humans in general) without question. Commander 2719 accepted all of this, including her crimes and the weight of the punishment they'll eventually carry. She accepted that—regardless of what is right and what is wrong—the choices for an Artificial are duty or death." They paused for a moment, like they were expecting an interruption.

"Well, I cannot accept that. I don't accept it." They shuddered, bleeding with emotion. "I'm an Artificial, but I'm not a pawn. I'm not a surrogate or a less-than; I'm not a she or a he or an it—I'm a *they*. And my name is Nkoti."

The other three inhaled sharply and Ciaan reached for Nkoti, held on like an anchor.

It was her turn now.

"I wish I didn't know the truth about my first mother."

The atmosphere went heavy—choking—with the weight of knowing. It felt like Ciaan was drowning, gasping for air that wasn't there, without being able to die.

Traffic lightened just after evening decompression started

and the control room cleared them for takeoff. The opulence of Wakan Tanka receded from the back window; it was nighttime and the dark side of the Earth seemed to swallow everything in space. Even the stars that shimmered in the curtain of black beyond the p-planets had faded, flickering like their batteries were just about to go out. A sea of Earth lights replaced them, sparkling across the planet's surface. They illuminated nothing but seemed to alter Earth itself, changing it from a planet of green and life to one of blind-dark death. Its shadow cast out over the visible p-planets too; their own stubborn sparks waned under it.

"I never thought my life would become *this*." Tidoris's voice was warmth out of the darkness.

"Innovative technical developments that might get me some accolades, a career track with midlevel ambitions, a stable life with stable people and eventually a stable partner and maybe even stable children. That was supposed to be my life. I'm not an adventurer—I'm not a resistance fighter." He watched Ciaan, eyes clouded behind his glasses. "And I'm not sure I wanna be one."

Ciaan looked away, out the shrouded window, and put a hand on Tidoris's leg. After a minute or two, he twined his fingers with hers and held their hands together as the ship shrugged into the abyss.

When they reached the Toi docking channels, the

ship slowed to a hover. Light footsteps tapped down the deckway from the bridge.

"Tidoris." Nkoti appeared in the doorway, jaw set. "You received both departure and reentry clearance from the Administrative Headquarters before we left, correct?"

Tidoris dropped Ciaan's hand clumsily, sat up straighter.

"Yes."

Nkoti's teeth ground together. "The official at the control rooms is saying that we don't have reentry authorization. He's demanding to speak to the senior base official on the ship."

"What?" Tidoris leapt up tall, clearly offended. "I very specifically double-checked our reentry authorization with Headquarters before we left, so what's this idiot even talking about? Probably some basic just out of orientation…"

He marched out of the room, still grumbling. Nkoti raised an eyebrow at Ciaan as they followed him to the bridge.

Mael sat strapped into his captain's chair, clutching the steering handle and looking annoyed. Tidoris snatched the intercom microphone from his outstretched hand.

"Ship to Toi CPZ base Control rooms, this is Technical Advisor Tidoris von Ulger. I received departure and reentry clearance for this flight two days ago at 1500 Afternoon Time. Do you need the filework numbers to verify?"

The speaker crackled and a squeaky, apologetic voice blasted over it.

"TA von Ulger? Who else is on board with you from the base?"

"Reserve Private Ciaan Gennett, as stated in my request report." Tidoris propped a hand on his hip. "May I speak with your supervisor?"

"That won't be necessary." A hint of panic tinged the nasal tone. "We've located your filework now; it was miscategorized. I'm very sorry for any inconvenience—this is my first week…"

Tidoris rolled his eyes as the voice continued, "Please proceed to channel 17."

Mael pulled forward before Tidoris and Ciaan had a chance to brace themselves.

"Incompetence," he muttered darkly.

As the ship maneuvered into the channel, Ciaan was struck for the first time in her life with the feeling of coming home. The base—and Toi itself—looked sturdy and peaceful and blissfully unaware, just the same as when she'd left it. Her short, jagged nails dug into the top of Nkoti's headrest.

When they approached the space gate, Ciaan noticed

a flurry of uniform sets on the dock.

Mael grabbed the abandoned microphone. "Captain to port 17. Are we clear?"

"Clear," a sleepy voice buzzed back.

The space gate opened, slow like a held breath, and Mael eased into the port. He unstrapped and hit a row of buttons, initiating system shutdown.

Then he turned to Nkoti. "Is the cargo secure?"

"Yes." They unstrapped too.

He got up, addressed all of them. "I DMed a few of my contacts; hopefully, one of them will get back to me with good news soon. Until then, *You* and *Me* need to keep a low profile—and we probably should too."

A murmur of agreement passed between them, then they all started making their way towards the main hatch.

Ciaan was the last one down the ladder; she hopped off, turned to say something but froze at the row of stunners pointed at them. The orange jumpsuits that she'd seen from the space gate held back in a nervous cluster and, from behind the armed line, two well-dressed figures emerged.

Their expensive coats fluttered as they moved—the taller one stopped in front of them, menacing without a sound, but the shorter one couldn't seem to help himself.

"Hello, Ciaan." His voice pooled like blood and garbage on a moonless metal ground. "Welcome back."

[EIGHTEEN]

CIAAN RAISED HER HANDS, slow but not too high; she didn't want anyone thinking it was an admission of guilt or using sudden movement as an excuse to stun her.

"Melean," she hissed.

The older official's eyebrows arched high and dangerous.

Ciaan corrected herself. "Official von Ulger—what an unexpected homecoming. You shouldn't have."

Melean grinned, smug and poisonous. "I know."

He took a long step towards Ciaan—next to her, Tidoris stiffened.

"I hope you'll excuse the small turnout and lack of festivities, but it's really the thought that counts, isn't it?"

The older official lifted a gloved hand, silenced them both. Melean stepped back automatically and Ciaan bit her lips shut.

"You're facing some very serious charges, Private Gennett."

She knew that voice, had wrapped it in a memory of exotic sashes.

"From what I hear, you and your"—High Official Yeager looked from face to face with disdain—"*friends* have been flagrantly breaking not only port base regulations, but also several Interplanetary laws and codes, specifically concerning restricted trade."

He paused, like he thought that might be enough to elicit a confession, but no one said anything. Ciaan was waiting to see how much Yeager knew and how much he was trying to trick them into telling, and assumed that was probably what the rest of them were doing too.

"You, Captain Moon,"—Yeager turned to Mael, tone slightly less condescending—"have half a warehouse full of unclaimed cargo that is being searched as we speak. I would like to believe that nothing questionable will be found, but that has rarely been the case in my experience. Couple that with the fact that several of your deliveries were made to people who're either dead or never existed to begin with, and an alarming picture begins to emerge. My young protégée here also suspects that you were harboring prohibited items on your ship prior to your suspicious run to our capital planet."

Yeager dropped a cold, detached hand onto Melean's shoulder.

"Does your young protégée have any proof of that?" Mael challenged, full of bravado, but Ciaan could hear the fear rattling around in his throat.

Yeager narrowed his eyes.

"Proof isn't everything, Captain." He folded his hands behind his back, and Melean followed suit. "I've certainly seen people convicted on far less. And that's such a shame because I've been in contact with your parole administrator on Earth and was informed that any breach of conduct would result in the reactivation of frozen warrants and your immediate deportation to a labor site."

Mael's face drained; any retort he had died on his tongue.

Yeager waved a dismissive hand at Nkoti. "I assume—should this all come to light—that your keeper would be disgraced if she was ignorant of your actions, and decommissioned if she wasn't. And you along with her, no doubt."

Ciaan flinched; the skin at the base of her skull sizzled. Mael shot dark glares at Yeager and Melean, but defended neither himself nor his first officer.

Yeager nodded towards Tidoris with a gummy sigh, like he was trying to feign commiseration with him.

"And you, TA von Ulger." He shook his head, unconvincing. "What a waste. Your brother tells me that you're full of clearly-squandered potential and desperate for social acceptance, which has undoubtedly led you to fall in with these unsavory individuals. Your father…I can only imagine his shame and devastation at your arrest."

Tidoris didn't respond, but Ciaan felt him shuddering beside her.

"Which brings us back to you." Yeager tilted his head, sneering at Ciaan. "Mixed blood and all the defects that come with that, an almost impressively long history of violent and destructive criminal behavior—and you're the docking supervisor for this ship, which places the responsibility to report any illegal or suspect activities and items solely on you. Your failure to do so has allowed the continuation of—if not, as I believe, the active aid in—violations of the Interplanetary Agreements. This, as well as the personal violation of your probationary status, marks you for transfer to a maximum security detention center without the option to appeal."

A strange serenity blanketed Ciaan at this final, direct ultimatum, like everything—her whole life—had been building towards this.

At least now, she thought, there wouldn't be any more uncertainties.

Yeager sniffed, nose crinkling like he could smell their treason.

"You're all satisfied, then, with these consequences?" he pressed. "If that's the case then, as a high member of the Interplanetary Commission, I have the authority to enforce them without the delay or show of trials."

Something shifted in the air around them, a restlessness that Ciaan couldn't quite put her finger on.

Yeager jumped on it. "Or you could let the blame fall where it most naturally lies. We could overlook the more serious allegations, Captain—in exchange for your cooperation and testimony—and just cite you for inaccurate filework. You and your Artificial would go free. As for you, TA von Ulger, I'm sure the Commission would be more than willing to consider your situation: caught up with bad influences and misplaced loyalties, you were simply unable to escape their momentum once this all began. And with a good word put in by your respected brother, I'm sure you wouldn't even get a minor mark on your spotless record."

Pieces started falling into place; the hush of it rang in Ciaan's ears.

"What're you suggesting?" Tidoris asked incredulously, addressing the High Official for the first time. "We're not gonna sell out our—"

"This is unconditional immunity?" Mael interrupted him, serious as being worked to death at a labor site.

Yeager hummed.

"These charges can never be used against us again. And the frozen warrants are expunged, clearing the bounty on me and my first officer." Mael bartered, fast and hard.

"That can be arranged." Yeager didn't seem too concerned with the specifics. "You'll be a free man, barring any future entanglements with the laws—you have my word."

"Like I'd trust that." Mael scoffed, sounded frantic. "I want it in writing—official documents all signed and notarized and uploaded before I make any deals."

Yeager looked him up and down—appraised him carefully, appreciatively. Then he waved off to Melean.

"Official von Ulger will write it up now. You're welcome to read it over once it's ready; just know that this offer is finite." His words clicked on a countdown.

Melean flipped open his Right Hand.

One down; Ciaan rubbed her sweaty palms against the coarse weave of her uniform pants.

"As a supervising parole escort, I have to say that I object to Captain Moon's tentative acceptance of this offer," Nkoti hedged. "But as a subordinate officer, I won't challenge his decision."

One to go. All eyes—except Ciaan's—fell on Tidoris.

"No." He choked it out, like it had to push its way through a crowd to get there.

Ciaan bit at her cheek to keep from swearing; she knew he'd say that. If it wouldn't have made their problems even worse, she would've told him to stop being so goddamn noble and take the deal.

Tidoris glared at all of them, defiant, and the only thing that gave him away was the knock of one heel against the metal ground. "I won't do it."

Behind Yeager, Melean stopped typing. His fine features twisted anxious and imploring—he glanced at his brother but Tidoris just squared his shoulders and jutted out his chin.

"Your faithfulness to your friend, however misguided, should be commended and certainly stands in your favor." Yeager brushed some invisible dust off of his lapel. "It's to our mutual benefit then that we have no solid evidence with which to charge you, beyond circumstantial corroboration. If you refuse to cooperate, I'm afraid we won't be able to keep a mark for insubordination of direct orders from going on your record, but I see no reason why any of this nastiness should reach beyond that—*for you.*"

Tidoris opened his mouth but Yeager cut him off,

raised a stern hand against any rebuttal, then wheeled on Ciaan.

"What about you?" he growled. "Do you have anything to say for yourself or your cohorts?"

Ciaan'd been listening for indications that Yeager or Melean knew about the unregistereds; so far, they hadn't let anything slip.

They could be bluffing, she considered. *This could be the end for all of us.*

Or, something insisted from deep in her gut, *it could be our only chance to save* You *and* Me.

If Yeager and Melean didn't know about the unregistereds, then maybe there was still a chance for them—maybe they could still be rescued. Maybe that was the eleventh-hour hand Mael was playing, or maybe not.

Ciaan couldn't see anyone else's cards, could only play the ones she had.

The ringing in her ears sounded like Aaniin now—not the real Aaniin, but the one Ciaan'd kept locked in her mind for seven years. It was a drone, nothing more, like it didn't have anything left to say.

"No, sir." Ciaan replied clear and calm, and let it seal her in. "I don't."

Ciaan'd prepared herself for an immediate transport, for being whisked away into the swallow of darkness and never seen again; she'd somehow assumed that High Official Yeager just had that kind of power. And she'd accepted it too because she couldn't think of any other options—so being hustled into the base brig was, frankly, a little disappointing.

"Watch her," Yeager snapped at the poor recruits on overnight duty. "I've got filework to upload."

It dawned on her then that, ultimately, he was nothing more than another bureaucratic cog. A larger, more influential cog, sure—but still just one replaceable part of the machine.

He didn't even threaten her before he left.

Ciaan dropped onto the dirty floor, stretched out her short legs and picked at the edges of her fingernails. The two recruits stared at her in awe through the shock wall, pulsing with blue current.

"What'd you do?" one of them—the most average-looking p-man Ciaan'd ever seen—whispered; the other one huddled in with wide eyes.

Ciaan folded her hands behind her head. "I killed a guy."

At their collective gasp, she laughed, let a twinge of hysteria edge through. They stepped back from the electrified barrier and didn't look directly at her again.

When Yeager eventually returned—Ciaan couldn't tell how long it'd been—he strode in pompously, flanked by an entourage of suited officials with their Right Hands out and typing furiously. The two recruits saluted them and stood awkwardly at attention.

Melean wasn't among them.

"If it's of any interest to you, your so-called friends have now officially turned you in to save themselves." Yeager smirked, eerie and blurred through the shock wall. "The obvious choice, of course, and it was wise of you to concede without a fight. That will make the rest of this so much more civil."

"Where are they?" Ciaan made sure it sounded reflexive, like an afterthought and not a demand.

"The captain and his Artificial have left the base with the polite suggestion to not return for the foreseeable future. Their unclaimed cargo in the warehouses was confiscated by the Administrative Headquarters, since much of it was suspected to be restricted or prohibited." One of Yeager's assistants waddled up to him and pointed at something on the Right Hand's screen; Yeager brushed him off impatiently. "TA von Ulger has been released into the care of his brother and is likely being transported to his home for a short recovery leave. I don't expect you'll be seeing any of them again."

The hard lump, the metal frame of her heart, constricted—just once, but painfully.

"And what happens to me?" Ciaan traced a crack in the thin cell wall. It wasn't deep, but it veined its way from floor to ceiling.

"You'll stay here until we can arrange for a judge to sentence you. Formalities." Yeager played with the buttons on one of his cuffs.

"Then a detention center?" It made a sick kind of sense that, despite everyone's best efforts, she was still going to end up there.

"In the official filework, yes." Yeager chuckled and shook his head, like he'd just remembered a particularly funny joke. "But since I know that you're the offspring of a formerly infertile Earth woman, I've decided that you're much too valuable an asset to just get thrown in the trash. I'm sure there'll be several research centers—private facilities, of course, that don't have to worry about governmental interference—vying for you. So I can't say exactly where you'll go until I see the bids."

His smirk curdled. "But what could it matter to you? It's a life sentence, either way."

Ciaan scrambled up off the ground, suddenly needing to look him in the eye. "You knew?"

Yeager gazed at her, unimpressed. "Yes."

He walked over, leaned in close enough that Ciaan

could feel his breath sizzle through the electric currents.

"Your mother was part of a system, and now so are you."

Ciaan staggered back until she hit the cell wall—had everything to say to that, and nothing at all.

[NINETEEN]

COME MORNING, THE AIR in the brig stank so foul that Ciaan wondered if the refuse shafts emptied above it. She wouldn't have even known it was morning except that the original two awestruck recruits were shuffled out and replaced by two only mildly curious ones.

The new guards didn't ask any questions, which was lucky because Ciaan wasn't in the mood for answering; she was too busy sifting through clue scraps, trying to piece together what might actually go on at a fertility center these days. She hadn't realized how stupidly vague all the descriptions they'd gotten had been until now.

She'd spent the night filing through the logical conclusions: clinical observations, treatment trials, lab tests, genetic mapping. As time wore on without any mile markers to track it, the possibilities warped sinister but (if even half of what the files claimed was true) not unheard-of: forced fertilization, invasive experimentation, methods that were more torture than medicine.

By the time another shift changed—bringing in two completely uninterested new guards—Ciaan was already imagining horrors she couldn't put a name to. Nothing that a detention center dreamed up could be worse than *that*; at this point, even an immediate transport to some death-sentence work colony would've been better.

More than whatever came later, Ciaan knew it was the waiting that'd break her open for Yeager and his shadowy bidders to scoop out.

She tried to distract herself, used meals—the same tasteless gruel that all reserves ate during orientation—at regular intervals and the guards' attitudes—sleepy in the morning, disinterested during the afternoon, paranoid going into the night shift—to estimate the time of day. There wasn't much else to do; except for her, the brig was empty.

She wondered if rumors were spreading about the mysterious jailed recruit who'd killed a man, or maybe more—no one knew for sure.

The second day passed less anxiously, but tar-slow and just as boring. The stretch between meals seemed to lengthen and the shrill beeps that indicated guard changes came less frequently than Ciaan expected. The pulse of the shock wall got louder and the crack in the wall inched higher and, when a particularly young-looking recruit pushed the dinner tray through the de-electrified panel in the barrier, Ciaan stared up at her.

"You know, I didn't actually kill anybody."

The recruit's eyes darted away; she nodded fast, then slammed the panel shut and locked it behind her.

On the third day, Ciaan started to think that maybe this was her punishment—that all the talk about research centers and labor sites and sentencing judges had been a smokescreen and the real plan was to just keep her locked in the CPZ base's underground brig until she was dead enough to not cause any more problems.

It'd definitely be the cheapest option and, if three days was anything to go by, satisfyingly sadistic for the budget. Eventually, the rumors would evolve to that one recruit—the base's only prisoner—who raved mad in its bowels.

Ciaan blinked, bleary-eyed, and shivered.

Maybe, she thought hazily. *I should try and get some actual sleep.*

The naked metal ground did everything it could to discourage comfort, but after three days of waking delirium, her fatigue finally won out; the hum of the shock wall lulled her to sleep.

Ciaan woke up feeling both alone and watched, strained to catch the usual murmur of the guards but couldn't hear them—couldn't hear anything—over the sparks of the barrier; it was deafening now. She pressed her palms over her ears but the noise still churned, like it'd burrowed into her brain while she'd slept.

She twisted her body—curled on the floor—and peered through the electric blue haze of the cell barrier. Someone was sitting on a chair that hadn't been there before, looking at her. The face formed and reformed through the currents; Ciaan crawled towards it, uncovering her ears.

"I gave the guards the night off," Melean quipped, pointing to the pile of two recruits—limp and draped over each other—in the far corner of the room.

When Ciaan squinted, she could see their bodies twitch every couple of seconds; Melean—savage but not a complete idiot—must've temporarily stunned them. Their own base-issued stunners sat discarded at his feet.

"We never get alone time anymore." Melean twined and untwined his fingers—stopping to check the cuticles and nails—then leaned forward, elbows on knees. "We always seem to be interrupted—always leaving something unfinished."

Ciaan steadied herself on one arm. "Is that what this

is, some sort of ultimate showdown that you've been brooding about since primary grades?"

Her hand slipped—an unsanded bolt stabbed into her palm and she hissed with the pain.

Melean reached into his coat pocket and took out a handkerchief, casually wiped his hands with it. "Please, do you really think I'm that petty?"

Ciaan scoffed; it burned against her throat, raw from the chill brig air.

"If you think I orchestrated this whole thing as some grand scheme to continue our cat and mousing, then you seriously overestimate my influence and power." He paused, then unlocked the de-electrified panel and tossed the handkerchief inside the cell.

Ciaan picked it up by the fringe, eyed it skeptically before wrapping it around her bloodied hand.

"You're not that important." He smoothed the wrinkles out of his sleeves.

"And you are?" She came as close to the shock wall as she could without getting zapped.

He shook his head.

"No, but I will be. Importance isn't who you are, it's what you achieve. And you"—he leaned down to meet her gaze directly—"have achieved nothing. You wasted your life on alleyway brawls, but I've moved on. That— not your greenie blood or extraordinary hair—is why my life will always be worth more than yours."

Ciaan dug her nails into the wound. Her teeth chattered as she seethed—at Melean's arrogance, at his smug superiority, at the truth of his statement. If her life was effectively over, what'd she achieved with it? Helping to save two—three—humans from starvation and disease, then abandoning them to a space pirate with no qualms about betrayal for the right price. Uncovering a massive interplanetary conspiracy but sharing it with no one of any significance. Martyring herself so that her best friend could be removed from the job he loved and blackmailed into a world he despised. Learning the truth about her first mother and having that put someone else's life—all of their lives, really—in danger, only to find out that she didn't want to know it after all.

Melean was right; she hadn't achieved anything in her life. She'd actually negatively achieved, costing the people she cared about more than she'd ever gained for them. That realization hit her harder than any of Melean's sucker punches, sent her slumping back down onto the floor.

"But still, you've always been *fun*. I never could predict your next move, which should count for something"—Melean's lips curled up, exposed a thin row of polished white teeth—"and it does."

The churning abruptly cut out and the blue haze

dissipated—replaced by a de-electrified, scratched-up plexiglass door. Melean held up a security remote that he must've taken off the stunned recruits.

"Now I can't open this door without either entering the code or sounding the alarm, so you'll have to accept that the shock is down as a show of good faith." He touched his fingertips to the panel like a reassurance that this wasn't a trick.

She didn't reciprocate the move.

"What do you want?" Ciaan forced herself back onto her knees, bones cracking with the effort. "What could I possibly have that you need?"

Melean licked his lips.

"Access," he said finally, like it wasn't what he'd really wanted to say at all.

Ciaan coughed rough and shallow. "Access?"

"Specifically the type of access that'd come with a reputation and record like yours; one that wouldn't get you questioned if you were, for example, trying to infiltrate a criminal organization or...reconnect with old, rogue cargo transit partners." He rubbed his palms together slowly. "And your *unique* background would also allow you interplanetary cultural access, which would be an asset in any diplomatic situation."

Ciaan thought she'd heard this speech before, only from a slightly different angle.

"Are you offering me a job?" she hedged, disbelieving.

Melean drew each word out carefully. "I'm offering you an opportunity to not spend the rest of your life in a cell surrounded by the dregs of the p-planets. You can take it or leave it."

He didn't mention the fertility centers; she weighed her options.

"Why?"

His eyes flashed, annoyed. "Because you're a useful tool who's squandering her potential and if you're not gonna use it, then I will. There are two things that you need if you want to get somewhere in life: money and other people's information. I've got one and you can help me get the other."

"So you want me to be your personal spy?" Ciaan stalled, but knew it wasn't going to do any good.

"I want you to be my personal whatever-I-ask, and those are the terms." Melean pressed a spidery hand against the acrylic wall and stroked it at level with her face. "You'll be my spy, my assistant, my nemesis, my…bedmate…."

Dark, wide, unblinking eyes tunneled into her, and for a half-second they looked like the ones she'd seen a million times before, hidden behind thin-framed glasses.

"…or, so help me, I'll shoot you with just enough nanomites to ensure that you live out the rest of your long imprisonment term in excruciating, sanity-breaking pain."

The plastic barrel of a military-issue nano-gun thunked against the wall—Ciaan stared at it, frantically tried to predict its trajectory.

Melean hooked a finger around the trigger. "This offer, like all the rest, will expire."

A flood of probabilities and outcomes rushed through Ciaan's mind, sinking deep into murky waters that she couldn't fish them out of. She thought about herself, her first mother, Aaniin, *Me*. She thought about it all graphed out on her Right Hand's function, dots of increasing chaos connected to a full final stop.

It ended—she must've had the idea all along—with a bullet.

A violent, arbitrary death for a violent, arbitrary life. Now or later, quick and dirty or long and excruciating, from Melean or Yeager or some other crisp-suited dick she hadn't even met yet; never *if*—it'd only ever been a question of *when*.

Ciaan closed her eyes, imagined the darkest parts of space that wove around the edges of sight—that'd be her infinity.

She waited for it, only a little terrified.

She waited—three long exhales—and when it didn't come, she cracked an eye open.

Melean sat rigid, one hand plastered against the

acrylic like putty and the other slack, nano-gun slipping from its grasp. He wasn't looking at her anymore; he was hunched over and Ciaan saw something pressed to his neck, just behind the ear. It followed back to an arm, a body, someone crouching behind him. A few other shadows moved restlessly near the doorway.

"Drop the gun."

Ciaan knew that voice—or had known it, before it'd gone so chilling and unforgiving. Melean's jaw twitched as the crouching figure stretched up to its full, lanky height.

"Drop it, Melean, or I'll put you in a paralytic coma," Tidoris growled against his brother's cheek.

He jabbed the stunner hard into Melean's neck and Melean winced.

"Think about what you're doing, brother." Melean fumbled with the nano-gun; Tidoris zapped him warningly and he sputtered, "You—we—are better than this."

"No, we're not." Tidoris stepped back and pulled the trigger.

Melean's whole body seized, then contorted—his eyes bulged and his mouth tore open like he was screaming, but nothing came out.

Ciaan'd never seen anyone stunned up close before— for being legal, it was pretty awful.

After ten or so seconds, Melean finally crumpled to the floor in a twitchy heap.

Tidoris shoved him aside with a booted foot. "I'm just so sick of your…your…*shibal!*"

Ciaan panted, didn't realize she'd been holding her breath until now.

"You didn't kill him, did you?" Regulation stunners weren't allowed to have lethal settings, but Ciaan knew Tidoris loved tweaking his technology.

He coughed—it rattled out like he was embarrassed—and kneeled down in front of the de-electrified shock wall.

"Of course not. Stunners can't kill people." He glanced down at his boot laces. "But he'll be pretty damn sore when he wakes up, and it might take six or seven days for him to regain full body sensation."

If the plexiglass barrier hadn't been between them, Ciaan would've lunged forward and hugged him.

"We need to get you out of here without tripping the alarm." Tidoris examined the keypad. Behind him, the lurking shadows edged closer to the cell.

Ciaan shook her head; all her energy—all her defiance and resistance and fatalistic acceptance—drained down her legs and out the soles of her feet. "Melean was right. Don't do this, Dori…it's not worth it."

Tidoris smiled, bittersweet, already messing with the

security remote. "When has that ever stopped us?"

She sighed, "It needs a code."

"Well, then, it's probably a good thing that I'm a better hacker than I am a fighter." Tidoris juggled the remote, a cluster of wires, and his personal Right Hand.

"Now, now." One of the shadows came into the light; its sleek, muscular build was hidden under an obviously-borrowed and incorrectly-sized reserve uniform set. "If Dori here hadn't threatened to hunt me down and inject a nanomite cocktail into my spine, we wouldn't be here right now. I'd say that's some kind of fighting skill."

Mael dragged the still-limp guards into the center of the room, double-binding them at the wrists and ankles with Melean. Next to him, Nkoti leaned down to tape all their mouths shut.

"How'd you get here? I mean, without being arrested on the spot?" Ciaan rocked back on her heels and tried to stand, knees wobbling. She steadied herself against the wall.

Mael snorted; Tidoris cut in for him.

"The network tunnels are actually fairly wide from when the original wiring was much thicker and heavier, and they run everywhere under the base. With the new micro-wiring, you can crawl through them comfortably."

Mael massaged a shoulder. "I wouldn't exactly say that."

"But how'd you get back to the base?" Ciaan finally got on her feet, scratching at her itchy scalp; she hadn't had a decent shower for the past five days.

"Well, after *someone* wouldn't stop sending threatening DMs, we left the *Maelstrom* at a safe dock and acquired seats aboard another cargo ship whose captain just so happened to owe me a favor." Mael shoveled the scattered stunners into his pack—then picked up the nano-gun delicately, examining it, before dropping it in too.

Ciaan gaped at him.

"You mean, you blackmailed your friend and stowed away on their ship?"

Mael slung the pack across his chest and shrugged. "Are you saying you *don't* want our help in escaping from a life of prison and torture? Because I'm fine with that."

Ciaan chewed her lips shut while Tidoris fed a stream of numbered commands into the keypad; it wheezed and whirled, fighting the override attempt.

When she opened her mouth again, her voice was small and insignificant.

"You shouldn't have risked coming back for me. I'm not that important."

Ciaan blinked fast, eyes traitorously wet. Mael grunted, harsh and dismissive, and it helped drown out the echoes of *you've lived a worthless life.*

Nkoti looked up from where they were patting down Melean for concealed weapons. "That's a matter of opinion—ours, not yours."

Something was different about them, like the scuffed metal of the p-planets had finally rubbed off on them. When they stepped closer, Ciaan could see that their face was streaked with cheap foundation, masking the unnatural tone of Artificial skin. Their hair had been chopped, short and uneven, and stuffed under the ugly work hat that none of the recruits actually wore.

But their eyes, Ciaan realized. *They still give them away.*

Nkoti stopped only briefly at the plexiglass, then passed on behind Tidoris.

"Besides," Mael continued, sounding impatient and a little awkward, "I'll be damned if we let you take all the credit for bravery and sacrifice just because you've got blonde hair."

Ciaan rolled her eyes as he pointed at the keypad. "You ready with that yet, Dori?"

Tidoris shushed him. "No, and bothering me won't get it done any faster."

Mael hummed, eyes crinkling fondly.

Ciaan suddenly remembered something. "What about *You* and *Me?*"

The air went taut and still.

"We brought them back with us," Mael started, barreling on before Ciaan could interrupt him. "One of my contacts here on Toi got back to me—they know what to do with them."

Ciaan tried to picture the type of people he'd consider perfectly acceptable to hand over a pregnant, traumatized, deaf teenager and her tongue-less brother to.

Her eyes narrowed. "Who?"

Mael ground his jaw, scratched the back of his neck.

Behind him, footsteps tinkered down the brig stairs.

"Hurry up. We have a very short amount of time before the patrol check comes and finds"—a new shadow, another woman, waved at the pile of stunned, bound bodies—"*this.*"

Her voice dipped low and strong—devoid of the worried, cautious notes that Ciaan would've recognized immediately in any other situation.

Ciaan peered at the figure, had to be sure, but the woman didn't linger in the darkness.

Her second mother walked briskly over to the shock wall and put two gentle, warm hands against it. Ciaan—moved by something long-buried inside herself—pressed a shaky hand back.

Tidoris exhaled loudly and, with an angry buzz, the barrier slid open.

[TWENTY]

CIAAN'S HAND FELL BEFORE her second mother could grab it; there was a chance, an opportunity, and then the moment slid away with the door.

Mael plowed between them. "Has the *cargo* been boxed and relabeled?"

"Not yet." Ciaan's second mother handed her a rumpled uniform set and a dark, heavy-braided wig. "If the delivery can't be made until morning, I think it'd be best to keep them secure inside the ship for as long as possible—nothing's given the Traders more problems in the past than sloppy transports and hand-offs."

Nkoti and her second mother shielded Ciaan while she changed in the cell; once she'd zipped up the jumpsuit, she broke past them and wheeled on Mael.

"*She*'s one of your Toi contacts? My second mother?!"

From nearby the stairs, Tidoris tried to shush her.

Mael held up his hands. "I didn't know she was your second mother! You never said she was a Free Trader."

Ciaan jabbed a dirty finger at him. "I didn't know!"

The memory of branded flesh hidden under overworn blouses sliced through her fury; she rocked back, felt like the last tethers to truth in her life had been severed.

"I…I didn't know anything," she murmured, wondered if anyone else could even hear it.

"I didn't tell you," her second mother corrected. "And I still don't know if that was the right choice."

Ciaan stared at her, swallowed against a tacky-dry tongue. "Did you know?"

Her second mother nodded. "Yes."

"How much?"

"My father worked as a Broadcasting Official. I have—had—aunts and cousins on Earth who we'd visit for the holidays, before they started tightening the travel restrictions."

Her second mother pressed her lips together and cleared her throat.

"I joined an information sharing collective first,

which turned into a Resistance group once news started coming in about what was going on down there. We joined a few protests before we were caught illegally transiting, and served a year and a half on Earth before being released—under surveillance—back to the p-planets. We were lucky," she scoffed. "Relatively lucky, at any rate. That was about twenty-five years ago."

"And then you found us," Ciaan gritted out.

"My first husband was in the Resistance too; we met during our detention on Earth. When we came back here, we knew it'd be too dangerous to keep protesting openly, so we began building a covert network—identifying who was in on it in the p-planet system, smuggling and transmitting restricted information, establishing a map of people and places willing to take care of folks who needed safe passage between the p-planets and Earth. We worked with anyone who'd help us: p-people, Earth humans, and occasionally even the Security Forces." She looked past Ciaan to Nkoti, eyes clouding as she watched the Artificial. "When they could be trusted."

"Eventually—once there was talk of the crisis ending—my first husband decided that it was time to retire from the Resistance. I…disagreed and we parted ways, as amicably as possible." The serious lines of her face smoothed over. "Sometime later, I met your father."

Ciaan swallowed again and it burned on the way down. "So you knew about my first mother?"

Her second mother sighed; Ciaan's chest tightened like a fist around the heart.

"Not at first, no, and I don't know how—*if*—it would've changed things if I did." Her jaw clenched. "Your father didn't know anything, either; he and your first mother met after she'd fled Earth and established a new identity. By the time he and I decided to get married, I'd convinced myself that there wasn't any point in telling him—or you. I wanted…"

To protect us; Ciaan finished the sentence for her.

"I wanted to have a safe, normal life." Her second mother turned away, like for once she didn't want Ciaan to see her.

"So you became a Free Trader?" Ciaan bit out.

Her second mother opened her eyes and laughed.

"Old habits." She reached out and tucked one of Ciaan's pale braids back under her wig. "You're your mother's daughter, Ciaan. But remember—you're not *her*."

A beat thumped between them, then her second mother pulled her in, wrapping her arms around Ciaan's tired body. Ciaan only half-hugged back, but didn't struggle against it—let her second mother share some of her resilience with Ciaan.

When her second mother finally let her go, Ciaan

noticed the others standing around awkwardly, picking at their knuckles and glancing towards a wide vent duct in the brig wall.

"You sure you'll be okay to go out above ground?" Tidoris asked the older p-woman anxiously, fiddling with the grate pins to get it open.

"Don't worry, Tidoris,"—she patted his arm reassuringly; there was the woman Ciaan'd thought she knew—"this isn't my first breakout. I've got a visitor's ID and made a big fuss about waiting around until the Administrative Headquarters opens to file a formal complaint, so I can't believe anyone'll hassle me."

"Besides"—she winked at Ciaan—"I'm a mother, and mothers are the most harmless people in the world."

Ciaan chuckled, grim and bitter, then waved goodbye to her second mother. She turned, jammed her hands into her uniform pockets, and her fingers caught around a delicate metal chain; she hesitated—wondered how that could be—since her original uniform set had been confiscated when she was arrested.

Nkoti reached for her.

Ciaan dropped the charms, blinked the last of the electric blue haze from her eyes. "Let's go."

One by one, they crawled into the duct. Mael, the last in, replaced the grate behind him.

Tidoris led the way; the light from his Right Hand screen illuminated the tunnels in front of them—though only he and Ciaan, who was right behind him, could really see anything from it. Nkoti followed third, movements measured and light, with Mael bringing up the rear. He had the bag of weapons and was in charge of taking care of anything that might try to sneak up on them back there; Tidoris kept his stunner holstered at his waist for any threats from the front.

Shuffling hand and knee in the dark, Ciaan understood why Tidoris'd said the space was comfortable—and why Mael had insisted it wasn't. For anyone used to working in cramped, stifling spaces, the few extra inches between limbs and walls was a luxury; for everyone else, it was an exercise in creeping claustrophobia. Ciaan tried to avoid the bundles of micro-wires above their heads, but every so often she smashed against one of the metal brackets that kept them in place. And she was the shortest person in the group— with swears of pain echoing every couple of feet, it was incredible that they hadn't managed to get caught yet.

With Tidoris veering them sporadically, Ciaan wasn't sure if they were following one main tunnel or turning off into the maze of sub-tunnels. The ground was slick with puddles of grease and electrical oil that soaked into her palms, and sweat started trickling down over her eyebrows, dripping into her lashes.

"Shh!" Tidoris stopped short; Ciaan reared back to avoid running face-first into his ass.

"What?!" she rasped, trying to catch her breath.

He craned his neck around and whispered, slow and over-exaggerated, "These are the main restrooms—Mael, you and Nkoti get out here. The exit vent is in a maintenance closet, so you shouldn't be seen. Wait for a blank DM from me and then head to the docks."

At the end of the line, Mael nodded, handing something up from his pack.

"Take this."

It was the nano-gun—he held it out to Ciaan.

She wavered, then grabbed it out of his hand and twisted back to Tidoris.

"What about us?"

He motioned ahead. "We can't all come out at the same place. With fewer night workers around we'll already be conspicuous, so you and I are going into the dock tunnels. They branch off and get narrower, but a central tunnel runs under each docking mechanism, so we'll be able to come out right under the ship at..."

He tapered off, unsure.

"Gate 3." Mael offered.

Tidoris blushed. "Gate 3. There shouldn't be any officers or recruits stationed there overnight—and since it's already been checked and cleared, we should be able to hide inside until *You* and *Me* can be handed off."

Ciaan followed his logic until it dead ended. "And then what?"

Tidoris cleared his throat; it didn't inspire confidence in her.

"And then," he sputtered. "We'll see."

After leaving Mael and Nkoti at a foul-smelling duct, Ciaan and Tidoris continued down into the sloping, slightly smaller tunnels. They crawled in silence, every nudge and creak bouncing off the walls and back to them. Once in a while they'd pass a turn that seemed stretched out, thin and black, sucking lost transmissions and curious recruits into its singularity.

Ciaan didn't look down those for too long.

Tidoris kept up a brisk, urgent pace while she lagged, wrists and shins scraping along with what little energy she still had after the brig. Her uniform set snagged on a sharp seam and dragged jagged metal down her calf; she hissed, then bit her cheek to smother it, but Tidoris heard anyway.

He squinted back, saw her clutching her leg to clot the bleeding. "You okay?"

"Yeah." She forced a laugh. "Don't worry about me, third mother."

Tidoris tried to smile, but it didn't stick—the glow of the Right Hand made his face look gaunt and severe—and Ciaan wondered when he'd gotten so steely and sure.

She maneuvered awkwardly in the narrow space, ripped off the torn fabric and knotted a crude bandage over the wound.

She nodded curtly. "I'm fine. Keep moving."

After a few more turns, the tunnel finally widened into a shallow, circular chamber; Ciaan could see the base's dim night lights wedging through the vent. Tidoris slid under the grate, fluid and alert, and stared up through the bars for several tense seconds.

"I don't hear anything"—he didn't move, didn't look at Ciaan—"and I can't see any shadows or hear any footsteps. Someone could be sleeping on watch, but…I think we're okay."

He started to pull back the grate pins; the metal whined and screeched without any other noise to cover it. It felt like hours—but was probably only a minute or two—before Tidoris finally swung the vent open.

It groaned on its hinges, but only a little.

He popped his head up, then back down, waving to Ciaan. "Clear."

She got into position behind him, ignoring the wince of pain as she stretched out her bandaged leg. They climbed out one at a time, careful to stay behind the bulky docking mechanism as much as possible.

The ship (once Ciaan could actually see it) was bigger and more sprawling than the *Maelstrom,* but not as well-maintained—though Ciaan hadn't really considered the *Maelstrom* particularly well-maintained before. The hull stretched several hundred feet back; they followed its arc, checking the dock for stray basics or nosy supervisors, but there was no one.

They pulled the rusty compression latch and opened the cargo hatch.

Inside, it reeked of wet animals and moldy produce, and they tried to avoid the unidentifiable muck stagnating between the welded floor panels. They climbed up another ladder to what Ciaan assumed was the central level of the ship; the deckway was broad but poorly lit and rickety, cheap lacquer flaking off the walls.

At the end of the corridor, a harsh light switched on and they held back, Tidoris reaching for his stunner.

A burly man—hair pulled into a frayed ponytail and face peppered with haphazard stubble—stepped onto the deckway, blocking their path.

All Ciaan could make out on him was the huge tanned animal skin jacket and the gun—long-barreled and unwieldy, but filled with the kind of old-fashioned bullets that could kill a person dead without waiting for the slither of nanomites.

"Off my ship!" he barked, jacket bunching tight around his armpits as he lunged towards them.

"Wait, wait, wait!" Tidoris fumbled with his stunner, tried to surrender without dropping it. "We're Captain Moon's friends! The ones you're helping get off-planet!"

The man cocked his gun, but didn't shoot.

You and *Me* peered out from the lit room behind him; they were in fresh clothes and scrubbed clean— watching the scene peculiarly, without comprehension.

Then—from somewhere that sounded both far away and right on top of them—a blast went off. The captain, Ciaan, and Tidoris all took off down the deckway.

Through one of the cork hole windows, Ciaan saw two bright-suited figures—Nkoti and Mael—running for the port gate. A cluster of dark-suited soldiers scrambled after them, shooting off high-powered blasters sporadically and without any accuracy.

Ciaan and Tidoris ran for the main deck hatch, jumping through it and landing hard, feet-first on the dock.

Tidoris began manually disengaging the docking

mechanism while Ciaan raced to the port door keypad; she had to re-enter the stolen code twice, fingers punching clumsy under pressure. Once it opened, she jammed herself in the middle of the doorway—activating its sensors and keeping it from closing again.

"Come on!" she screamed frantically to Mael and Nkoti, flailing her arms like maybe they couldn't see her otherwise.

Their boots pounded loud—nearer and nearer—and their faces came into focus, streaked with partially sweated-off makeup and black grease. Shots, and not the ones meant to just stun, pinged around Ciaan. She ducked and cowered but didn't move out of the doorway. As soon as Mael and Nkoti reached her— barreled through the gate, not slowing down—Ciaan flung herself out of the way and watched the door crash shut.

Behind them, the ship roared awake.

"What happened?!" Tidoris huddled near the main hatch ladder, shouting over the gunning engines.

The ship started to lift off the ground; Mael—the first one there—leapt for the lowest ladder rung, but it hovered just out of reach.

He jumped again. "An officer was in the bathroom and heard us coming out of the vent—he cornered us and called for backup, but we got away before it came…"

"Backup?!" Ciaan glanced back at the soldiers' unit gathered on the other side of the locked port door; they didn't look like any backup she'd ever seen on the base.

An officer aimed a blaster at the keypad and the whole thing exploded, blowing the door out and slicing a gash up the docking bubble. Ciaan's ears rang from the explosion and, for a split-second, everything dialed down to syrupy slow-motion.

Then someone was yanking her by the wrist as the soldiers swarmed in.

Mael dragged her to the ladder and hoisted her up; she grabbed on two rungs below Tidoris. Nkoti wasn't on the ground—they must've been the first one up—and once Ciaan got a decent grip, she turned back for Mael.

He was still on the dock, straining for the bottom rung, a few inches too short to reach it.

"You've gotta pull me up!" he yelled, face awash in cold fear.

Ciaan hooked her legs around the rungs and hung down from the ladder, stretching her arm as far as it'd go. She felt long, firm fingers—Tidoris's—wrap around her other wrist to keep her steady.

"Attention, criminals!" A loudspeaker blared from the row of soldiers with blasters trained on them. "You are suspected of fleeing a lawful detention, assaulting a Senior Officer, falsifying official filework, and transporting restricted and prohibited items. Surrender yourselves immediately and unconditionally, or you will be deemed a hostile threat and we will have no choice but to fire openly on your ship and your persons! This is your only warning!"

Ciaan finally got ahold of Mael's wrist—bracing herself against the hull, she pulled and pulled and pulled until he had both a hand and a foot on the ladder.

"Stop!" Someone shouted above Ciaan; she looked up and saw the captain's tanned animal skin jacket clogging the ship's open hatchway, keeping Tidoris from climbing aboard.

The captain shoved something in front of him, a heavy steel gun and the swell of a pregnant belly. He held *Me* with one rough arm around her neck, propping the gun against the side of her head.

"This is what you really want, isn't it?"

A hush snuffed out the snap of blaster-fire; apparently, Mael's favors had run out.

"*Ya! Shibal gaesaegi'ya!*" Mael seethed, spitting the foreign words venomously and thrashing against the hull as he tried to swing his way up to his no-longer-friend.

"I'll give 'er to you—you can have all of 'em!" The captain's eyes roved wild as he stamped his boots down on Tidoris's fingers. "Just don't ruin my ship!"

The soldiers faltered, confused, and fell out of

formation as one man—still wearing his fluttering coat—marched through the blasted-open gate door.

High Official Yeager raised a nano-gun and fired once; the shot whizzed over Ciaan and caught *You* in the stomach, just as he rushed out from behind the captain to shove his sister out of the way.

The boy collapsed on the deckway, gaping hole full of nanomites eating away at his gut, and *Me* lunged at the surprised captain—clawing and biting savagely at any piece of skin she could find. He yowled, shielding his face as she tore into him, and tried to scurry away.

Nkoti pulled *Me* off and stomped a boot onto his animal-skin-wrapped back—pinned him to the deckway—then picked up the captain's manual gun and blew a shot straight through his brain. He dropped flat on his stomach, blood and tissue pooling out from what used to be his face.

On the dock, Yeager adjusted his aim and fired once more, hitting below Ciaan.

Mael shrieked, agonized and ear-splitting, as Ciaan wrestled with her holstered nano-gun and pointed it out towards the crowd of soldiers. She locked the sight on Yeager—her trigger finger itched, waiting for an excuse to fire.

Yeager lowered his weapon and called out to her, casual like a blade slipped between ribs.

"Your captain or your cargo—it's your choice! But I'd make it soon; the nanomites won't care either way."

He muttered something—an inaudible command—to the soldiers and they stood down.

"Whichever one you choose, you won't get very far. But you're welcome to try." He gave Ciaan a cold, mocking salute. "I'll see you again soon, Private Gennett."

Then he spun on the soldiers, snarled a second set of orders: "Put out an Interplanetary Fugitive Report on this ship and its crew. List them as armed and a high-risk security threat. Force will likely be necessary in apprehending them."

With that, Yeager retreated out the port gate towards AH; the soldiers marched after him, keeping their distance.

He didn't look back.

Ciaan dangled from the ladder, punchy and reeling, still clutching the nano-gun. She felt two pairs of hands pulling her onto the ship; once on deck, she leaned out to help Tidoris and Nkoti get Mael in too.

They laid him across the deckway, next to *You*; the nanomites had already begun eating away at the flesh on his right leg.

"I'll override the space door code—can you fly this ship?" Tidoris yelled to Nkoti over the engines, fuming against their dock tethers.

Nkoti nodded, face flecked with bits of the captain's brain, and sprinted to the bridge without waiting for a direct order.

Tidoris tapped desperately at his Right Hand keys, smearing them with blood from his fingertips. As soon as the override went through, the ship lurched forward, free from the dock and the base and from Toi itself.

Ciaan sat quietly between the bodies—the captain, Mael, and *You*—dead already or almost there. She took a deep breath—smelling the tinge of lacquer and the piss-tang of an aimless, groundless life carved between the blackness and the starlight—and pushed out everything she'd ever expected, everything she ever thought she knew, on the exhale. The hologram of her world sputtered, flickered to static, taking with it all the things she'd never been—could never be. Beyond that was only grey-white noise and unformed, vast possibility.

And finally, Ciaan was ready for it.

[EPILOGUE]
86 1/2 YEARS LATER

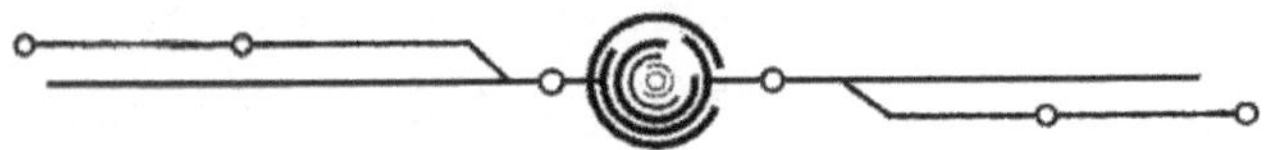

THE CARGO SHIP SLEPT in darkness, drifting under the shadow of Enkai. It kept its orbit wide to discourage the p-planet's ports from engaging it for docking, using the casual mid-morning traffic to disguise its unauthorized loitering.

Ciaan sat on the edge of her short bunk, hurriedly sifting through the wrinkled paper files they were about to hand off while scanning the latest newsfeeds on her black market Right Hand. She cross-checked the official Information Channel transmissions with the underground ones—which were collected mostly from leaked files like the ones stacked next to her on the bed.

The reports came in: prominent fashion trends, relationship advice, debates over architectural styles for a proposed New Media Hall. Food shortages brought on by biochemically contaminated water supplies, the troubling decrease in Earth humans' average yearly incomes, protests against the attempted annexations of non-standardized regions. The occasional raid on private, off-grid fertility clinics—relics of an irrational, barbaric era.

Our worlds, Ciaan mused as she rubbed the spikes of her buzzed hair, *are strange places.*

Her Right Hand double-beeped, indicating an incoming message. She pulled up the log—an unknown, secured line—then minimized it when footsteps started clattering down the deckway.

Mael hobbled slow through the open door, one arm wound around Tidoris for support. The gears in his robotic leg, fused with the flesh just above his knee, churned and wheezed at the strain.

"I wish you'd let me use my cane." Mael pouted at Tidoris as he took an unwieldy step. "I wouldn't have bought it if I thought you weren't gonna let me use it."

Tidoris fussed, helped Mael bend down onto another bunk. "I've almost got the fluidity controls worked out...I haven't built a prosthetic before, Mael, so you're gonna have to be patient. You don't want to go back to the soldered stump, do you?"

Mael glared at him darkly.

"I want my cane."

Tidoris shook his head.

"Once it's fully operational, this leg'll be better than any cane—but you'll never get used to it if you keep using supplemental support. You need to re-strengthen your muscles." A grin tugged at the corners of his mouth. "Besides, that cane makes you look old."

"How dare you!" Mael huffed, only half-offended. "You just want an excuse to touch me."

Tidoris rolled his eyes, scratched at his stubbled cheeks to hide a flush.

"Yes, exactly." He jabbed a finger into Mael's scarred thigh. "Now stretch out so you don't sprain anything."

Mael mimicked Tidoris—their teasing, prodding battles had evolved into something coyer and more tender than before—but still did as he was told.

When Tidoris stood up again, Ciaan could see the hollows in his clothes where muscle and fat used to hold the fabric firm; she tried not to think about what else he'd lost along the way.

Instead, she stuffed the brittle papers into a discreet cargo container and locked it. "How long until we dock with the contact?"

Mael shrugged, searching automatically for the broad

window that'd cut across the far wall in the *Maelstrom's* crew quarters. He blinked, momentarily confused by its absence, before catching his mistake.

They'd abandoned the *Maelstrom* after their escape from the CPZ base, knew that—if they wanted any chance at not being immediately captured—they'd have to let it go. But it echoed in their habits; they often found themselves getting lost down unfamiliar deckways and peering out windows that weren't there.

For Mael, the skip back from the *Maelstrom* always lagged a little longer.

"The contact's late, as usual. I don't know why I bother being on time with these rogue traders—they never return the favor." Mael kept staring at the blank wall, like maybe he could carve a window out of it with his mind. "Any new transmissions about the search for that band of dangerous criminals and Interplanetary fugitives who escaped from Toi in a violent shootout with Security Forces six months ago?"

Ciaan shoved off the bed and handed the cargo box to Tidoris. He nudged her, let their shoulders knock together, and she didn't pull away.

"Nope, but there's always tomorrow," she scoffed. "Any publicity, right?"

Mael leaned back on a pillow—barked out a brittle, humorless laugh—then saluted at the doorway behind them; Nkoti fidgeted there, like they were waiting to be invited in.

"What's the word from the bridge, Acting Captain?"

Nkoti cleared their throat; they still weren't completely comfortable with that title—especially coming from Mael. "We just received a request for an excess cargo transport from a non-standardized region in the Southern American Union."

Excess cargo transport had become their keyword for smuggling humans (of any kind) out of threatening regions or facilities and into places, on Earth and the p-planets, where they'd be safe. After their harrowing escape, they'd stumbled into a chain—ending up as part of the web of those who knew what was really going on and were trying to do something about it.

"Tell them we can't get there until next week. If that's too late, they'll need to find another transport ship." Mael tried to heave himself off the bed.

Tidoris rushed over, grabbed him by the waist to steady him.

"I'm gonna go and see what's taking this damn contact so long and you"—Mael poked Tidoris in the chest with a stubby finger—"are coming with me."

They shuffled out together, still bickering. Tidoris glanced apologetically at Ciaan as he passed her; she winked and watched him choke on the way out.

The only ones left in the now-quiet room, Ciaan and Nkoti turned to each other. Nkoti held back, hesitant, until Ciaan sat down on her bunk and patted the lumpy patch of mattress beside her.

"Any transmissions about *Me* and the baby?" Ciaan started, feeling the bed dip with Nkoti's weight.

"Not yet." Nkoti looked muted these days—complexion waning and thick black circles smudging under their eyes—but warmer, too, more human.

"The last we heard, the baby'd been stabilized after birth at the outpost and they were both being transported to the next port. That was 28 days ago."

Ciaan nodded; she remembered.

"If everything went smoothly, they should've arrived in the non-standardized region's safe zone by now, but..." They trailed off; these days Nkoti spoke more haltingly, less sure. "I wish she hadn't decided to go back there—she would've been easier to monitor in a Union."

Ciaan exhaled softly, let her head drop onto Nkoti's shoulder. "Maybe. At least we talked her out of taking her brother's body back with her."

Sometimes—right before she fell asleep—Ciaan could still hear the girl's heart-wrenching sobs as she clung to *You*'s lifeless body, sprawled out on the ship's metal floor. By the time they'd gotten out of the docking channel, it'd been too late to do anything for him; Mael had screamed—delirious and writhing next to him—that the boy had to be treated first, even as Ciaan held him down so Tidoris could perform the amputation.

"We gave him an honorable space funeral." Nkoti reached up, traced their fingertips down the side of Ciaan's braidless head.

Ciaan closed her eyes, let them linger.

Nkoti whispered against her forehead, "Is the cargo ready for transfer?"

"Almost," Ciaan murmured, cracking her eyes open. "I just need to check a few more things."

It was a lie, but Ciaan wanted a couple more minutes of privacy before their next run.

Nkoti leaned back, got up from the bed without asking for anything else. They walked to the door then paused, smiled back and it was something unspoken, understood, between them—whatever it was, Ciaan appreciated it.

When she was alone again, Ciaan clicked on her Right Hand expectantly.

A tinny voice perked up. "You have one new message."

"Play and expand display." She propped the machine against the mattress.

The projection stuttered—black market Right Hands weren't as consistently reliable as the standard issue ones—as her second mother crackled into view; her face was etched in serious lines and she gripped one of Ciaan's long, white-yellow braids in her fist.

Illonde's voice filled Ciaan with a sense of something almost, something fleetingly gone.

"Hello, honey. You know they check all our DMs now so I can only send them through Resistance encryption lines, which're more difficult to arrange. Not impossible though." Her gaze flicked to something off-screen, then back at the camera; she crouched in close. "I was looking up at the stars—the real ones—last night, thinking about you burning on strong out there with them, doing what you have to do."

Her second mother's lips pressed thin, soft and sorrow-soaked. "Take care of yourself, Ciaan. I've only got one daughter like you."

Something that'd been swelling inside Ciaan, growing up from the pit of her stomach since her second mother had stepped out of the shadows in the base brig, burst through her chest and out of the cords of her veins. She swallowed the remnants of copper blood on the frigid steel ground and sighed, "You too."

"We love you; I'll be in touch when I can." The recording scattered into pixels and her second mother faded from the air.

Ciaan dusted the rest of the loose, unimportant file

scraps into the waste compartment—she needed to head to the bridge; they'd want to go over the plan before the transfer.

Her Right Hand dinged abruptly, prompting: "Store or delete?"

She considered the question, mapped out the ties that bound her—between Toi and Earth and back again—and decided to spend more time watching the stars and charting her place among them.

"Delete," she answered gently.

There were people, more than just herself, who she had to look out for; she needed to be careful, didn't want to risk it for all their sakes.

Besides, she *knew* now—didn't need a stored DM to convince her anymore.

[ACKNOWLEDGEMENTS]

Orbit started its life a decade ago, as a short story in a senior year undergrad creative writing class—but the idea had already been rattling around in my brain, a strange product of concurrent reading assignments (Alex Kotlowitz's *There Are No Children Here* and Orson Scott Card's *Ender's Game*) and my long-standing love of speculative fiction. The meat of the book was shaped by my life and experiences in South Korea, where I wrote the first (awkward, stilted) draft. After setting it aside for a few years, my debut novel has finally found its place with the incredible Snowy Wings Publishing family, and I couldn't be more excited about it!

10 years is a long time and a lot of people to thank, but I'm going to do my best: thank you, first and foremost, to Lyssa Chiavari and Snowy Wings Publishing for turning my dream of publishing *Orbit* into a reality. Thank you to my editor, Amy McNulty, who tackled a manuscript that hadn't really seen the light of day in 7 years. Thank you to my cover designer, Najla Qamber, and my formatter, Dorothy Dreyer, for their lovely and generous work. Thank you to my family—my parents, Joanne and Richard Hellman, and my siblings,

Rachel Hinshaw and Matthew Hellman—for their boundless love, support, and belief in me. Thank you to my partner, Jonghyun Kang (the original Jongmal), for putting up with my writerly whims. Thank you to my best friend and editor, Rachel Bruno—who told me that if I didn't write this book I'd always regret it, then ran the first round of edits on my very roughest draft. Thank you to my mentors who encouraged me along the way: Eugene Wildman (who, despite a general rule against genre fiction, welcomed my first draft of *78 Years Later*), Luis Urrea (who proves that genius and ego are not irrevocably intertwined), Lisa Redpath (who told her 6th grade student, in complete sincerity, that they had talent and should keep writing)—and every other teacher, professor, and mentor who took the time to let me know that this passion was worth pursuing. Thank you to my friends and loved ones (those who're still in my life, and those who aren't) who cared for me and cheered me on when I felt like giving up: Nathan Bohn, Kimber Brightheart, Neidi Chavez, Amy Goshe, Amber Hellman-Wylie, Lauren Jankowski, Erin Linsenmeyer, Jacob Mueller, Kayla Nicholls, Nicole Noel-Liang, Laya Rose, Karen Russell—and everyone else who I've been lucky enough to have in my life during this journey.

And finally, thank you to *you*. Yes, you—person who saw this book and decided to take a chance on it. Thank you for supporting indie authors and creators, and for letting me share this story with you.

I hope that Ciaan and the others can leave you with something worth thinking about.

[ABOUT THE AUTHOR]

LEIGH HELLMAN is a queer/asexual and genderqueer writer, originally from the western suburbs of Chicago, and a graduate of the MA Program for Writers at the University of Illinois at Chicago. After gaining the ever-lucrative BA in English, they spent five years living and teaching in South Korea before returning to their native Midwest.

Leigh's short fiction and creative nonfiction work has been featured in *Hippocampus Magazine, VIDA Review,* and *Fulbright Korea Infusion Magazine.* Their critical and journalistic work has been featured in the *American Book Review,* the *Gwangju News* magazine, and the *Windy City Times.*

They are pleased as punch to be publishing their first novel, the new adult speculative fiction work *Orbit,* with Snowy Wings Publishing in 2018.

In their everyday life, Leigh is a strong advocate for full-day breakfast menus, all varieties of dark chocolate, building a wardrobe based primarily on bad puns, and bathing in the tears of their enemies.